NEWARK PUBLIC LIBRARY-NEWARK OHIO 43055
W9-BYQ-324

14 DAY
LOAN

The Trap At Comanche Bend

Also by Max Brand
in Thorndike Large Print ®

Alcatraz
Galloping Broncos
The Iron Trail
Seven of Diamonds
Speedy
Trouble Trail
Valley Vultures
Riders of the Silences

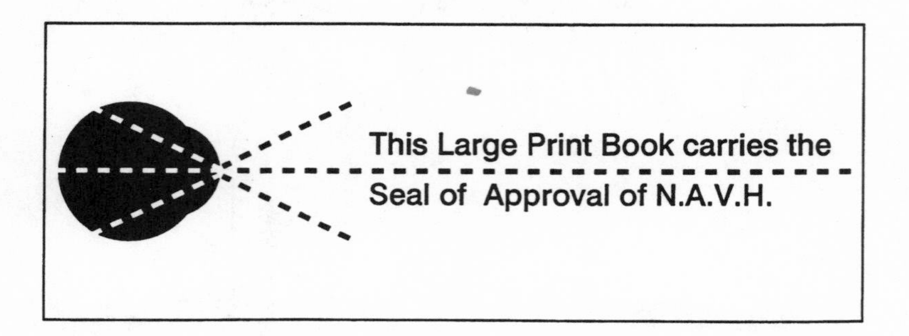

The Trap at Comanche Bend

Max Brand

Thorndike Press • Thorndike, Maine

Library of Congress Cataloging in Publication Data:

Brand, Max, 1892-1944.
The trap at Commanche Bend / Max Brand.
p. cm.
ISBN 1-56054-700-6 (alk. paper : lg. print)
1. Large type books. I. Title.
[PS3511.A87T745 1993] 93-7031
813'.54—dc20 CIP

Thorndike Large Print® Western Series edition published in 1993 by arrangement with Golden West Literary Agency.

Cover design by Ron Walotsky.

The tree indicium is a trademark of Thorndike Press.

This book is printed on acid-free, high opacity paper. ♾

CONTENTS

CHAPTER I

One Hundred Fahrenheit

The black shadow in the thermometer on the back veranda climbed steadily from ninety-five to ninety-six, to ninety-seven, and then hesitated. But it made up for the hesitation by lunging suddenly toward one hundred. John Scovil watched the ascension happily.

"Billy," he said to the cook, at that moment shaking out grimy dishrags and hanging them on the line, "Billy, there's nothing like this dry air of the mountain desert."

"Huh!" grunted Billy, and paused to wipe the sweat from his forehead and stare at Scovil.

"When the mercury hits ninety in old Manhattan," went on the jovial Scovil, "your drinking man wilts like a rose in an oven; when it goes to ninety-one the laborers drop beside their shovels; at ninety-two the fire hose is turned loose on the tenements; at ninety-three strong men begin to babble of green fields, and at ninety-four the whole town is filled with raving maniacs. But out here my muscles just about begin to loosen up at a hundred in the shade."

"Hell!" said Billy. And lunged back into the treble hell of the kitchen.

But the smile persisted upon the large face of Scovil. His million-dollar smile, men called it on the Street. Neither Bull nor Bear could dim its radiance. Amid the crashing of falling stocks and in the dull fog of financial confusion the smile of John Scovil glimmered still, a beacon whereby lesser speculators steered their perilous way to safety from the storm.

Providence built the man as a background for his smile. His waistline bulged so comfortably that one chuckled at the very sight; his bald head shone pink, worn smooth by the many rains of disaster which had splashed harmlessly off it; his rosy cheeks bulged about that capacious grin, so that his eyes appeared and anon disappeared like stars twinkling through a cloudy night.

John Scovil looked down on the twoscore scattered buildings of Comanche Bend; then his gaze wandered with an approving chuckle past the village to the lank-sided mountains which leaped toward the sky and sprawled mightily off toward the gray-blue haze of the distance.

"By the eternal God!" said John Scovil. "This is the country God made and man forgot!"

"The horses, Mr. Scovil," broke in a voice near by, and he turned upon a man who led two saddled cattle ponies around the side of the veranda leading from the corral.

"Good!" nodded the big man. "We'll be with you in a jiffy, my friend!"

He turned. His smile went out. The famous smile of John Scovil which time and danger and the assaults of crooked fortune could not dim — that smile went altogether out and left his face as blank and grim as a December landscape when a cloud blots the cheery sunshine.

This is what he saw.

A hammock stretched between two trees near the house — a broad, deeply cushioned hammock so perfectly poised on the ropes that when the air puffed lazily up the valley it swayed slumberously to and fro; and in the hammock lay Scovil's daughter, Nancy. It is hard to describe Nancy. The first temptation is to descend to details like a Cellini in prose, and consider one by one her perfect hands, and the line running from finger tips to elbow, and the round, perfect throat, and the dark, dark hair, and the darker eyes — but dealing with Nancy's face, it is as well to spring at once into Homeric superlatives. For instance: the face of Helen launched the armament of the Achæans; the face of Nancy put out John Scovil's smile. Why should he be so grave at the vision? In dumb pride and enjoyment, no doubt.

A best seller lay face downward beside her; and near it an open box of bonbons. She selected one without looking, raised it, nibbled, looked thoughtfully up to the whispering foliage of the shade trees, and then flicked the half-tasted chocolate away, where it rolled in the sand. The lower jaw of John Scovil thrust out; he mentioned a forbidden name, and started for his daughter.

At a little distance from her, however, he slackened his pace, shrugged his shoulders, and with a frowning effort summoned up again his famous smile. In this wise he swaggered jovially up to the girl.

"All right, Nan," he invited, "the horses are saddled and waiting for us."

She lifted her eyes slowly, as though the lids were weighted.

"For us?" she queried.

"Right-o!"

She selected another bonbon and nibbled it thoughtfully.

"And where should we go?"

John Scovil's smile faltered, but he sustained it, as one might say, with an iron will; and shrugged his shoulders like a prize fighter waiting for the bell and making sure that every muscle is fit.

"Where do we go?" he echoed. "To a bit of heaven, Nan, that's fallen to earth just on the other side of that range!"

Nancy Scovil covered a careful yawn with careful fingers.

"It's awfully out of place, then, isn't it?" she murmured.

Signs of increasing temperature appeared in her father's face.

"A stream," he went on courageously, "jumps out of the ground up the valley and goes sliding and slithering over the rocks, ducking between the boulders, slipping out into broad, cool pools. I have the fishing tackle in the saddlebags. Nan, the trout are so thick we can jump in and kick 'em out with our boots!"

His daughter surveyed him with a trace of concern from the sombrero on his head to the spurs on his heels — for when in Rome, John Scovil always dressed like a Roman — and having ascertained that outwardly, at least, her sire was normal, she allowed her graceful head to sink back once more in the cushion.

"My dear," sighed Nancy Scovil, "you know that I never wear boots."

"I'll be — hum!" stated John Scovil. He pointed an accusing finger. The famous smile was gone, alas, for all that day. "For Heaven's sake, Nan, who ever heard of wearing dancing pumps in the mountain desert?"

She opened her lips to answer, and let them remain parted, while her eyes followed the fluttering fall of a leaf.

John Scovil raised both of his long arms to heaven.

He groaned. "Why did I ever bring you out here? Why?"

"I haven't the least idea," admitted the girl, and removed the corner from a butter chocolate.

John Scovil loosened his bandanna; he grasped the box of candy and held it behind his back.

"Nan," he said hoarsely, "I hoped to keep the truth from you, but I'm at the end of my rope. I'm going to tell you why I brought you along with me here — why I saddled myself with you when I came here — here!" He gestured nobly around him. "Where ten thousand-foot mountains walk down to your backyard and nod good morning to you — where men speak from the heart — where the very air is an elixir of life — where every day is a poem, strong, swift, and free!"

He paused and glared at her.

"Nan!"

She started slightly, and the heavy lashes flickered up a little.

"Nancy Scovil, have you been asleep?"

"Certainly not."

"Repeat my last words," he demanded suspiciously.

She thought an instant.

"I am going to tell you why," she answered.

"Those were the last words I said?"

"Yes."

For answer John Scovil gestured to the giant mountains to bear witness to his patience and his sufferings. Then he dropped his big fists upon his hips and continued: "Do you remember when Doctor Romney examined you?"

"Of course. There wasn't a thing wrong with me. Silly idea of yours, dad."

"Was it?" echoed her father sardonically. "Now, young woman, I'll tell you exactly what Romney reported to me." He extended his arm and with a rigid forefinger sent each point stabbing home at her. "Your blood pressure is subnormal; your heart action lethargic; your mind somnolent; your nerves torpescent!"

One of her rare smiles slowly lightened her face.

"Why," she sighed, "I had no idea he found me so interesting!"

"And the result," thundered John Scovil, his temperature leaping to a hundred and ten, "is that before you're thirty you will inevitably fall a prey to — er — galloping senility —

by heavens! Inevitably, unless something is done about it immediately."

"Dear me, dad," said the girl, "it makes me quite warm just to watch your face."

Scovil's attempt at answer was merely a burst of stuttering. He managed to say at length: "There is only one hope for you. In this electric air — among these splendid mountains — it is barely possible, if you take advantage of what lies about you, that you may be restored to the normal. Heaven knows, I did not wish to bring you here.

"For ten years I've yearned to get back to this land of giants and breathe this keen air; and now, when I finally succeeded in taking one long vacation, I put a burden around my neck — dear heavens, traveling with you is like trying to make thirty knots dragging a sea anchor. But where's your gratitude? Where? I ask you, what single thing have you noted about the desert?"

She considered a moment.

"Sand!" she said at length.

John Scovil could not speak. But, somewhat alarmed by the swelling arteries in his temples, he removed his sombrero and began to fan himself violently.

He managed to say at length: "If the change made you miserable it would be something. But you don't even miss the city. Where you are means nothing to you. Point-blank, Nancy, tell me what you had in the city which you miss the most here?"

Once more she pondered, laying a forefinger beside her head. Inspiration lightened dimly in her eyes at last.

"My morning bath," she smiled.

"Good heavens!" gasped Scovil, and again with profound emotion, "Good heavens!"

He turned his back on her and began to pace up and down, breathing quick and deep, like one who has been running hard uphill. Then he paused beside her again. She had placed one hand under her head, her face was turned, she was sound asleep!

One who did not know that this was an anxious father leaning over his only child might have rashly surmised that John Scovil was about to strangle a helpless woman; yet in an instant his face softened. For she was marvelously lovely as she lay there, the great, black lashes sweeping softly across her cheek, almost too beautiful for earthly uses. And as Scovil stared the smile returned gradually to his lips; a mist of tenderness dimmed his eyes. Now her lips parted, stirred. She seemed to be speaking in her dream.

He leaned tenderly down, close and closer, and he heard: "With cocktail sauce!"

John Scovil stood erect. He pulled his sombrero villainously low over his eyes. He rolled up his right sleeve to his big, fat elbow. What might have happened then no man can tell, for at this ominous moment a voice called behind him: "Oh, Mr. Scovil, a gent here to see you!"

Still he remained staring down for an instant upon the lovely form of his child. The parted lips changed; she smiled, she was speaking again in her deep sleep.

Then he turned suddenly upon his heel, and walked slowly toward the house, his heels striking hard, his knees sagging, his head lowered, the very picture of one bowed by the burden of a great thought.

CHAPTER II

The Rubicon

It was Billy, the cook, who called.

"The boss wants to see you," said Billy, hooking a thumb over his shoulder. "He's with another gent in the parlor. Step right in."

Benson, the boss, parted his yellow-stained mustache and spat emphatically as Scovil entered the parlor — that sanctuary sacred to Saturday night calls and Sunday socials. And partly because of his host's solemnity of manner, and partly because no ordinary visitor ever trod the parlor carpet with his dusty boots, Scovil looked attentively at the "other gent."

His hat tilted far back on his head, and he himself tilted far back in the chair, one could not tell whether he were about to fall to the floor or spring to his feet. He was in no wise remarkable. He had thick, athletic shoulders, a very broad smile, and a pair of very bright eyes. Yet John Scovil's burden of soul weariness lightened mysteriously as he looked upon the stranger.

"You folks come from the same town back East," said Benson. "I thought maybe you might know each other. No?"

He concluded the introduction: "Mr. Jerry Aiken, Mr. John Scovil; shake hands, gents!"

While the ceremony was being performed he continued genially: "Kind of queer you ain't met up with each other back in your home town, seein' you both come from New York."

The ghost of his usual smile reappeared on Scovil's mouth.

"You're taking an outing?" he queried. "Just from Manhattan?"

And he surveyed the deep tan of Jerry Aiken approvingly.

"No," answered Aiken, "I'm just going back to it."

"Well," sighed Scovil, and he glanced down at his own rather bulging waistline, "you look mighty fit. The mountain desert has agreed with you."

"I'll tell a man it has," nodded Aiken. "I came out here five years ago with only one lung to the good, and that one only doing half time; my legs twisted up with rheumatism; glasses half an inch thick on my nose, and an armor-plated grouch."

"And now look at you!" smiled Scovil. "But

how can you give up the West after five solid years — lucky dog!"

"Too expensive for me," ran on Aiken easily. "Took me two years and several thousand to learn how to play poker, and then I decided that I'd break the bank in the cattle business; but the weather and the stock market stacked the cards on me, and now I'm going back to New York, where people are simple, and pick up some of their spare change."

"But you hate to leave the mountains, eh?"

"Not a bit of it. There are plenty of mountains in Manhattan, as I remember it; but I had a wrong point of view when I was there. Fun? Why, if a man can cut out a calf in a round-up, he ought to be able to cut out a calf on the Street; and a cattle stampede has nothing on the subway rush. Am I right?"

"You're an optimist," sighed John Scovil. "I wish —"

His face grew suddenly gloomy.

"Jerry runs himself down all the time. That's his way," put in Benson, for fear that Scovil might think too hardly of the self-confessed failures of Aiken. "Give him an even break, and he'll make good with cows or with hosses. I say he ought to stick with the mountains and the range, but I can't convince him. Besides, Jerry, you picked out the worst range in the country. Why didn't you open up around here?"

"I don't know," murmured Jerry Aiken. "Things looked good to me down there. I'll tell you the trouble, Benson. You know it as well as I do. I like the country, but the country doesn't like me. I like the cow-punchers, but they don't like me. They're different, and I like 'em for it. I'm different, and they fight shy of me for it. There you are. No matter where you cut the deck, you run into a crimp. It's stacked, partner!"

But Benson shook his head sturdily.

"When they get to know you, it's different. I didn't quite size you up when I first met you, Jerry. But that time we forded the Platte — Mr. Scovil, I want you to hear this. I want to tell you how my life was —"

Jerry Aiken showed signs of distress.

"None of that, Benson," he cut in rather sharply. "Mr. Scovil is like the rest of New Yorkers. He burns up to-day, slaps a mortgage on to-morrow, and forgets yesterday. And I'm with the rest of 'em. Forget it, Benson! What are you doing for amusement out here, Mr. Scovil?"

The shades of night swept across the ruddy face of Scovil. But the singular, frank communicativeness of Jerry Aiken had its effect. He rose and drew the curtain from the window. To Aiken, who followed him, he pointed out his daughter, still sound asleep in the hammock.

"There," said Scovil darkly, "is my good time. Mr. Aiken, I brought my daughter West with me!"

"What of it?" asked Jerry Aiken cheerily.

"She won't ride, she won't walk; she won't fish, she won't shoot."

"Why don't you make her?"

John Scovil shaded his eyes, for the sun streamed brilliantly through the window.

"Eh?" he grunted.

"Oh, is she sick?" asked Jerry Aiken.

"Not sick, but dead on her feet. The only activity she's strong for is eating, and her trump card is sleep."

"Then," said Jerry Aiken, "do as you'd do on a lazy horse. Use the spur."

"That," said Scovil with some coldness, "is easy to say; but when it comes to practice — well, I'm her father."

"Nonsense," breezed Jerry Aiken. "A horse is exactly like a woman."

"Young man," said Scovil severely, "that sounds very clever, but what sense is there in it?"

"Think it over. A horse has no sense. Even a mule has more. Exactly like women. You can tell a horse by the way it stands and a woman by the way she sits. A horse shies at a bit of paper, and a woman jumps for a mouse. Give a horse the reins, and it breaks its neck. Give a woman the reins, and she breaks her heart. Let a horse run loose, and it bucks you off when you try to ride; keep it in harness and it works every day. Give a woman a low-necked dress and a ballroom for a pasture, and she'll make her husband pull leather if he wants to keep his place; corral her in the kitchen and curse out the coffee in the morning, and she lives for you and for you only."

"My young, my very young friend," said John Scovil acidly, "there are exceptions which break every rule. Look at the girl in that hammock. She's the exception."

"Put a Mexican curb on her and throw a blanket over her head," nodded Jerry Aiken, "and the worst mustang on the range can be handled."

"H'm," said Scovil. "It's easy to talk, but it takes a Columbus to find land."

"Mr. Scovil," said Aiken, warming to the argument, "in twenty days on conscientious work your daughter could be saddle broke, come running when you whistle, bark for a piece of bread, and feel like a queen in gingham."

John Scovil burst into ironic laughter.

"My dear boy," he said, "you talk very well, but talk proves nothing."

"If you want action," said Aiken instantly, "I'll give it to you — at my own price."

A wild light came in the eyes of John Scovil, but it went out miserably.

"If this were the year one thousand," he muttered, "by the Eternal, I'd try you out. But we live a thousand years or so too late."

"Rot!" exploded Aiken. "Men don't change with time. Homer was the twin of any blind beggar on Broadway; and I'll show you Helen of Troy in a dance hall five hundred miles south. What worked in the old days works now."

"People may be a good deal the same," agreed Scovil, "but customs change. High-handed methods won't work. Not in this century."

"My dear Mr. Scovil," chuckled Aiken, "it's plain that you've never been in Mexico. Here's the laboratory, Mr. Scovil, where men and women are made — these mountains and this air. Give me a specimen to start on, I'll guarantee the thing can be made into a human being."

"There's something about you, Mr. Aiken," smiled Scovil, "that gives me confidence. If you were a doctor you'd have a panacea; and if you'd lived in the seventeenth century you'd have had a Universal Parry. But — where did you crowd so much experience into a rather short life?"

The irony did not in the least disturb the good cheer of the other.

"I've crowded a great deal into my life," he nodded. "In the first place, I was born; in the second place, I've eaten and laughed and talked; in the third place, I've learned how to sleep. And I haven't the slightest doubt I could set up a new school of philosophy on these original grounds."

"And your great lore concerning women?" laughed Scovil, falling in the same bantering mood.

"I have a mother and a sister," said Jerry Aiken, "and therefore I know everything there is to know about women, from Eve to Queen Bess. Remove the skin and they're the same underneath."

But the twinkle went out of John Scovil's eyes. For a long moment he stared fixedly at the smiling face of Jerry Aiken. Then he turned abruptly upon Benson.

"Mr. Benson," he said, "I'd like to have about two minutes alone with your friend Aiken."

Benson left the room amicably, but at the door he fired a word of advice.

"Go as far as you like with Jerry," he grinned, "but don't play cards with him, and salt what he says before you use it."

"There you are," chuckled Aiken. "West of the Rockies they see through talk the way you and I see through a plate-glass window and look at the show inside. Now, fire away, Mr. Scovil. I'm leaving in a moment. I only slid up into these parts to say good-by to my old friend Benson."

"Young man," said Scovil, partly stern and partly wistful, "I like you and I think I can trust you. And — I have a wild idea. Wouldn't have come to me if I hadn't talked with you.

"I wouldn't consider it for a moment if I weren't desperate. But I've come to the Rubicon. If I turn back, I go into a long life of misery carrying a burden on my shoulders. If I cross the river — well, it can't be any worse than that. The time has come for a show-down. This afternoon that girl out there called my hand. Now, Aiken, if I were to give you carte blanche with her, just what would you do?"

"Just what I've already told you. I'd get her to an open space, put on a saddle with a double cinch, put a Spanish bit in her teeth, and — send home the spurs!"

John Scovil looked afar and set his teeth; his lips twitched into an ill-savored smile.

"Could it be done?" he murmured.

"Easily. Take her out for a trip through the mountains, and let me go along."

"She'd never go."

"Then take her by force."

"By force? Put my hands on her? Gad, Aiken!"

"I'll do it for you."

"Impossible."

"Are you turning back from the Rubicon?"

"Damn me!"

"It's the crisis; buck up. The crisis: Banquo's ghost —"

"By the Lord, you mean to kidnap her. But then how could I be with her — I —"

"Kidnap you both."

"There's something Napoleonic about you, young man!"

"Bah! Napoleon was an antique. I'll give you an up-to-date version. I'll roll you Austerlitz, Lodi, Friedland, and Marengo into one pill, and hold the match for you."

"I'm mad to think of it."

"Opportunity knocks only once."

"But if the farce should ever be known —"

"If you begin to weaken now, it would be foolish to go ahead with the thing. Good-by, Mr. Scovil."

"One minute! Wait! By heavens, I think I'll do it! Could you take us out here in the mountains?"

"I could."

"Do you know the people around here?"

"Not one of 'em except old Benson."

"Eh? Then you know the country, at least?"

"Not an inch of it."

"But where the devil could you guide us, then?"

"To happiness, Mr. Scovil. And bring you back with a living woman instead of an animated corpse. You're going about with a modern Frankenstein, a sleeping demon; I'll wake her up. She'll eat out of your hand before she's through with this little course of study."

"A crazy experiment — but somehow I have a bit of faith in you, Aiken. Take her out in the mountains with a man I don't know — and — but a gentleman is a gentleman. I *do* trust you, Aiken — absolutely. Shall we shake on it?"

"Not before we come to terms."

"Eh? Terms? Of course."

"I'm not in this for my health. Look at me! One hundred a week is all I ask for — and a bonus, say, if I'm successful."

"One hundred a week!" gasped the millionaire.

"You misunderstood me," answered Jerry Aiken blithely. "I said one hundred and twenty-five."

"But, good heavens, Mr. Aiken, that's the fee of a business expert in —"

"Don't mention finance. This is to deal with

women. Much harder. One and hundred and fifty dollars a week, Mr. Scovil. I'll shake on those terms."

John Scovil was famous for something more than his smile.

"And the bonus?" he queried rather grimly.

"That," said Aiken, bowing, "I leave to your own sense of justice. That, and the hospital bills."

"Shake hands," said John Scovil.

They shook.

CHAPTER III

Tenderfoot

In spite of superstitions to the contrary, the man of the mountain desert dislikes frivolity. He is accustomed to silences, and he loves silent men. One accustomed to fence-riding falls out of the habit of speech, and noise irritates him. When he is drunk he may go to another extreme, but aside from those inspired by booze there is nothing which the desert mountaineer hates so much as the loud mouth.

Which explains why, when Jerry Aiken entered Steve Lawler's saloon in Comanche Bend whistling to the top of his bent, a number of heads turned slowly toward him and a number of eyes narrowed to slits. This is the manner in which the cow-puncher looks at a cattle pony before he says: "It's a no-good, high-headed, blankety-blank." And in this manner he looks before he says: "That man talks too much."

But the stranger gave no more heed to those keen stares than a man in plate armor might give to a rapier. He stood correctly garbed, according to the ideas of Comanche Bend, in a vest without a coat, a ragged-rimmed sombrero, spurred boots, and well-worn overalls. Yet when he slapped his hand down upon the bar it became apparent at once that he did not belong. A man carefully dressed as a girl can deceive even the keen eye and the hair-trigger instinct of a woman; but all the chaps and spurs and sombreros and slang in the world cannot make a cow-puncher out of a tenderfoot.

That hand which he slapped upon the bar, for instance, though tanned to a berry brown, lacked the distinguishing characteristic; for constant wearing of gloves bleaches the back of the cow-puncher's hand and leaves it often freckled, with a sort of parboiled appearance. Also, when a man's eyes are not framed by a myriad of crowfoot wrinkles from squinting over sun-white sands — and when a man's fingernails, instead of being broken off square with the tip of the finger, round to careful points — when such details as these are lacking, all the make-up in the world will not deceive the eye of the range rider. And the instant that hand slapped down on the bar the eye of the bartender perceived, and telegraphed his information to every corner of the barroom with a single glance.

The attentive eyes narrowed still further.

Strange that the man should make so unfavorable an impression. It was not a handsome face, to be sure, but open, made for smiling, irresistibly good-natured. He stood an average, or even less than average, height; but the set of his thick shoulders and the spring of his step proclaimed an abundance of trained muscle.

"Are you drinking with me, boys?" queried this jovial stranger, and a spinning five-dollar gold piece winked swiftly on the bar. He turned and glanced up and down the row. Many a blank eye met his and looked through and beyond him. He might have been a pillar of mist in the form of a human.

"Not drinking with me," translated Jerry, with grin unabated. "How about you, my friend?"

"Jest liquored," grunted the bartender, and mopped the bar with surly, downward eye.

"Whisky," ordered the newcomer, still cheery, and then, poising his glass: "This is an unexpected pleasure, gentlemen; I never expected to drink alone this far West. Here's to many returns of the day," And he downed the brimming glass.

Vague surmises loomed, ghostlike, in the eyes of the cattlemen. Somewhere in that remark was an insult, or a pseudo-insult; yet it was impossible to pin down the point of the speech and name the sting. They ruminated with bull-like solemnity.

In the mean time: "Mr. Bartender," said the amiable stranger, "may I have a word with you alone?"

"Kind of busy," replied Steve Lawler gloomily.

"Business," said the other, "is my middle name. I won't take much of your time. Don't believe in a lot of talk without a point. Inside of thirty seconds, Mr. Bartender, I could sell you a thousand dollars worth of stock, learn the maiden name of your first wife, and get your signature on a blank note."

"H'm!" murmured Steve Lawler, and, finding no other objection handy, he went to the end of the bar, a sufficient distance from the remainder of his patrons. The stranger at once leaned confidentially close.

"My motto," he began, "is — find headquarters and talk to 'em from the shoulder. You're headquarters for Comanche Bend and this is what I have to say: I have a little job ahead, and I need two men who can ride hard, shoot straight, think quick, and keep their mouths shut. Where are they?"

"In the —" began the bartender, and then realizing that he had spoken too suddenly, jerked down the arm with which he was pointing, and reddened.

"In the back room?" nodded the stranger. "Thanks, very much!"

"Wait!" cautioned the bartender, and though his voice was low, it had a little obscure ring to it that stopped the stranger as he turned.

"Waiting," said the latter, "is the worst thing I do. You're a busy man; I'm a busy man. You have no time to listen; I have no time to talk. Here's a present for your wife. Good-by!"

The bartender found himself holding a five-dollar bill and blinking at the back of the stranger as it disappeared into the back room. He started to follow — but, changing his mind, he stood quite still, with a rather evilly expectant smile, and canted his head to one side as one waiting for a loud sound. But no sound came. So he went thoughtfully back behind the bar.

Inside the back room this is what the stranger saw:

Two men sat on opposite sides of a small table playing cards. One had his sombrero drawn far down over his eyes; the stack of coin and bills in front of him was imposing. The other had pushed his hat back on his head, and his own stack was not half so interesting.

A brush of two-days-old, fiery-red hair obscured the face of the winner like a sunset glow; his companion was dark as a Mexican. And contrast moved back and forth between the two like the shuttle of the weaver working in dark and gay at once.

Both were tall, indeed, but the bones seemed about to burst through the parchment skin of the auburn gentleman; when he spoke his Adam's apple rolled notably up and down above and below his bandanna. He had a very lean face with small, buried eyes; indeed, his face reminded one of a greyhound's — and he had the same narrow, fighting jaw. His comrade, even taller than he, bulked amazingly broad across the chest, with a bull-throat above it, and a face as solemnly savage as a good-looking image of Buddha; when he stirred the chair groaned beneath the burden of massive bones and solid muscles.

They played silently, earnestly, with a cunning and subtle ferocity of purpose, as though life itself were at stake in the end of the game. And none, surely, could dream that these were those noted inseparables — "Red" Mack and "Pete the Runt" — who for ten years had ranged the mountain desert side by side through labor and deviltry unending.

At the coming of the stranger they turned their heads, Red Mack with a sharp, ferretlike motion, Pete with a surge of his entire, vast body. The newcomer stood smilingly before them, arms akimbo.

"Gentlemen," he announced, "I have been looking for you for thirty-five minutes" — he drew up a chair, sat down, pushed his hat far back on his head, and perched his heels on the very edge of the table — "and I'm as glad to find you as a calf to find his mother."

Red Mack looked at the feet upon the table and then at Pete. Pete looked at the feet upon the table and then at Red Mack. They said nothing. And the thunder of their silence fell harmless and unheeded upon the ears of the rash stranger.

"I need," he went on, "two men who can ride hard, shoot straight, and keep their mouths shut. In other words, I need you, gentlemen. I have work which must be done; you are out of employment; the end is obvious. The only trifling detail is: What pay do you get? These three things must be clear to you."

Red Mack cleared his throat.

"M' frien'," he said, "these three things is clear to me: I like silence, I hate talk, and I hate a crowd."

And his small eyes fixed with much meaning upon Jerry.

"In all of which," nodded the blithe stranger, "I perfectly agree with you. There is nothing which irks me so much as a talking man; there is nothing which pleases me so much as silence; and above all things I detest a crowd. I see plainly that we are going to get along well together."

"H'm!" rumbled Pete. "Partner, we have money; we don't feel like work. That's all."

"Wrong," observed the other. "*He* has money — you are about to have none. And instead of being the end, this is only the beginning."

Red Mack blinked rapidly, and then squinted in surprise at his companion.

"And though either of you have some money now, the little party you have planned for to-night will clean you out."

"And where in hell," asked Pete the Runt, "did you hear we was goin' to have a party to-night?"

"Gentlemen," observed Jerry, "I could tell you a great many more things about yourselves which would surprise you — to put it mildly. And later on I may let a few of them drop. Just now I want to talk business."

Now, the patience of the man of the mountain desert is as long enduring as the patience of the elephant, so that Pete, after brooding for a moment on the feet upon the table, said calmly: "What business?"

"I can put it in a dozen words," said the newcomer. "In a house on the outskirts of this town are two persons: a man and a woman.

Their names are John Scovil and Nancy Scovil, his daughter. Their characteristics are, money. My purposes are three. First, to kidnap them; second, to take them into the mountains; third, to squeeze old Scovil dry. My needs are: two men who know the country, can fight in a pinch, ride hard, and keep their tongues in place. The plan is simple, you are the men, and it only remains to turn the trick."

Red Mack opened his lips to speak, but Pete raised a hand for silence.

"And what split," he said, "do we make on the coin you get from this Scovil?"

"Very simple," nodded the stranger. "I see you are a practical mind, and practical minds are what I like to deal with. You will get what I pay you by the day. What I squeeze out of Scovil I put in my own pocket."

Pete sighed deeply.

"Well," he said, "I'll be damned!"

Red Mack was more lucid.

"Partner," he said, "maybe my beard ain't long enough for you to see, but take it straight from me: I wasn't born yesterday. We do the work, you get the profits, eh?"

"You understand me perfectly," nodded the stranger brightly. "You supply the brawn and I supply the brains. The division of the spoils is perfectly square."

"H'm!" remarked Pete.

"And now," ran on the other, "since we understand each other so well, the little matter of pay. I will give you — let me see — forty-nine dollars a week — seven dollars a day. To translate: *per diem,* seventy whiskies or one hundred and forty beers. And, moreover, I pay in advance."

Forthwith, he produced a roll of bills. The first gleam of intelligence flared in the eyes of both Red Mack and Pete. The former moistened his ever dry lips carefully while the stranger counted — from a seemingly inexhaustible store — six twenty-dollar bills. He tossed three to each of them.

"I haven't exact change about me," he said breezily, "and so you'll both start ten bucks to the good."

Red Mack counted the bills and folded and thrust them into a breast pocket.

"Wait!" said Pete anxiously. "D'ye mean to say, Red —"

He stopped midway in his sentence, for one of Red's eyes closed in a solemn and portentous wink.

"As for security," went on the stranger, rising to his feet, "I know that I can trust both of you to do your work. As for details, tomorrow morning I shall call on you and tell you exactly what must be done. Finally: my name is Jerry."

"And mine," said Mack, "is Mack. And this is Pete. Some call him Pete the Runt."

"Glad to know you," said the other. "As for me, you'll get to know me by degrees." And he turned on his heel and left the room.

"Now what in hell," mused the Runt, "did he mean by that?"

"I dunno," said Red Mack, frowning. "They's something about that gent more'n seems right off."

"And what," pursued Pete, "d'ye mean by hooking up with a damned tenderfoot with no gun on his hip and a callus under his tongue from talkin' foolishness?"

"Wait till we get to our hangout," said Red Mack, "and I'll tell you why."

So they rose, pocketed their money, and retired to their room in the hotel. Pete occupied the one chair and rolled a cigarette. Red Mack sat on the bed and counted off his points on the tips of his fingers.

"Now," he began, "I leave it to you: Does it rain fools every day?"

"It doesn't," admitted Pete.

"And does fools with a wad of coin that would choke a cayuse come around knockin' at your door once a week beggin' you to take their money?"

Like a winter sunrise, understanding slowly dawned over the dark face of the Runt.

CHAPTER IV

Time Up

Early the next morning, true to his promise, the tenderfoot rapped at the door of Pete and Red and stepped inside in response to their call. A cigar of enormous length jutted at a jaunty angle from one corner of his mouth; his hat perched precariously on the very back of his head. And around the cigar his generous smile curled like a wreath of sunshine.

"Good morning, gentlemen," he said. "Here I am!"

"Good!" said the others of one voice. "What about to-night?"

"We shall meet just outside of town as soon as it is dark. Each of you ride to the meeting place separately so that no suspicion will attach. Then we shall ride to the house where John Scovil and his daughter are living. As soon as we reach it we shall dismount and I shall hold the horses —"

"H'm!" said Pete.

"While you two slip softly into the house."

"And what if they's a house full of men, eh?"

"Shoot 'em down, of course," said the tenderfoot blithely. "When you have emptied your guns I shall be behind you to give you two more."

"H'm!" said Pete.

"But," said Jerry, "you will find no one at the house except the two you want. Every other person is riding over to the Falls today."

"That makes it simple."

"It will be necessary, if the girl is to ride with us," said Jerry, "that she wear man's clothes. I have purchased a small outfit for her! I'll tend to her, and you two get the old man. If he puts up a fight — treat him gently. He's our purse, you know, and must be handled well."

"Leave him to me," said Mack. "I'll take care of him."

"All right, boys. Keep your courage up. Depend on me. If we get in a tight place, I'll bring you through. Don't be afraid. When the crisis comes, just keep your eyes on me. So long!"

His adieu left them mute and gaping, but as the door closed behind him speech came to Red Mack.

"Of all the outlyingest, sneakingest, lowest,

dirtiest, snakiest, crookedest, outtalkingest damn fools I ever see," began Red, "he is —"

"The worst, the crookedest, the yellerest —" started Pete.

"Shut up, Pete. I got to talk. I'm bustin' inside. Pete, when I get through with this big-mouthed, white-livered, fat-headed, soft-handed, hard-tongued liar and crook —"

"I'll bust him in two and throw the pieces away," burst out Pete.

"Lemme talk, Pete!" pleaded Red Mack.

"Gimme room!" commanded Pete. "I got enough steam inside me to bust a boiler wide open. And think of me sittin' here grinning like a scared kid while that schoolmarm in pants was talkin' —"

"He ain't a woman; he's worse 'n a woman."

And Red Mack rose and began to pace the floor hurriedly.

The supper which the expert hands of John Scovil had cooked and served — in the absence of all servants from the house — had swiftly disappeared under the sustained attacks of himself and Nancy. For in this one point she was a true daughter of her father. All languor dropped from her the moment she looked a well-piled plate in the face, and the touch of a knife and fork was to Nancy like the touch of his Stradivarius to the violinist.

Tonight she had done ample justice to the meal her father cooked and served; he knew by old experience that her presence in the kitchen would be worse than useless, but when he had finished the work his heart could not but warm with a thrill of paternal pride when he watched her notable inroads upon the food.

She was very graceful, and she ate with the sham leisure of the cat toying with a mouse — she seemed to disdain sleepily, everything which appeared before her — and yet the things disappeared. If her execution delighted John Scovil, her manner made him want to wring her neck.

Mutton chops in geometrical progression disappeared under her negligent gestures. With an absent-minded smile she demolished a side dish of hashed-brown potatoes and turned a towering glass of milk into a hollow shell.

Carelessly she conjured a heaping dish of canned peas and several crisply browned trout into the realm of the departed. Her father watched and then labored in turn. He covertly let out his belt and returned to the attack; and when he had reached the utter limit of his capacity she still went leisurely on her destructive way.

"Nan!" cried her father enthusiastically, when at last a period came to this invasion;

"you certainly do justice to my cooking."

"Yes," murmured Nan Scovil; "this thin air makes me want quantity and close my eyes to quality."

"Eh?" grunted John Scovil, and blinked. But, his curiosity overmastering him, he broke out: "Where do you put it, Nan? Where does it go?"

And he stared in amazement at the rounded but decidedly slender figure of his daughter.

"This rough, active life," yawned the girl, "makes one need nourishment."

"This rough, active — good heavens, Nan —" He rose abruptly. "Well, let's do up the dishes."

His daughter raised her eyebrows slowly.

"I say, let's wash the dishes now, Nan."

"My dear dad," she murmured, "how perfectly absurd you are!"

He stared silently on her.

"Do you mean to say," he said slowly, "that you wouldn't even clear off the table — leave all this mess standing for the cook?"

"Well, he's had his vacation to-day. And you know you say yourself, dad, that we have to pay for the good things in life."

Her father stared into space.

"How long?" he murmured faintly. "How long?"

"Besides," concluded Nancy Scovil, "you know that I always have a nap after dinner."

And she rose and sauntered slowly into her bedroom, which opened off the dining room of the ranch house.

"Nancy!"

She turned, stifling a yawn.

"What in the name of Heaven would come of you if I died and left no money to take care of you."

"I never worry about impossible things," she answered.

"I believe, I honestly believe, that you'd sit down in one place and starve to death."

"Oh, no. I'd send for Bobby."

"You'd marry that impossible young cad?"

"He isn't so annoying when one doesn't listen to his chatter," said Nan. "Besides, he has a comfortable house."

"You'd sell yourself?" muttered Scovil hoarsely.

"I'd be sensible, dad; that's all."

And she was gone through the door of her room.

Her father stood speechless, choking, for a long moment. He made an impulsive gesture to follow her, but checked himself as if he feared for his own self-control. At length he strode to the door and cast it wide.

But the anger speech withered upon his lips.

She lay upon her bed. Already her eyes were closed, and the smile which was always hers as she slept touched her lips. John Scovil struck his knuckles hard again his forehead, and turned slowly back into the dining room.

"Partner," said a heavy voice from the opposite door, "stick up your hands — pronto!"

John Scovil whirled into the face of a leveled revolver held by a swarthy giant. Behind this fellow, another man, with fiery-red hair, was gliding into the room, a broad grin splitting his lean face into two unprepossessing halves. Behind him, still a third stepped into view, smaller than the others — an alert, smiling fellow.

"He's got no gun, Runt," said the red-haired man. "No use searching him."

"You got your own technik, and I got mine," said the Runt coldly. "Get them hands up, friend, or I'll blow your heart out."

John Scovil slowly raised his arms.

"If you've come for money, lads," he said perfectly cool, "you'll find a tidy bit of it in a wallet in that coat which hangs from the wall yonder. Help yourself; no hard feelings about it."

"Shut yer face," said Pete. "You talk when you're asked questions."

He swiftly patted the hips of his quarry.

"All right," he conceded. "Put your hands

down ag'in — but don't try no funny stuff with 'em. I got an eye on you, friend."

"Easy, Runt, easy," said the red-haired man.

"Shut up, Mack," answered Pete gruffly. "This job has got to be done according to the right form or not at all."

"And now the girl?" suggested the third member of the party.

"That's your own job, Jerry."

"I suppose she's in this other room," remarked Jerry.

John Scovil leaped in front of the door to his daughter's apartment, and blocked the way to Jerry, who approached with a large bundle under his arm. The gun in Pete's hand tightened around the trigger.

"Men," said Scovil hoarsely, "what do you want with my girl?"

"Stand out of the way," commanded Jerry coldly, "or I'll have my men tie you up and take you away like a big side of pork."

"I will not move," said John Scovil firmly, "until I know that she —"

"Is due for a long ride, and you with her. Stand off there. Runt, throw this big bum in the corner and sit on him."

Pete obeyed with cruel thoroughness. John Scovil was a large man, and a strong one in spite of his middle age, but he struggled as vainly in the arms of Pete as a child struggles in the grasp of his mother. Seized by one arm and one leg, he was heaved up and flung bodily into the corner of the room. The weight of Pete followed him, and the strong man pinned down his victim securely by sitting upon him. He drew forth the "makings" and leisurely rolled a cigarette.

"This is going too far — d'ye hear?" roared the poor victim, struggling futilely. And he pointed as ominously as his position allowed toward Jerry Aiken.

"What do you mean — going too far?" sneered Jerry Aiken. "I'll do the leading in this game, and you follow suit." He turned to the Runt. "If he opens his face again," said Jerry Aiken calmly, "gag the fat fool. Now I'll tend to his kid."

"If you —" began Scovil in a bellow, but his talk turned into vague, choking utterance, for the Runt dropped his vast brown hand upon the throat of the millionaire and leaned — ever so slightly.

Jerry bestowed a final grin upon the scene and opened the door to Nancy's room.

He did it carefully. The girl must surely have been alarmed by the struggle in the outer room before this, and either she was now in hiding or she had armed herself and might act rashly in self-defense. Slowly, slowly, he pushed the door ajar, an inch at a time, until he heard a thin, small, soft sound, no louder than a whisper, but of a character utterly unmistakable. The lady slept, and she was snoring in her sleep.

Jerry threw the door wide, stepped in, and closed it behind him.

Yes, there she slept, with one arm beneath her head, smiling in her sleep. On the table in the corner burned a lamp with the wick turned very low, yet casting enough light to show the girl to him plainly, and all the curving graces of her beauty. Yet no gleam of admiration came in the eyes of Jerry. He chuckled loudly as he shook her by the shoulder — no easy touch, but such a touch as the hay-press foreman uses to rouse his men at four a. m. of a weary morning. The smile left her lips, but her eyes did not unclose.

"Wake up!" shouted the bandit, and, seizing her by the hand, he tugged her to a sitting posture on the bed.

She stared at him, her eyes wrinkling with a great yawn. Absent-mindedly, she rubbed the place on her wrist where his grasp had fallen. Presently a glimmer of surprise lighted her face.

"Who are you?" she asked, drawing the coverlet closer about her shoulders.

"I'm the fellow who's going to take you and

your dad for a ride."

"Oh," she murmured through a ready yawn. "Is that it? Tell dad I'm not interested in riding."

She lay back on the cushions.

"But I am," said Jerry Aiken. "You're not going to ride because you want to, but because you have to; and the same holds for your father."

"A — kidnaper!" she cried softly.

"Whatever you want to call it. You've got five minutes. Here are some togs. They're for you to wear. Hop into 'em, and be damned quick about it. I've no time to waste on you. Five minutes, or we'll take you as you are."

"Take me where?" The girl sat up again in the bed, rested her chin on her palm, and blinked a sleepy inquiry at him.

"Where we please," frowned Jerry. "I'll turn my back while you dress. At the end of five minutes if you haven't these clothes on, I'll throw a tarp over you and take you as you are!"

With that he turned away and took out his watch.

No protests, no screams, no feminine tears and exclamations. His head fairly rang with the silence. Presently he heard the rustling of clothes behind him, which announced that she was dressing.

Then a little cry: "Men's clothes!" After a moment: "Rose would give her teeth to be in these trousers."

"Your five minutes is nearly up. Have you anything on?"

"The trousers and the shirt. Why?"

He turned. The whipcord riding trousers were still unlaced at the bottom, and the blue flannel shirt was open at the throat. Above it appeared a flushed face and bright eyes under a great mop of dark, tangled hair.

"Look here!" exclaimed Jerry Aiken. "This isn't a masquerade party. Hurry up! Jump into the rest of your clothes."

But she was viewing herself with side glances in the mirror.

"Where did you get my measurements?" she asked. "This is a perfect fit!"

"Good!"

He caught her by the shoulders and plumped her down in the chair. With one hand he gripped her left ankle tightly; with the other he caught up one of the riding boots he had brought and drew it on. He duplicated the work with the other boot, caught up the sombrero, and jerked it into place upon her head.

"The time's up!" said Jerry. "Come along!" And he dragged her to her feet.

"But," cried the girl, "you don't mean to

say that you're going to take me without so much as a single trunk? Without any of the necessities of life?"

She had taken all that went before so calmly that his heart relented. He released the wrist by which he was drawing her toward the door.

"What d'you want? Two minutes to pack one bag — that bag yonder. Where's your stuff?"

"All through that chest of drawers."

"I'll run through it!"

He ran to the chest and jerked the drawers out onto the floor.

"Turn up the lamp!"

She obeyed, and he dumped the first drawer load upon the floor.

"No, no!" cried Nancy. "I'll need every bit of that drawer full!'

"Bunk!" grunted Jerry. "Silks! What good are silks in the mountains?" He heaved a whole armful of priceless lingerie toward the window. "And this drawer? My dear, these aren't clothes — they're fine feathers. What is there that you *have* to have?"

"Very well," she sighed. "If I can only take the necessities, let me pick them out."

He watched her with interest; and she worked now actively enough. Into the little bag which he had designated she transferred one by one from the bureau little vials with peculiarly wrought stoppers, small boxes, tiny cans and glass jars whose colored contents varied through rose and blue to pure white. And from the drawers below she brought out articles of dress — filmy, transparent, edged with ruffles or lace.

"Time's up!" snapped her abductor.

She closed the bag and locked it. Then, catching sight of herself in the mirror again, she changed the angle of the sombrero, and did something mysterious to the broad brim.

"I've been perfectly foolish," said Nancy, "to keep away from broad brims so long. Don't you think so?"

And she turned her lazy smile upon Jerry Aiken.

"Out through the door!" he commanded, frowning.

"Carry that bag carefully, please," she pleaded.

"I carry it?" thundered Jerry. "Carry it yourself if you want it. And now start on the jump."

She obeyed without a word, but at the door she stopped short and then burst into a peal of clear laughter. For she saw her father lying, wriggling slightly, under the full weight of Pete the Runt, whose swarthy face scowled back at her.

"Ready!" called Jerry.

Pete the Runt stood up and brought the millionaire to his feet by the simple expedient of fixing a hand on the collar of his shirt and giving one prodigious jerk. It landed Scovil, gasping and blinking, on his feet.

"Nancy!" he roared. "Stop that laughing, or I'll be —"

"You houn' dog!" cut in Red Mack, who had been staring agape upon the lovely vision of Nancy Scovil at the door. "Is that the way you talk to a lady? Shut up, or I'll jam my fist down your throat."

"Young man," stuttered Scovil to Jerry, "this has gone too far. I warn you solemnly that if you go another step in the matter the full vigor of the law shall be called in to —"

"Kick that old fool out of the room and throw him on a horse," ordered Aiken calmly.

Unfortunately the mind of Pete the Runt was to the last degree literal. He started the millionaire on his way by a thrust from behind with his hand, but he furnished the chief impulsion through a tremendous swing of his stanch right leg. The foot landed with a thudding impact, and John Scovil shot toward the door. Here Red Mack awaited him, and with a vicious grin caught him and hustled him out into the dark of the night.

"Now you," said Jerry, "follow 'em, and step smart!"

There, before the house, stood five horses with the reins hanging over their heads, and behind them were two pack mules, low-headed, flopping their awkward ears at the strange procession which tumbled out of the house.

"But," protested Nancy, as she saw her father lifted bodily and flung into a saddle, "are we to —"

"Get into the saddle and talk afterward," he commanded.

She obeyed without a word, and with surprising agility. In an instant the cavalcade was off at a swinging gallop.

"But," panted Nancy, reining her mount a little closer to Jerry's, "I don't see why you didn't let me — have — my nap out — before the party started!"

CHAPTER V

The Flight

Red Mack led the way. In the light breeze of the night the brim of his ancient sombrero flopped into a dozen queer and constantly changing forms, and sometimes it seemed as if they followed a Hermes, with winged helmet. John Scovil, now fallen into silence, rode at the side of his daughter immediately behind Red; Jerry Aiken followed close thereafter, and the rear guard consisted of Pete the Runt, who drove two pack mules ahead of him.

They climbed steadily up the boulder-strewn floor of the ravine, until they broke out of the deadly darkness onto the floor of a high plateau at whose distant edges the mountains sprang up again, ghostly pyramids against the horizon. They had really cut through the first range of mountains.

Jerry could see the girl with a degree of clearness. The procession began to gallop as they reached the sharp down pitch of a slope, and he saw that Nancy rode well.

There are few things which try the powers

of a rider so much as a hand gallop down a grade. Usually there is much flopping of shoulders and arms, and a great deal of swinging about in the saddle, but Nancy Scovil bounced not at all.

Here and there, winding among the rocks of the slope, the sure-footed cattle pony picked its way like an expert football player dodging his course through a broken field, but Nancy swayed gracefully with the rapid alterations of the pony. Never once, so far as Jerry could judge, did she pull leather, and the rhythm of her riding pleased him like the rhythm of music. Her father, good rider though he was, grunted and swore at the jolting gallop, but when they struck out on the level again Jerry heard the girl singing softly to herself.

Singing while she was being borne away she knew not whither, strange men leading her to a destination and a purpose unknown! Jerry swore gently to himself.

Now the gait settled to a steady dogtrot. Pete the Runt had by this time convinced his mules that they might as well reconcile themselves to the inevitable, and they lowered their heads and jogged with grunts at Jerry's heels. Silence fell over the party.

It may have been weariness which stopped all tongues. It may have been the awe of the solemn mountains about them, or the great, gray arch of the sky overhead; but there was not a sound except the scuffle of hoofs through gravel, or the sharp ring of iron against a loose rock, the panting of the horses, and the inevitable creak of straining or chafing leather. Always the dogtrot, except when a steep slope compelled them to a walk, or when a sudden down slope sent them into a brief, lurching gallop; and so the miles rolled back behind them, and the mountains through which they had first passed became glimmering ghosts far, far behind.

Then Red Mack held up his arm in the gloom, and the cavalcade halted. It was a solemn moment, for reasons they could not name, that instant of deadly silence while Red Mack kept his arm stiffly above his head. And then they heard a musical and stealthy sound. It was like a human whisper at first, rising and falling suddenly, as if in distant, murmured conversation; but presently they knew that it was the noise of running water. Red Mack dropped his arm and turned straight for the sound until they came to the side of a little stream of water.

It was very narrow — hardly a step across — and so shallow that the rocks of the bottom glinted even in the starlight. Far away, on either side into the night, the silver surface stretched and went out in a dwindling chalk mark. Red Mack swung from the saddle; Pete the Runt was tugging at the ropes of the packs. Jerry slipped to the ground and approached the girl.

"Here, you!" he ordered. "Hop off your horse. That's a saddle — not a rocking chair."

"But," argued Nancy, "it's the only place I see where I can sit."

"Sit on the ground," suggested Jerry harshly. "Off with you!"

She turned her head, cast one long glance at him, and then said to John Scovil: "Dad, are you going to sit your horse quietly and let a man talk to me like that?"

"He'll answer for it!" cried her father hotly. "He'll answer for this and for a lot of other things, or I —"

"You!" snapped Jerry. "Close your face, or I'll put a gag in it. As for you —" This was to Nancy, and he used actions instead of words. There was a rock beside her horse, and upon this Aiken stepped, slipped his hands under the pits of her arms, and half lifted, half dragged her to the ground.

He released her before she had quite regained her balance, and she staggered several steps away. Jerry went to her father, who had stepped from the saddle.

"Now," he said rapidly, lowering his voice

so as to keep it from carrying to any of the others, "it's up to you to keep quiet and let me do the talking. Understand?"

Following, perhaps unconsciously, the example of Aiken, Scovil answered softly: "Young man, I am helpless in the hands of you and your two ruffians. But this is not the end of the story. You'll pay for it, by the eternal! I'm a mass of bruises where that brute — ah — sat upon me, and if it takes me to the end of time I'll —"

"Keep quiet and do what I tell you to do," cut in Jerry. "You've made me a business proposition, and now you'll keep it."

"It was a mad idea in the first place," said Scovil. "And the manner in which you've carried out the crazy scheme has destroyed the contract utterly. There is only one thing for you to do. Turn the heads of the horses back toward Comanche Bend, and, when we get there, clear out of the country. That's the one safe bet for you, my young friend!"

Jerry laid a strong hand upon Scovil's shoulder.

"Listen to me," he said, "and let every word soak in to bed rock. You've started this party, and I'm going to see it finished. It's a habit with me to put through anything I begin. I'm going to take you with us. If you'll come of your own accord, well and good. If you won't,

I'll have you tied on the back of your horse and driven. Don't forget it!"

He turned on his heel and strode away.

Two men working with absolute precision and in perfect harmony can accomplish astonishing results, and by the time Jerry finished his brief conversation with Scovil he found that Red Mack and Pete the Runt had already undone the packs, cared for their mules and horses, and were even now laying down the bed rolls. He began to direct at once.

"Your bed is over here, Scovil; and here's yours, girl. Time to turn in, both of you."

Nancy had not stirred from the spot to which she staggered when Aiken dragged her from the horse. Now she protested in her usual quiet voice. "But where do I undress?"

"Bah!" cut in Jerry. "Pull off your boots and roll up in the blankets. Do you think we carry along a dressing room with a camping outfit? Hurry up — you have work to do tomorrow."

"Work?" she echoed blankly.

Her father gradually worked his way closer. Off to a little distance Red and the Runt worked over their own bunks, and their lantern cast a dim, flickering light over the group; yet there was a sufficient illumination to show Jerry the unmistakable signs of interest in the face of Scovil.

"Work? Certainly!" repeated Jerry. "Don't you know that every one on the trail follows the Indian custom? The women do the work, and you'll have your hands full with four men to take care of. Roll in; you'll need your sleep."

Something like a muffled chuckle came from John Scovil; his daughter, after an instant's pause, walked deliberately to her bed and then felt of it carefully.

"It's too rocky and pebbly underneath," she said, "and too hard. I could never sleep in that."

"What will you do?" asked Aiken.

"I'll sit up."

"You will not. Off with those boots and into those blankets, or I'll roll you up in them with your boots on."

A dim light came in the eyes of Nancy Scovil.

"Dad," she said, a little ring snapping into her voice, "are you going to allow this — fellow — to lay hands on me?"

A singular sound exploded in the throat of Scovil. It surely could not have been a choked laugh!

"My dear," he said, with a gesture of resignation, "you certainly see that I am helpless in the hands of this ruffian."

"Speed, Miss Nancy — that's the thing,"

insisted Aiken, and he snapped his fingers.

She drew herself up.

"This is both absurd and impossible," she said coldly. "I shall sit on this rock to-night, and go to bed if I see fit. That is final."

"Quite wrong," announced Jerry. "It's not even the beginning. I'll count to three. If you don't start for bed by that time, I'll help you on your way."

"You mean you would dare to compel me by force?"

"One —"

"Dad, if you're a man, you'll stand between him and me!"

"My dear, I am unarmed. How can I protect you from the scoundrel?"

"Two —"

"If I were only a man for a single second," murmured Nancy Scovil.

"Three —"

"You dare not!"

But Jerry, with neither mirth nor anger, swept her suddenly from the rock, and in the most businesslike manner possible carried her to the bed which he had designated as hers, laid her down, and then rolled her in the blankets as one might bundle up a carpet.

He had expected a struggle, from that light in her eyes as he approached her, but the moment he lifted her she became a dead-weight, unmoving either of hand or foot. A dead-weight he laid down upon the blankets, and a dead-weight he rolled unceremoniously over and over till she was swathed like a papoose. And last of all, he found himself staring down into blank, emotionless eyes which looked through and beyond him — perhaps to the unconcerned stars above.

"Good night," said Jerry Aiken, "and when you hear me call in the morning jump out of those blankets — on the jump!"

She made no answer. Her face was that of a Hindu devotee contemplating Nirvana. Jerry Aiken turned away, when something in the expression of John Scovil arrested him. It was the slow beginning of a vast smile which spread and spread until the eyes of the big man literally went out, and the wrinkles of silent joy ran out and outward like the waves around the stone dropped into still water.

"Aiken!" called Scovil softly.

He approached the older man.

"My boy," said Scovil, "I've an apology to offer. I've been blind — sulky like a small youngster when some one steps on his toes — but now my eyes are opened. Jerry, you're a great man!" And his large, fat hand fairly swallowed the lean brown fingers of Aiken.

"I knew you'd come to in time," chuckled

Jerry. "Sorry I had to let the boys muss you up a bit when we started, but I couldn't let them see that it was a fixed up job."

"Hereafter," murmured Scovil, with an almost tearfully earnest voice, "I follow where you lead — without question. Jerry, I didn't think it was possible! But I've seen it done!"

"Forget it," said Jerry. "Turn in. This is only the beginning. And don't mind it if I bark at you once in a while to-morrow."

"But what's the use of all this if she never fights back? She has no more spirit than a spaniel!"

"Mr. Scovil," answered Jerry, "I'm like death. All I need is time." And he went toward the bunks of the two guides.

They had their blankets laid down almost touching each other, and now they were both half in bed, their boots standing near by, while they sat up and smoked the farewell pipe of the day. The lantern smoked fraternally between them. Two pairs of solemn, disparaging eyes stared gloomily up at Jerry as he approached; but he perched himself jauntily on a rock near by and smiled at them.

"Well, boys," he said, "you've done well. The party is started as smoothly as oil."

No answer.

"And," continued Jerry, "if things keep

running like this, you may be in for a sizable bonus when we're done."

The heads of Mack and Pete turned to each other; silent glances were exchanged; but not a sound from either.

"And so," concluded Jerry, "good night to you both."

He rose, but Red Mack called after him in a guarded voice. He turned back.

"I got jest one thing to say," said Mack deliberately.

"Which is this," continued Pete the Runt. "Be as hard as you want on the fat gent, but don't muss up that gal again. That's all!"

But Jerry waved the warning away.

"Pure bunk!" he insisted. "That's what she needs. She's like a mustang, boys. Needs the curb and the spur at the same time. Oh, I know women. They're an open book, if you know the language they're written in."

"Then —" began Mack, with some heat, but Pete the Runt cut in with his deep voice:

"Let it go. Only, my frien', before you get through with this, maybe you'll want to write a new endin' onto your book on women. S' long!"

"If you have any footnotes to offer," said Jerry airily, "I'll be glad to use 'em. S' long."

When he was gone Pete the Runt muttered in a voice like a groan: "How long are we goin' to stand it, Mack?"

"I got cramps all up and down my right arm from keepin' from hittin' him," answered Red Mack gloomily. "Did you see the way he picked up that girl?"

"And the way he rolled her in them blankets like a sack of oats?"

"Funny she didn't make no sound," mused Mack. "Maybe the tenderfoot is right; Maybe she *does* need to be manhandled that way."

"Ugh!" Pete the Runt shook his vast shoulders with suppressed emotion. "You don't know nothin' about women, Mack. Most like it's your face that keeps you away from 'em — I dunno. But no lady wouldn't holler nor make a noise when she seen it wasn't no use. What d' you think Miss Scovil is? She's got blue blood, I'll say!"

"And she knows a gentleman when she sees one," added Red Mack. "When that low houn' pulled her offn her hoss she turned right around and looked at me!"

"That so?" murmured the Runt.

And he slipped down with a chuckle into his blankets. He knew perfectly well that that glance of appeal had been sent to him, not to Mack. What girl would waste a second glance on the ugly face of Mack? But if the poor fellow didn't understand, why make him miserable? Yet the Runt chuckled himself to sleep over the absurdity.

CHAPTER VI

Desertion

It was rarely indeed that more than one idea possessed the brain of Nancy Scovil. The present ever swallowed up both past and future, so, as she lay in her blankets on this night, she forgot all the excitement of the abduction, and all the cruel and selfish indifference of her father, and all the frank brutality of Jerry Aiken.

She forgot all these things because of the pebbles beneath the blankets. At first they were hardly noticeable, but after a moment or so the hardness began to work through, as though each rock were impelled by a separate and malignant force. With a good deal of difficulty she twisted over on her side to seek greater comfort in the new position, but a new pebble at once jabbed her in the ribs. She wiggled up a little into comparative comfort. But it did not last. Separate hardnesses began to pry at her knee, at her hip, at her shoulder. It called for a continual shifting.

Finally the insistent annoyance brought

back to her the picture of the grinning, happy Jerry Aiken; a little pang went through her and brought in its trail a vague sort of desire to wipe out the fellow's smile. But the picture of Jerry did not persist. She turned upon her back, and all the wide, star-touched dimness of the heavens fell like a coolness about her face.

One of the mules snorted; the familiar snore of her father commenced fitfully and then swung out upon a deep serenade. She knew by dread experience that it was deadly unless one could fall asleep before that snoring began. But presently she found herself looking up among the stars again. They tangled into odd, geometric figures, vaster than thought, triangles with points ten billion miles apart; and the cool peace slid down upon her soul.

She forgot the snoring of her father; the crisp air of the night bit sharply at her cheeks, her throat was cold. The water whispered reassuringly near by, and then, in a wave of star-lighted darkness, profound sleep moved over her.

Only an instant, it seemed, before a voice ran in upon her dreams, ringing:

"Haloo! All up! All up! Haloo!"

Her eyes opened; the sky above her was a vast, transparent crystal with delicate pink and rose hues buried in the glass. She sat up in her blankets.

"All up! All up!" repeated the voice.

Then she saw him coming, swinging up the slope from the creek, his shirt open at the throat, busily plying a towel over his tangled hair. A cold plunge, and on a morning like this!

She grew suddenly and shudderingly aware of a chill numbness which chained her limbs from head to toe. A cold plunge! The thought stabbed her. Then she grew aware of a thousand little aches and pains. Her shoulders and hips and knees ached as if she had been beaten.

"You there — Nancy!" called that tormenting voice. "Out of your blankets!"

Her father, with tousled hair, sat on his bed pulling on his boots. Red Mack and Pete the Runt were already caring for their horses and the mules. She stood up, dizzy, and shook the blankets from about her. All the rest were gloomy faces, in tune with her own feelings, all except Jerry Aiken, and now he burst into a song. Song! It was like a blow in the face.

"All right," continued that demoniacally cheerful voice. "Run down to the water and have a wash. Then trot back here on the double. Breakfast in five minutes!"

Breakfast! A pang of hunger thrust her through, and with moistening mouth she hobbled down to the creek with her toilet bag in her hand. She bent over a pool of clear water, expecting a swollen-eyed, pale ghost to stare back at her; instead, she saw rosy cheeks and almost artificially bright eyes. Very strange!

Her fingers grew numb as she washed in that snow water, but as she combed her hair into some semblance of order the blood began to thump hotly through her veins. The most fragrant perfume she had ever scented in her life blew down to her — it was from the camp fire, where the coffee already steamed, and Nancy Scovil almost ran toward it.

She was stiff indeed, but the stiffness was already beginning to disappear; every instant the freshness of the morning air drew deeply down into her lungs. Her father had picked up a hatchet and was starting toward a dead stump not far away.

"Wait!" commanded Aiken. "Give that hatchet to the girl and let her chop the wood. An old man like you and still working for your daughter? Not on this trail, Scovil! Hey, you, pick up that hatchet and hustle us an armful of wood. Hop to it!"

Her father turned upon her a smile brighter than the rising sun and tossed the hatchet so that it kicked up the sand at her feet.

"Good idea, Jerry," he nodded. "All right,

Nan. Rustle the wood before the fire goes out."

She looked at the rough handle of the hatchet; she looked at the delicate, pink palm of her hand; she stared dumbly at her father; what on earth could it mean? Work?

"I haven't the slightest idea how wood can be chopped," murmured Nancy. "You ought to know that, dad."

"Right enough," nodded John Scovil. "I'll teach you how it's done."

"You'll do nothing of the kind," cut in the tyrant. "If she can't cut wood, she can't eat. No work, no food, in this camp."

Nancy looked strangely at Jerry. She picked up the hatchet, but as some sense of the indignity came home to her she threw it down again.

She said quietly to the leader of the band:

"Mr. Aiken, you have the brute power to abduct us and bring us here; but you have not the power to make me work like a common ranch hand!"

"Look here!" said the Runt darkly to Jerry. "This has got —"

"Do you hear that?" cut in Jerry in a sad voice, and he shook his head solemnly. "Do you see what you've brought your daughter to, Scovil? Proud and idle! What's she good for? I ask you that! To spend another man's money. Look at her! She won't even work for her breakfast — even a common tramp has better sense than that. All right, Scovil, go ahead and get the wood, but your daughter goes without food till noon."

She turned haughtily away and sauntered down to the edge of the water, where she sat on a rock and tried to enjoy the colors of dawn reflected before her. It was not possible that they would allow him to carry out his inhuman threat. No food until noon? No food for a thousand years, he might as well have said, for that spreading hollowness within her would be fatal long before. But it was all a bluff; in a moment he would send one of them to bring her back.

Then, as a wave of sullen resentment boiled up in her, she determined that she would of her own accord utterly refuse to touch food even when it was urged upon her. That was it — a hunger strike! They dared not murder her, and to escape from that they would have to bring her back to some town quickly. And she pictured herself carried, hollow-cheeked, empty-eyed, into some village, at the very door of death. She would do it, if only to spite that unspeakable Jerry.

But, no, her father would intercede for her. That was plain. He would, at least, smuggle food for her, but work she could not and she would not! The strength of her new resolve spread a pleasant warmth through her.

And then — she would not believe it at first — a sound of singing boomed down to her from the camp fire. She listened — she shook her head and canted her ear to make sure. It was beyond all doubt the voice of her father. He sang while his daughter starved beneath his very eyes!

"It's no use, Jerry." John Scovil stood beside his horse after breakfast, with the cavalcade ready to depart. "She's as stubborn as the very devil. It's her only strength. You can't break her will. She'll sit down there by the water till she dies, and never ask you for a crust of bread."

"Will she?" Jerry noncommittally busied himself with his girths.

"Besides," went on Scovil; "Mack and Pete begin to look rather black at you. I don't think they'll stand it if you treat her too roughly."

"H'm!" remarked Jerry.

"Besides," Scovil frowned, "there is a limit to all things, and you've gone too far!"

"You said that last night," answered Jerry.

"By heavens," cried the other, "I mean it, man! I can't let the child starve herself to death!"

"You'll stand more than this before we're

through," said Jerry grimly. "There is some flint in every one, and I'm going to keep hammering that girl till I get a spark from her."

Scovil hesitated a moment.

"If you don't watch your two men, you are liable to strike a spark that will burn you to a cinder," he suggested. "But that is your business."

"It is," responded Jerry curtly. He raised his voice. "Hey, you, Nancy. Are you going with us, or are you going to stay here?"

No answer.

"This is no beaten trail," he continued. "There'll be no other party along to pick you up. But stay here and starve if you will!"

No answer.

"All right, boys, start!"

"By Heaven!" muttered the Runt to Mack. "I think the yaller houn' really means to ride away and leave the gal here to die!"

"Give him a try," suggested Mack, his lips twisting, wolflike, back from his teeth. "And if he really rides right off from her — well, that's all the ridin' he'll ever do!"

Instinctively, his right hand wandered toward the butt of his .45.

The procession formed and started at a slow walk. There was no further call to the girl, but the creaking of the saddle leather shouted to her with a voice louder than any human accent.

She looked up. Before her stretched the cruel desert, and at its verge the naked, blue mountains, scores of miles away. The sun was still young and comparatively feeble, but every instant its heat increased with a promise of that furnace intensity which would scorch the sun toward midday. And not even a shrub under which she could lie to escape. It would be like burning at the stake, but more terrible, more slow. Yet — it could not be that they would leave her!

The creak of the saddle leather grew louder, louder, and then commenced to fade away. She stood up; she cast one look around her.

"Wait! Wait!" cried Nancy. "I'm coming!"

But the slow walk broke into a dogtrot which was hardly any faster; Nancy commenced to run frantically.

Certainly they did not slacken the pace at which they traveled because she was chasing them so frantically; yet neither did they increase that dogtrot, and only one head turned to watch her. It was her father's rubicund countenance which faced her, and she came to a sudden halt, frozen with astonishment, when she saw that he was actually smiling — nay, grinning with inexplicable joy!

It was only an instant that she paused in

her bewilderment, for during that precious instant the cavalcade jogged on several more yards into the lead. Then she began to run in real earnest; a cold, sharp fear had caught at her heart like the dread of insanity.

What had come to her father? It was sufficiently strange that he should have calmly submitted to leave his daughter behind him in the desert, though that might have been explained through his natural dread of that laughing demon, Jerry Aiken, but that John Scovil could actually grin in such a terrible moment was beyond conception.

So Nancy Scovil drew a deep breath and started running like the wind. She had never dreamed that her legs could carry her so swiftly, so untiringly, so surely over smooth and rough. The wind of her running whipped the hat from her head; her hair tumbled down; her breath came hot and fast, and tears of excitement dimmed her eyes.

Vaguely, through a mist, she was aware of John Scovil in his new madness, reeling to and fro in his saddle, in imminent peril of a fall, while he held his shaking sides, and the roar of his laughter blew back to her. But at last she had regained the company, passed Pete the Runt in the rear, and now trotted, panting, beside her horse, which Aiken led.

Through her bewilderment cut his relentless

voice: "Let go of that stirrup! Get back with you and pick up your hat. Do you think I'll let you throw away my good money on sombreros?"

She released the stirrup and stood still, a sudden desire to take him by the throat almost mastering her. But there he sat in his saddle, high above her and grinning complacently down. The fresh roar of her father's laughter thundered at her ear, and once more the company trotted past her.

There was nothing for it but to obey. Luckily the hat lay only a few steps behind her; she regained it in a moment, and again raced until, almost exhausted, she reached her horse once more.

"Stop the horse!" she cried frantically to Jerry. "Don't you see I can't get on?"

"Climb on or stay behind," said Aiken, still grinning. "It makes no difference to me."

Desperation gave her strength. She clapped the sombrero more firmly upon her head, seized the horn of the saddle, and dragged herself up; but when she was almost to safety her arms gave way as if she had been paralyzed above the elbows. Down she came, and nearly stumbled under the feet of the horse.

Her teeth flashed as she cast a glance toward Aiken — the grinning demon — and then she essayed again. Perhaps hate gave her added power; at any rate, she managed to swing herself up, and a moment later her leg swung into place; then a black haze, from the exhaustion, swept across her eyes; she had to seize the pommel of the saddle and cling blindly to keep from falling from her place. And when she raised her head the voice of her father boomed near her:

"Circus stuff, Nan! Ha, ha, ha! I've never seen a better exhibition of running and — ha, ha, ha — jumping. Wouldn't have believed it of you!"

"Very graceful, too," murmured Aiken.

"It was, especially when her hat blew off."

"And when her hair came down."

"And when she ran —"

"Like Atalanta — a regular new Atalanta!"

They rode on either side of her, and when she looked from one to the other she was met by derisive laughter; tears veiled the sight of Nancy Scovil, but when her eyes cleared again she was aware that Red Mack had turned in the saddle and was watching Jerry Aiken with a somber interest. His glance turned to her, and she felt the electric sympathy of his look. It was a marvelous stimulant.

Aiken, too, saw those plainly labeled glances. He fell back to the rear with Pete the Runt and beckoned Mack to join them. He came willingly enough, with a brow like a thunderstorm. They slackened their pace until they were well to the rear and out of hearing of the rest.

"My frien'," muttered Pete the Runt, and he fixed a glittering eye upon Aiken, "you come back here just in time. I was pretty near to coming up to have a talk with you."

"Runt," growled Red Mack, "you and me has got jest one and the same thought, then. I got a whole mouthful to spill to this gent."

Jerry observed them with a slightly thoughtful air. Plainly matters had come to a crisis. Red Mack's hand gripped his bridle rein as though he were strangling a living thing; he slouched a little forward in the saddle, and his free hand was perpetually busy arranging and patting with soft touches the holster on his hip. Pete the Runt, on the other hand, rode perfectly erect. His large nostrils quivered now and again like a hound on a scent, and his great jaw muscles bulged rhythmically as he held some passion in leash. Thunderclouds rolled, manifestly, about the head of Aiken, and lightning was not far away.

"First," broke out Red Mack, and his jaw stood out like that of a bulldog as he spoke, "I got this to say. It ain't any long speech, but they's a pile o' meanin' in it for them as has got the brains to study it out. Partner" — he swung full around in the saddle — "I dunno what part of the country you come from, but I'll lay ten to one that it was a rotten part!"

"In the opinion of a great many people," replied Aiken blithely, "it is."

"I knowed it," went on Red Mack, "because the ideas you took out of it are rotten ideas! Around these parts —"

"Wait a minute," cut in Pete the Runt. "They ain't no use making a long yarn to a gent like him. I'll put it straight and snappy. Partner, they's jest two things I ain't goin' to stand by and watch. One is, when a feller begins beatin' a hoss up around the head."

"Very true," nodded Jerry. "A detestable practice. Moreover, I understand why horses are so tenderly treated out here in the desert. They're very useful."

"My frien'," said the Runt darkly, "which maybe it would be better if you didn't cut loose till I get through talkin' and you have all my ideas corralled inside your head."

But Jerry's smile was invincible.

"The other thing I can't stand to watch," pursued the Runt, as he automatically swerved his horse closer to that of Aiken, so that his own great bulk towered above that of the smaller man — "the other thing is, bad treatin' of a woman, bullyin', and things like that. I dunno where you was brung up, but I was brung up to *keep my hands off a girl.*"

His voice lowered with the last few words, and his eyes filled with an evil light. On the other side of Jerry, Red Mack was moistening his lips with terrible eagerness, and his right hand glued itself about the butt of his gun.

But Jerry nodded to them both with grave understanding.

"You have my ideas absolutely," he said. "Women have to be handled with gloves out here — they're so scarce!"

Red Mack snorted. When he spoke his voice rose up the scale into an angry whine like that of an angered puma which has missed its kill.

"Maybe I'm blind," he said. "Maybe I ain't been seein' you treat that pore girl like a yaller dog all this while? But if I'm blind, partner, you ain't the doctor that can fix my eyes. Don't forget it!"

"Do you mean to say" — Jerry was apparently astonished — "that you fellows are making all this fuss about — that?"

And he indicated the girl who rode before them with a jerk of his hand.

Now, there is nothing so terrible to the man of the mountain desert as a sneer. He meets satire with satire, and mirth with mirth, and in his rage he fears no man; but the hidden deeps of scorn make his soul shrivel like a cut cactus on a hot day.

The heads of both Pete the Runt and Red Mack jerked to the front and stared inquiringly toward Nancy. She was putting up her hair. The sombrero dangled from the horn of the saddle, and under her flashing white hands the masses of black hair fell swiftly into a great braid, glittering in the sunlight, and as she rode, with her arms raised, her body gave with wonderful subtlety to the sway of the horse.

The two heads confronted Aiken, glowering and hostile again. In such wise two stern fronted bulls might turn together to crush a single foe.

"What's wrong with her, I'd like to know?"

"What's wrong with her?" cried Jerry. Suddenly he threw up his hands and burst into hearty laughter. He seemed to have great difficulty in controlling his mirth.

"Do you mean to say that you haven't seen after all these hours — what's wrong with her?"

He was wiping the tears of his laughter away while he spoke; and crimson flooded the swarthy face of Pete the Runt. In his heart of hearts there was an almost religious desire to slay.

"Jest fool laughin' don't mean nothing," he asserted doggedly, and his glance sought Red Mack with a plea for arguments and assistance.

"An' her father sits by and laughs at the poor girl," cut in Red Mack. "Which it looks to me like a put-up job on her, between you and old Scovil."

"A put-up job?" chuckled Jerry. "If it's a put-up job, he'll pay through the nose for the work!"

"What," persisted Mack, "is the reason he seems so damn chummy with you? He don't seem no way put out because he was took away into the hills without no leave asked."

"I'll tell you why he's rather friendly," Jerry explained smoothly. "I was talking with him last night for a moment, and he began to tell me about his daughter. It seems that up to five years ago she was just like any other girl, when one day —"

He stopped short, and caught his hand up across his mouth.

"What was I saying!" he cried. "Boys, I forgot that I gave Scovil my word of honor that I wouldn't repeat the thing he told me. But watch her for yourself, and maybe you'll understand what I mean."

"Partner," asked Red Mack hungrily, "can't you gimme jest one word of a hint? Maybe I'm simple, but I don't see nothin' wrong with her."

"Between you and me," admitted Jerry frankly, "I didn't see anything wrong with her, either, until her father spoke to me last night. But now it's as clear as glass. I see right through her."

With corrugated brows Pete the Runt and Red Mack pondered.

"They ain't no doubt she's different," Red Mack thought aloud. "I seen that the minute I laid eyes on her."

"Me, too," nodded the Runt. "Anybody with eyes can see she ain't quite ordinary. But just where she's wrong — that's the only thing I can't quite make out."

"Gentlemen," said Jerry suddenly, "I *shall* give you just a hint. Have you noticed that she is very silent?"

"Ain't hardly said a word. Yep, I noticed that, all right."

"Except something impertinent?"

"She's sure sassy."

"And that she has a peculiar way of looking into the empty air as if she saw something in it?"

"Yes, yes! Go on," muttered Red Mack, edging closer.

"Well, gentlemen," said Jerry solemnly, "still waters run deep, as the old saying goes. And this poor girl, my friends — is not in her right mind."

"Now, what d' you mean by that?" queried the Runt.

"In a word," sighed Jerry, "Nancy Scovil is crazy!"

"Hell!" groaned Red Mack. "Nutty? Her?"

"Sees things in the air," muttered Pete the Runt, and he heaved a long and dolorous sigh. "Ain't it terrible, Mack?"

"Pretty as a picture," nodded Red Mack, "but I seen that something was wrong with her right off. She didn't have no comeback when she was manhandled. Say, if you'd treated my girl like that, she'd have turned loose a whole dictionary full of words at you and follered it up with bullets."

They both lowered their heads, and when Jerry examined them covertly a moment later he discovered that the face of each was lined with solemn thought.

CHAPTER VII

Jerry Cooks

The air was dull this day; not that the sky was overcast, for the rare clouds skirted swiftly from horizon to horizon, attesting the movement of the upper air currents; but the crispness which is usual in the air of the mountain desert was lacking. The mountains were no longer brown-sided, clearly drawn giants, but instead, dim, wavering shapes of blue which lost themselves against the pale background.

They had intended to travel steadily until noon, but a little before that time they reached a spot designated and planned by Providence for campers. It was a little hollow whose sides cut away the rising wind, and in the exact center of the depression lay a deep water hole with straggling shrubbery stretched a short distance on all sides of it; and there was plenty of dead wood to make a quick, hot fire. So they dismounted to make the noonday halt.

A scene of bustle, with Jerry Aiken firing directions on all sides, Scovil taking care of his horse and Pete and Mack busy with the packs. But Nancy Scovil stretched herself with feline luxuriousness and sat down upon the sand to watch the work.

John Scovil looked at Jerry, and Jerry winked broadly in return and then walked briskly to the girl.

"Are you giving an afternoon tea?" he asked caustically. "Or are you sitting at the seashore watching the waves!"

The dark, soft eyes blinked sleepily up at him. They always made Jerry think of the dark eyes of a cat drowsing in the sun and dreaming, perhaps, of the last mouse it ate — or of the milk it would steal that night from the pantry. The gentle, lazy voice of Nancy Scovil answered:

"No; I've never had any suave gentlemen at tea."

"The next gentleman you'll entertain is your horse," said Jerry curtly. "Would you leave him standing there for two hours with the saddle on his back?"

Her leisurely gaze still rested upon Aiken. It was hard to meet those inscrutable eyes, for she might he contemplating murder, or the dinner she was in danger of missing if she disobeyed — even as she had missed the breakfast — but now she rose and yawned delicately.

"I'll be very glad to take care of my horse,"

she said. "He seems to know his place."

No mockery in her glance as she said it; merely a straightforward statement of fact. She drew up the stirrup and tossed it across the saddle to get at the knot of the girth. She examined it carelessly.

"Hurry up!" snapped Aiken.

"Who saddled this horse?" inquired the girl.

"I did."

"I thought so," sighed Nancy.

"And what's wrong with it?"

"You could moor a ship with this knot."

"You can do your own saddling after this."

"Thank you."

She pulled the saddle from the back of her horse and swung it to the ground. It was a heavy saddle of Mexican work, built to carry any weight and stand the strain of infinite pitching by the most educated broncho on the range, yet the girl handled that mass of metal and leather as if it had been a feather.

Jerry Aiken watched her curiously as the slender shoulders swayed with the weight. There was strength in her, apparently, like the flexible endurance of fine spring steel. If only those chains of contemptuous indifference could be snapped and the spirit inside her awakened!

He tossed a hatchet to her feet.

"Chop up a pile of wood for us. You'll find

plenty of it over in that brush. Be careful to pick out the dead stuff."

There was, as always, the little pause before she obeyed, as if she were balancing thoughts vaguely in her mind.

"No work, no food," continued Jerry.

She leaned with another sigh and raised the hatchet and then sauntered slowly toward the brush about the water hole.

"Victory!" whispered John Scovil to Jerry.

But Jerry answered, frowning: "Not yet. We've a devil of a long way to go before we waken her. Look at her. She moves like a machine that you start going by winding up a spring. What's up now?"

She had struck a single blow with the hatchet and now she stood thumbing the edge of the implement.

"Are you posing for a statue or playing a guitar?" Jerry called angrily.

"Give me another hatchet," yawned Nancy. "This one wouldn't cut water."

Jerry ground his teeth. He said fiercely: "I sharpened that myself."

"It looks like it," she answered.

"Are you or are you not going to chop that wood?"

"I am not. I'm going to break it."

And she made her word good by laying dead branches across a stone and snapping them into suitable lengths with the hammer head of the hatchet. It was a ponderous hatchet, with a blade as wide and long and massive as the head of a splitting ax, but Nancy swung it easily with one hand.

Jerry Aiken watched with puckering brows. He recovered himself, however, at the sight of Red Mack bestirring himself among the cooking utensils.

"Heh," he called, "don't rush at that cooking, Mack, because you had your chance this morning."

Red Mack turned slowly toward the guide to happiness.

"Well?" he demanded.

"We want something more than jaw exercise, Mack," pursued Jerry. "We had enough of that at breakfast. Now we need food."

"And what's wrong with the breakfast I cooked?" demanded Mack.

"Those flapjacks you turned out this morning," continued Aiken breezily, as he kicked some sticks together to start the fire, "had uses of their own, I've no doubt. For instance, I suppose that as harness leather they'd compete with anything that a hungry coyote ever gnawed the middle of winter; but as food they weren't even a good excuse for chewing gum. There's a lump in my stomach where they've gathered."

"My frien'," grunted Red Mack, and he waved to Aiken in formal courtesy, though his jaw set in a hard line, "you can go the limit. I resign."

"Thanks," chuckled Jerry.

He rolled and twisted up a piece of paper so that it would burn more slowly, lighted it, and placed it on the ground. Over it he laid some of the small, dry twigs.

He continued: "As a cook, Red, you've good intentions, but that's about all. That coffee this morning was the nearest thing to lye I've ever drunk."

Here the Runt, in some alarm, caught the arm of Red Mack. His grip was iron.

"Don't do nothing rash, Red," he said anxiously. "You're keepin' hold on yourself, ain't you?"

"I'm tryin'," grunted Red.

"Words ain't bullets," persisted the Runt persuasively. "Let 'em go. This feller is jest a talkin' fool. Which you can get hanged for killin' even fools."

"Look at him now," groaned Red. "He's grinnin' to himself. If I could jest once take him by the neck and —"

"Hang onto yourself, Mack. Think of the easy money we get on this job."

"Is it worth it?"

"It sure is. Besides, don't forget that our

time is comin' later on, Red."

Red sighed profoundly. "It ain't what he says," he observed sadly to the Runt, "but it's the way he says it that makes me want to wring his neck."

Yet, however worthy he might have been, Jerry Aiken set about his work as if he were a past master of camp cooking. In a moment a pyramid of jumping yellow flame rose crackling above the dry brushwood which Nancy brought for the fire, and then he began the real business of cooking.

John Scovil helped him, but his duties were limited to the opening of cans and such servile work; the real effort remained solely in the hands of Aiken. He worked rapidly, as if he were perfectly at home in such duties.

A collapsible oven appeared and was set up over the first fire, and while it heated Scovil built a second blaze, Aiken being occupied in mixing with canned milk two tin pans filled shallowly with dough, and these were baking in the hot oven within five minutes from the beginning of the operations.

The sweet, pungent odor brought Nancy Scovil close. Next, with the remnants of the batter, mixed thin with water, he compounded corn fritters and set these sizzling over the second fire. Bacon, too, began to fry, and, like a trumpet sounding reveille, the sharp perfume touched the nostrils of the rest.

Nancy lounged nearer and nearer to the scene of cookery with something akin to interest flickering in her eyes while Jerry placed a coffeepot over the fire. Corn fritters, hot bread, coffee, bacon! And that was not all. The nimble fingers of Jerry, dexterous as when they flew among the cards, seized from the hands of the admiring Scovil two tins of red salmon. To be heated by frying? Or by boiling? No, no! Aiken lifted his hands in horror at the suggestion of Scovil, and the next instant he was swiftly grating cheese. With this he compounded the salmon and added seasoning before the salmon joined the baking bread in the oven. A feast!

Red Mack and the Runt held thoughtful communion in the background.

"Seems to me, Red," observed Pete, "that we kind of got our wires crossed about this Aiken gent. He don't handle them two fires like no tenderfoot. Why, I figure old Shorty, that was cook so long for the Circle Bar L, could of took lessons maybe from this Aiken. Smell that bread bakin' when he opened the oven door?"

"I did," nodded Red, "but I ain't makin' no remarks till I taste the food. Lots of hosses looks good, but they turn out high-headed fools when it comes to runnin' cattle, Runt."

Runt nodded at this profound truth.

"Like that pinto of mine," he suggested. "But they's something about this Aiken gent. You notice he don't wear no gun."

"Ain't that a sure sign of a tenderfoot?"

"I dunno, I dunno," said Pete hastily. "We got time to find out what he's like, ain't we? But don't go stackin' your coin on him bein' a fool till you see the way the cards are runnin'. Mack, look at that bread! Kind of crust ma used to have on hers!"

One by one the dishes were brought forth. And all together. By some sort of uncanny instinct Jerry had so managed that within the same moment the coffee steamed and lifted the lid of the pot; and when it was removed from the fire, the opened oven revealed the pans of bread browned to an even tone that might have delighted the heart of the best chef in Paris. There was the fish and grated cheese crisped perfectly, over which the cook now scattered a final coating of the newly grated cheese and another dash of seasoning. Moreover, the bacon lay in its tin in lean, symmetrical strips, wavering up and down to indicate that it was crisped to perfection.

They gathered. If a morning's riding had put an edge on their appetites, the sight of the viands increased those appetites to razor keenness. And even Nancy Scovil uttered a deep sigh as she took her place at the tarpaulin which served as the table. Jerry Aiken, the last to sit down, cast about him a final glance like a general about to charge into battle in the crisis, and he smiled with content as he surveyed the expectant faces.

Then he took his place, and he himself served them with the address and the same speed which had marked his cookery. Not only were the portions generous, but they were so arranged that the tin plates did not seem in the least crowded.

Huge slices of the "pone" neighbored heaping piles of the fish and cheese, and orderly pieces of bacon trimmed the side of the plate; while all were grouped around the corn fritter in the center. And such corn fritters! From a deep brown at the crisp, thin edges, they swelled toward the center a delicious yellow. But chief of all, each plate was flanked by a steaming cup of coffee.

You may take whisky and even tobacco from the man of the mountain desert, and he will endure and perhaps not complain overmuch, for he is accustomed to hardships; but take away his coffee, and no money can purchase his services, no force can divert the heavy hand of his wrath. They are forced to drink whatever brand of the drink is set before them, but each, in his heart of hearts, carries the thought of one perfect brand of coffee which he has drunk many and many a day ago — one and one only.

Yet it was not strange that when the Runt and Red Mack looked into the cups which Jerry Aiken had made for them, each thought his old dream was come true again. For the coffee was a dark brown, but so transparently clear, so free from any suspended particles of the ground beans, that they could see the bottom of their tin cup with the golden sunshine glinting on them; and from the cup arose a delicate and yet shrewd aroma that opened the heart.

Red Mack silently, with a trembling hand, poured a careful amount of canned milk into his portion. Pete the Runt cast a glance of utter scorn at his old comrade and raised his own portion undiluted with a baser liquid.

"Partner," he said in a deeply moved voice to Jerry Aiken, "they is coffee and coffee!"

Jerry Aiken nodded and prepared himself for the compliment with the usual foolish smile of the flattered.

"And from the smell of this, and the looks of this," went on Pete the Runt in his rather formal oration, "I'd say that —"

The voice of Nancy Scovil broke in, unhurried, soft: "This is about the worst coffee I've ever drunk."

They looked at her in amazement, and the Runt lowered his cup.

"You haven't even tasted it," said Jerry Aiken coldly.

"I don't have to," went on the purring voice of Nancy, and her filmed glance rested without either contempt or malice upon Jerry. "Like Mr. Peter, I can tell what it is by the looks." She raised the tin cup and tasted the drink. "But the taste is worse than the look. However, I suppose you're used to the vile stuff."

Jerry Aiken could not speak; the others hastily, covertly, raised their cups and drank, and then turned their eyes in a mute chorus one upon the other. Not one of them could find anything wrong with it. To the Runt, indeed, it was delicious beyond words, but it requires a dauntless spirit to praise where others have criticized. It seems to reflect an uneducated, provincial mind.

So the Runt muttered: "Seems to me you're right. I dunno what it is. They's something wrong with it."

"The worst coffee," said John Scovil, with heavy conviction, "that I've ever drunk."

Under these three blows, one after the other, Jerry Aiken sat stunned. He looked about him helplessly, but the eyes of all were lowered toward their plates. And, perhaps to prove that to him, at least, the coffee was perfect, Aiken drank a huge swallow of it and burned his throat.

He was still spluttering and choking when he saw the face of Red Mack as a generous chunk of bread disappeared into his mouth. The eyes of Mack glistened. He ate hurriedly and swallowed in haste, his eyes already speaking while his mouth was still too fully occupied to permit speech. Nancy Scovil, too, was nibbling a corner from her piece of bread.

"That *is* bread!" burst out Red Mack, his voice going out like an indrawn sigh. "Man, man, that *is* bread!"

"Solid, isn't it?" nodded Nancy Scovil calmly. "Good, durable bread. Just the thing for camping trips. But I don't understand, Mr. Aiken, why you didn't do your baking before you started. Your bread would be just as good after a month on the road as it is now."

"Why do you eat it, then?" snapped Jerry Aiken.

"For exercise," answered the unhurried voice. "It may give me an appetite for the rest of the things you've — cooked."

And she instantly disposed of another large morsel of the pone.

"But — it looks all right, don't it?" muttered Red Mack.

"Doesn't it!" agreed the girl. "It has that

advantage over the coffee."

"It's the last time," said Jerry Aiken hotly, "that I'll ever touch a frying pan while we're on the trip."

"It usually *is* better to stick to things we know how to do, isn't it?" suggested the girl, and something like a smile, ever so faint a hint of light, appeared, twinkled, and went out deep in the black shadow of her eyes. "Like cards," she added.

Jerry Aiken, anxious and perturbed, hurriedly broke off a bit of bread and ate it, his eyes going thoughtfully up like a music connoisseur listening to his favorite symphony.

"If this bread is bad," he began hotly, as soon as he had finished, "I'll —"

"It isn't bad at all," said the girl reassuringly. "Not bad at all, after you've tasted the fish. It looks like salmon; it has the same smell; but it's as dry as wood chips. You have a talent for spoiling things, Mr. Aiken."

Jerry Aiken breathed once, twice, and again before he trusted himself to speech.

"Appreciation in women," he observed, "is like gratitude in mules — it isn't there."

Red Mack recalled some of the disparaging remarks which Jerry Aiken had made concerning his own culinary efforts of that morning; he now brightened visibly.

"It ain't talk," he remarked, "that makes

a cook, and words don't take the place of salt and pepper. Anyway, Aiken, you *meant* well by us. They ain't no reasonable doubt of that."

Jerry Aiken glowered in silence, bolted the food which remained on his plate, and retired to a distance beyond earshot. There they saw his lips moving while he walked to and fro puffing on his cigarette, but no sound blew over to them.

CHAPTER VIII

Poker

From this distance, under the impression that he was strolling back and forth with the manner of one wholly detached and oblivious to his surroundings, Jerry Aiken now and again turned an angrily watchful eye upon the others, who still sat about the tarpaulin eating at their own lolling ease. Red Mack finished first, and Scovil second, with Pete the Runt considerably in the rear of these; but still Nancy Scovil ate on, unhurried, leisurely. There remained at last some of the salmon and cheese which she had stigmatized as "wooden chips," and even this she scooped onto her plate and finished it with the last crumbs of the bread.

Jerry Aiken, fascinated, watched her polish off the remnants. He drew nearer, like a bird caught by the eye of the snake. What was there about her? Was all this languor a sham? Was there, under the surface, a mind as keen as the tongue whose satire had transpierced him just the moment before? No; she seemed quite unaware that she had routed him and driven him to a distance. In his judgment, she had not opened her lips since he left them.

The last of the food was gone. It was not gluttony. No, there was nothing puffy or fat or flabby or weak about her. He remembered with what ease she had swung the heavy hatchet in her single hand, and the little grace with which her body gave to the motion of the horse all morning, and the speed and tirelessness with which she had run after them as they left the first camp.

Her eating reminded him of the eating of some beast of prey — some beautiful and dangerous panther which feeds heavily and then has a great reserve of energy which will sustain it through a long period of fast and effort. Or was she not more like some hibernating animal whose nourishment in the autumn must carry it through the lean, cold fast of the long winter? Winter, unquestionably, reigned in the soul and body of Nancy Scovil. She slept a long sleep. But what if she awakened?

That was the point! In the meantime she had baffled and scoffed at him; he quivered at the thought of it. He felt a touch of anger such as none but a man had ever called forth in him before.

Her dinner finished, she raised her head and

sent the first intelligent glance about her, not as one having enough, but rather because there was no more in sight which she could consume. Then she leaned back, straightened her legs, and stretched out her arms. Her head canted back and then a little to one side, and one by one Jerry Aiken watched the lithe muscles of her body curve out against her clothes.

Presently a new inspiration came to Jerry Aiken. Neither verbal abuse nor physical labor seemed to stir in her the faintest flicker of revolt or supply the least incentive to action; but he remembered hearing that no woman can lose money and retain her equanimity.

"Shove the dishes off the tarp, boys," he said, sitting down at his former place. "You have some cards, haven't you, Red? What about a little hand of poker? A five-handed game."

"You mean the lady to play?" queried the Runt.

"Why not?"

"I'd like to," murmured Nancy, "if I can keep awake."

And she covered a long, leisurely yawn. One of Nancy's yawns, indeed, was a marvelous thing to watch, for every inch of her body seemed to tingle with the pleasure of the stretching. It was like seeing a panther awaking from a long winter sleep, except that in the case of Nan Scovil the awakening was never quite completed.

So they knocked the dishes away, drew the tarpaulin taut, and Red Mack produced a pack of greasy, thick-edged cards. It was singular to watch the change of expressions on the faces of the men, for friendship ceases and Auld Lang Syne is not, when poker is the order of the day in the mountain desert.

They sized each other up cautiously, silently. The stolid face of the Runt grew yet more masklike; the small, shrewd eyes of Red Mack glittered with strange intentness; the confident smile of John Scovil seemed ominous; and then there were the nervous, swift fingers of Jerry Aiken as he shuffled the cards, for by the cut the first deal had fallen to him.

"Now's where we knife the tenderfoot," muttered Red Mack to the Runt. "Here's where we sink a prong into that wad Aiken carries. When it comes to my deal, Runt —"

He broke off the muttered communication by saying aloud: "This ain't half bad." He completed his survey of the circle, ending it with a needle-pointed scrutiny of Jerry Aiken.

The slender fingers of Jerry Aiken mixed the cards and began flicking them rapidly around the tarpaulin. His hands moved with such speed that the eye could not follow them, and there was a continual light, slipping sound as the pasteboards flicked from the top of the deck and flashed out in a continuous stream as they showered into place. There were never less than three cards in the air.

The poker face of Red Mack was disturbed as he watched this exhibition of consummate skill, and finally he cried out: "I'll tell a man, you can sure deal, partner."

His bright eyes twinkled as he strove in vain to follow the motion of each individual card. It was the first bit of genuine applause Jerry had earned, and he would have been more than human if he had not responded. A faint smile touched the corners of his lips, he met the admiring gaze of Red Mack with a benevolent glance, and — put a little too much power behind the last card he flipped. The very last card of the deal! The others had fallen like sentient winged things almost exactly in place, building a neat little pile in front of each player, but the last card whirled, skimmed past the top of the girl's cards, and shot into John Scovil's stack of five.

Jerry reached over and pulled it out.

"Sorry," he said to Scovil.

"You have the wrong card," remarked Nancy, letting her hand lie untouched while the others picked up their cards.

"That was the card, wasn't it?" asked Jerry of Scovil.

"Certainly," nodded the latter. "It stuck out

from the rest."

"I didn't see it that way," yawned Nan. "A new deal, please, Mr. Aiken."

The red increased in the face of Jerry Aiken, and then his lips drew straight.

"Do you insist?" he asked coldly.

"Of course, if the game is for pennies," began the girl, "it doesn't make any difference."

He flashed a single bodeful glance at her and then swept in the cards from the rest. Once more he looked at her and his lips stirred over soundless words while he mixed the cards, pouring them together with wonderful adroitness.

"Partner!" grunted Red Mack, shaking his head with astonished enjoyment. "You sure have the hang of cards. I couldn't never learn to slide 'em together like that; I ain't so bad in my own way; but I'm sure an amachoor compared with you, Aiken."

"If you made your living by the cards," suggested Nancy carelessly, "you might learn to do it just as well."

Jerry bit his lip, but once more restrained himself. Fortunately the point of the remark had escaped Red Mack.

"Never in the world," continued Red in his outspoken wonder. "My fingers is too stiff."

"Honest labor always stiffens a man's fingers," observed Nancy.

"And what do you mean by that?" asked the Runt, puzzled.

"Why, Miss Nancy," said Red, "you couldn't follow them cards when he dealt; you couldn't tell whether they was from the top or the bottom or the middle of the pack — they jest jumped out of their own free will."

"That's the point," said Nancy.

"Eh?" grunted the Runt.

"Oh!" murmured Red Mack softly, and his eyes narrowed upon Aiken.

The latter was speechless, but his eyes said many things as he began to deal the second time.

He was more deliberate now. Perhaps his anger made him so, or perhaps he wished to show the crowd that it was an honest deal. At any rate, each card came off the top of the pack with a sharp snap and whirled swiftly across the tarpaulin, fluttering down into place — even at that rate of speed, such expert dealing was a thing of beauty to watch — and the suspicion was slowly charmed from the eyes of Red Mack.

Once more Jerry came to the last card and paused before he dealt to the girl.

"I hope," he said with hidden irony, "that you have been able to follow every card?"

"Thank you," said Nancy, looking away

from him, "you have done much better."

"Thank *you,*" snapped Jerry, and sent the last card spinning toward its place.

It described a low arc, whirling rapidly, with the force of the vicious snap with which Jerry had launched it upon its journey. Straight and true it traveled. But alas! The very speed of its whirling made it descend slowly, slowly, and just before it landed a puff of wind caught it, tilted, and flipped it, face up, upon the tarpaulin, sliding out toward the center. A white spot of rage appeared in the center of each of Jerry Aiken's cheeks; but Nancy Scovil looked far off, and when she spoke she was struggling with a yawn.

"Dad," she murmured, "won't you be kind enough to deal for Mr. Aiken? Otherwise, I'm afraid we'll never get to our game."

Red Mack was grinning openly; John Scovil chuckled. "Of course, if you want me to, Jerry."

"I've put up my ante," remarked Jerry icily, "and I'll deal this hand."

And with set teeth he swept in the cards and dealt for the third time. In spite of his rage he took care to deal with the utmost caution. He almost reached across the tarpaulin to lay each one of the cards correctly and face downward upon its pile. And then, with a last venomous glance at the girl, he looked to the

Runt upon his left to wait for the bidding to commence.

It was an uneventful hand. They had settled back into the silence which usually hangs over the poker table, and the game progressed smoothly, frictionlessly, except when Nancy followed the Runt's example, and refused to draw to her hand. Jerry scowled, and after that the betting was short lived, and Jerry drew down the little pot with a miserable pair of queens. On the next deal — the Runt's — Nancy again withdrew, and Red Mack gathered a lonesome dollar with a queen-high straight. In his deal, which immediately followed, three good hands came out, and Jerry took the stake from Scovil and Mack with a flush.

When the deal came to Scovil, he and the Runt and Mack were earnest for revenge, with Jerry playing with the air of one who is in company under his usual speed, while Nancy, as always, paid more attention to the sky than to the cards. Scovil flicked out the cards with a brusque and businesslike decision.

The hand quickly settled down to a contest between Red Mack and the tenderfoot. The former was thoughtful — very. Not that the stakes were ever high, but it was more or less of a contest of wits, and he felt that the honor of the mountain desert must be vindicated and the shame of this tenderfoot who masqueraded as a bona fide Westerner established. Red Mack bet with a grim decision; Jerry carelessly, as if he were not at all interested in the result.

"Forty-five," drawled Jerry.

The forty-five stood for cents.

"See you and raise you five," said Red, with confidence that his hand was worth it.

Jerry glanced at the growing little pile of silver and seemed to grow suddenly excited. He leaned over. Eagerly he watched the face of Red. It was very poor etiquette for the poker table, and Red flashed a quick glance of scorn toward the Runt.

"See you and raise you ten," snapped Jerry.

Red Mack hesitated. He became more deeply thoughtful than before.

" 'Scuse me," he murmured, and slowly, deliberately, rolled a cigarette. The first lungful of smoke gave him decision.

"See you" — he hesitated, brooding on the face of Jerry — "and raise you five."

Jerry drew a breath of relief, as if he had dreaded that the betting might have stopped there.

"See you and raise you ten," he added instantly, and flipped out the dime.

Red Mack crushed his cigarette to shapelessness between thumb and forefinger. His eyes rested on the little, negligible scattering of coins.

"It's yours," said Red Mack slowly, and laid down his hand with a thoughtful frown. Jerry scooped in the stakes.

"Jest one minute," cut in Red Mack, as Nancy reached out to gather the cards for her deal.

Her hand was stayed.

"Mr. Aiken, they ain't nothin' to make you show your hand. Suppose we do it mutual?"

"Certainly," nodded Jerry. "What have you?"

"This," and Red Mack exposed three kings.

"Too bad you didn't stay with the betting," chuckled Jerry, and he tossed a pair of fives upon the board.

It was the rankest sort of a rank bluff. Now, there is nothing illegal about bluffing in poker, as every one knows. In fact, it provides half the charm of the game and gives the judicious but unlucky a chance to snare the spoils of the game. But the loser from a bit of bluffing always curses his opponent rather than his luck, so now Red Mack leaned forward with his hands tightly clasped together. He wanted blood money for that defeat. He had been defeated. Already he could guess at the grin which was gathering in the corners of the Runt's mouth. And afterward the Runt would have something to say.

"Suppose we raise the limit?" he asked.

"Anything you like," grunted John Scovil, who wanted action almost as badly as Red Mack.

"As high as you wish," nodded Jerry.

"The sky, then!" snapped Red Mack. "We'll see how the game runs when there's real money in it!"

And then he began to wait, silently, almost fiercely, for his cards.

But the wait was long, for far different was the dealing of Nancy Scovil from the lightning speed of Jerry Aiken. She shuffled like a bank clerk telling money. Each card was raised and flipped down separately by her conscientious thumb. Ten times, by Aiken's nervous count, she mixed the pack in that manner, and then she commenced to deal. One by one she dealt the cards and laid them carefully in front of each player.

With her glance far away toward the clouds, she moistened her thumb — abomination of all card players — and went methodically on with the deal. Red Mack closed his eyes and leaned back in a silent agony of endurance. John Scovil began muttering nameless things under his breath, and Jerry glared like a tiger about to spring.

The cards were finally out. Every one

stayed, and the draw was three all around. No big hands before the draw, then, but every one in the game. Jerry began by using the limit in a modest way and wagered five dollars. Red Mack saw it and so did the Runt, and Scovil raised it five. Nancy paused to consult the sky. The rest were merely sunk in irritated, hopeless silence during the pause, but Jerry watched her with a bitter interest, hungrily. If she were drawn into the betting — if she lost — surely that would rouse her. Women cannot stand defeat.

"See the ten," murmured Nancy at last. "And raise it five," she pursued.

Jerry flashed a glance at her and another at his hand.

"See that and raise it five," he snapped.

Sweat gleamed on the forehead of Mack, but he saw the bet, and then the Runt withdrew. Scovil followed by raising ten, and to the crowning astonishment of them all, Nancy raised the same amount.

Jerry hesitated, paused.

"Call you," he muttered at length, and Red Mack sat back, hanging his head in disgust, though whether with the others or himself it was hard to tell. A pile of bills now rustled in a rich promise in the center of the tarpaulin. Silently Mack and Scovil pushed in their money for the call.

"Well, gents," growled Mack, "I'm the sucker. It ain't my turn to show, but there's what I bet on. They won for you, Aiken, but look what they done to me!"

And he tossed down the pair of fives.

"Oh," said Nancy, looking with her first show of interest toward the pair, "is that all you have? Why, my hand is better than yours, Mr. Mack. See?"

And she laid down a pair of sevens.

"Nan," said her father benevolently, "I'm sorry to do this, but you need a few business lessons, and let this serve as one of them. I don't know who you've been playing with in New York, but if you've been winning anything, they ought to be in a hospital for the simple-minded. Listen to me, and never forget: One pair is never worth a bet in more than a three-handed game. Why, I even hesitated with *two* pairs, but they looked good against you and Red."

And he laid down a pair of treys and a pair of nines.

"What about you, Aiken?"

"Wait," drawled Nancy. "I have another pair, dad, and it's better than yours."

And she put down two kings.

"Nancy," said her father, reddening, "there are times when I'd like to turn you over on my knee and spank you."

"Kings over sevens," nodded Jerry. "That's not a bad layout — sometimes."

He smiled with cutting irony upon the girl.

"Am I going to lose?" sighed Nancy.

"It has that appearance," said Jerry. "You apparently didn't need the lesson your father gave you just now, but you *do* need this one: I want to show you that it pays to stay, at times, on the little ones."

"Lay down your hand and let's look at it," demanded Red Mack. "You've talked plenty."

"No hurry," Jerry grinned. "It takes a lot of time for Miss Scovil to see a thing, and I want this lesson to sink home. Watch your cards and watch your chances," he continued, "and when you think you know your company — and feel the run of the cards — then ride the little ones.

"Now, I opened this hand with a pair of little, measly deuces. Think of that! Yes, a pair of little ducats. *But* — when the draw came I got another one — another little deuce. Not much? Oh, no!" He laughed contentedly. "Not much at all, but how very, very small these three little deuces make two pairs look!"

He flipped them face upward upon the tarp.

"Deuce of spades, deuce of hearts, deuce of clubs," he continued gayly. "Look them over and learn them by heart, Nancy. They may help you to remember this little demonstration of how poker should be played."

He reached out and grasped the pile of bills; they gave out a crisp rustling.

"Music, Nancy, eh?"

And he drew them in.

"Three deuces?" said Nancy, who had listened to his speech with her usual blank inattention and faintly parted lips. "But three kings are better, aren't they?"

"Three kings?" cried Jerry. "Who the deuce said anything about three kings?"

In a panic he stared about at the exposed hands.

"Here's the third one," murmured Nancy, and she laid beside her other two kings a third one, the last card of her hand.

"Kings over sevens!" shouted Red Mack, as much overjoyed as if the victory had been his. "Miss Nancy, I'll say you know poker! Kings over sevens!"

"A full house!" echoed Jerry, aghast.

"Thank you so much," yawned Nancy Scovil, "for gathering the money for me."

And she held out her hand.

CHAPTER IX

The Holocaust

Jerry sat stunned, watching her gather up the coin and the bills. There was no triumph in her face or in her actions. Indeed, that made his irritation the more extreme. She acted as if such winning were the commonest part of the routine of daily living. It seemed to bore her to arrange the little stack of bills in order, fold them, and place them in her wallet. She struggled with a great yawn. In fact, sleep seemed brimming in her, and about to overflow her being.

John Scovil made a gesture of despair, and then Jerry rose slowly to his feet. He felt like retiring to a lonely spot and beating his head against a rock, but he knew that he must not surrender. Something must be done — before the girl fell asleep. And already her head was nodding in the warmth of the sunshine. His eyes fell upon the stack of dirty tin dishes. That would fill in the interval while he thought of something new.

"Get up," he commanded. "Here's a pile

of dishes to be washed."

She lifted her dark, meaningless eyes to his face — and rose. Why was her obedience more irritating than any open defiance?

"All right, Pete," continued Aiken, "you can make up the packs while Mr. Scovil and I take a walk around the hill. First we'll see if we can't get rid of some of the lady's glassware — that stuff always spoils the pack, and one of these days it'll be busting and spilling over everything."

So saying, he opened Nancy's bag. She ceased from her labors and watched; John Scovil, noting, indulged in a hopeful smile.

"What's this?" Jerry grunted. "Cold cream! Who the devil ever heard of taking cold cream for a trip through the hills? Bah!"

He hurled it into space, and it shattered to a thousand pieces on a distant rock.

"Perfume — violet scent for bathing — what's it for out here, drinking?"

The perfume followed the cold cream.

"Rouge? Made in France — Maison de la —"

It soared through the air after its fellows and smashed to splinters on the self-same rock. And after it a dozen other little jars and vials flew toward ruin. And still, though he kept half an eye upon the girl, she stood watching blankly and spoke not a word.

"Florida water!" he cried contemptuously, and rising with the last bottle, he tossed it carelessly upon the ground. By chance, it struck neither rock nor pebble, but landed in the soft sand. "What d'you want," cried Jerry sternly, "a beauty parlor?"

For answer, she walked quietly to the surviving bottle of Florida water and raised it from the sand.

It was unbroken, unspilled, and she sighed a little as she wiped away the dirt. That was her only token of emotion as she replaced it in the little traveling bag which Jerry had so ruthlessly rifled.

"Get busy," he commanded. "Those dishes are waiting."

And still there was no protest. Pete the Runt stood with his newly rolled cigarette between his lips, and the match burned unheeded down to his finger tips; Red Mack was frankly agape, his little eyes wandering hopelessly from the girl to her tormentor and back again. And John Scovil was red and shining with perspiration. As for Jerry he bit his lips nervously as watched the girl.

Still without a word Nancy began to clear up the dishes, knocking off her few uneaten fragments into the sand. Then making two trips to the water hole, she brought back first a bucket of water and then a large armful of wood. Soon a roaring blaze snapped viciously under the bucket, and very methodically she rolled up her sleeves from the white, rounded, flashing forearms and set about preparing the necessary suds to remove bacon grease. If she had spent a lifetime in the wilds cooking and caring for rough men, she could not have accepted the labors with less show of irritation. It was like watching a race horse submit tamely to the heavy collar of the Percheron.

Now Jerry motioned to John Scovil, and they walked together around the side of the hill. The heads of both were down, and as he walked, Jerry swore with increasing loudness and steadiness. And he kicked at the rocks which lay in his path.

In the meantime, as soon as their packing was finished, the Runt and Red Mack sat down together and rolled their cigarettes. The girl had stopped washing dishes and stood staring blankly into space.

"D'you see?" muttered Red Mack to the Runt. "Broodin' ag'in. Broodin' is always a sign of a nut."

"It is," agreed Pete solemnly, "and she's the most outbroodin'est girl I ever see. Which I wonder what's the point she's dippy on. She sure has her poker head workin' safe and sound."

"How d'you mean?"

"Well, most of the nuts is dippy on jest one point. I knew a gent once that was jest as common sense as you or me till some one mentioned 'mule' to him, and then he begun rarin' right off."

"Well," murmured Red Mack sympathetically, "mules was designed special to drive gents nutty. But they's something damned queer about Nancy. Gives you a creepy feelin', eh?"

"It's her eyes," decided the Runt, "like the eyes of a dead cow. Makes you feel like tryin' to do something to make her happy."

"Wonder," brooded Red Mack, "if it wouldn't sort of cheer her up to hear some jokes out of the almanac?"

The Runt glanced about in a panic and then cleared his throat.

"Don't you know what laughin' does to a nut?" he asked fiercely.

"What does it do?"

"Oh, nothin', except that they most generally keeps right on laughin', sort of helpless, till they kick out."

"The hell you say."

"The hell I don't."

"Where'd you see that happen, Runt?"

"Don't ask me, Mack. It cuts me up a pile, because I was the one that started the poor gent laughin' that time."

"The first time you ever made anybody laugh," grunted Red in deep suspicion.

"Look at the way she's starin'," said the Runt, "and —" He stopped with a gasp, for Nancy had buried her face in her hands. Her shoulders heaved; her whole body quivered.

"What's done it? Did she hear us talkin' about her bein' a nut?" groaned the Runt.

"God knows," echoed Mack, white of lips.

When a child weeps, it is an outburst of wailing ecstasy that sets it quivering and twisting from head to heels; when a man weeps, there is a frame-tearing, throat-choking quality to it that moves more horror than pity; but the weeping of a woman is a thing of art.

In a way, it is her natural expression. Like the atmosphere, she gets rid of her clouds by sending them down in an easy, gentle rain. Also, when a woman's face is hidden, it is nearly impossible to distinguish her laughter from her weeping. The muffled sounds are practically the same. But to Pete and Mack that musical murmur meant only one thing — tears!

One must have been born and reared in the mountain desert to appreciate how they felt as they watched her; for in that hard country a man may slay his fellow man with impunity, and even with applause, but if he lays so much as the weight of one finger on a woman, he is damned and exiled. And to make a girl weep is equivalent to patricide among the ancient Greeks. Taking this into consideration, the grim glances which Pete and Mack turned upon one another may be dimly understood. Then they approached her. The Runt laid his hand on the trembling shoulder.

"Ma'am —" he began, but a fresh convulsion shook her, and he shrank back.

"Runt," hissed Mack, "what d'ye mean by pawin' her like she was a sick hoss? You don't know nothin' — you never did know nothin' — you was born ignor'nt — you was raised without eddication. Stand back!"

Red Mack took off his sombrero, brushed its rim with one perturbed elbow, replaced it far on the back of his head, and asked: "Miss Nancy, if we've hurt your feelin's, tell us what you want."

She raised her face, and they saw the stains of the tears — strange tears, for her eyes were as bright as a rain-washed sky, and the corners of her mouth were tremulous with something which neither of the men could relate to grief. Indeed, it seemed almost as if she had been laughing until she wept!

"There is only one thing I want," she faltered.

"What?" they exploded in one voice.

"A man."

"Lady," asked Red hoarsely, "what can I do for you?"

"Oh," she murmured. "I don't mean you!"

The Runt came to life.

"She ain't got any job for a lightweight like you, Red. Miss Nancy, if you got any use for two hundred and ten pounds of muscle, jest tell me."

"Two hundred pounds of muscle are no use; I need two hundred pounds of manhood."

Red Mack suddenly took command of the situation.

"Runt," he said, "pitch into them dishes. I'll wipe 'em. Now, lady, you can talk free and easy."

"No, no!" protested Nancy, in apparent terror. "If they were to see you doing my work — they'd beat you!"

A deep-throated snarl came from Mack; Pete was already at work. The sight must have overcome her — and dread for them — because she buried her face in her hands and the musical murmur began again.

"Runt," hissed Mack, "if she's a nut, so am I!"

He turned his head, still busy with the dishes.

"Lady, speak out when you can. What can we do?"

As he turned back, the girl's fingers parted

just a hair's breadth in front of one eye, which peered out at them; then she raised her head again, her face suffused.

"Everything! You can give me freedom!"

She caught her breath suddenly. "But I forget. No, you seem kind — I don't want Mr. Aiken, that terrible Mr. Aiken to hurt you. Besides, I suppose you're paid well by my father."

"By the Lord!" burst out the Runt. "Is all this a put-up job between 'em? But what's your pa got agin' you, Nancy?"

"I don't know — he's never loved me — it's always been like this since my mother died."

"Jest plain bullyin' you?" snarled Red Mack. "I'd like to — Nancy, if you want to bust away from 'em, we'll take you anywhere in the world. We'll leave 'em to-night. Runt, think how they been pullin' the wool over our eyes! Nancy, we'll go anywhere you like and as far as you like."

They saw her breast rise and fall, gently, quickly; and then her voice, low as the voice of a man, and unspeakably soft, made them quiver.

"Would you do so much for me without any reward?" Suddenly she threw out her hands toward them. "Oh," she cried, "I need you so much — both of you!"

"Go take a little walk off by yourself and get quieted down before them two cowardly hounds comes back," suggested the Runt, "and leave everything to us."

"I'll do whatever you say," she murmured, and turned away.

"Look at her!" muttered Red Mack. "God A'mighty, Runt, they been breakin' her heart, them two swine! Look! She's cryin' ag'in while she walks — she ain't used to kindness. That's clear."

But in reality Nancy Scovil had bowed her head and raised her hands to stifle a great yawn.

The moment Jerry and Scovil had passed from sight around the corner of the hill toward which they directed their stroll, the younger man said bitterly: "You win, Scovil. You knew your game, and you bet on a sure thing. I'm done."

"For Heaven's sake, Jerry," pleaded Scovil in deep alarm. "Don't lay down on me! You're doing fine. See what you've made her do?"

"A machine could do what she's done, and do it faster."

"Including poker?"

He won a dark glance from Aiken, who continued: "Yes, I can *make* her do things — like an automaton. But we brought her out here to make her into a human being, and I can't even make her angry. I'd be happy if I could get just one rise out of her, but a shark, compared to her, is a warm-blooded animal."

He paused to wipe his forehead and flick the sweat away in his anger.

"Don't give up, lad," entreated Scovil. "I know it's hard, but there's still hope. If you fail, think what lies before me. It's hard enough to spend twenty-four hours with her; but think of a life near Nan!

"If I get up in the morning with a great scheme for a deal on the Street, when I sit down to breakfast with her I feel the idea begin to vanish away in a cloud of vapor. It isn't that she's merely a burden; she's a disease that's catching. I tell you, Aiken" — and he lowered his voice to solemnity — "I have brought home a party of half a dozen good fellows, live wires, in the hope that some one among them might strike a spark in her, but it's always like dropping a wet blanket over a fire. As soon as she turns those blank eyes on a man his wits go wandering. He begins to stammer; his talk fizzles off into sighs. Jerry, if you leave me, I'm lost."

"Scovil," Jerry replied, "it's dangerous for me to stay near her. If I'm with her for another twenty-four hours I'll be like putty in her hands — or else I'll wring her neck. But,

Scovil, I feel myself going under! When I bully her and look into those empty eyes I feel as if I were beating a dog which kept crawling to me in spite of the whip! Phaugh!"

He stopped, shuddering, and Scovil whispered sympathetically, "I know. When she was three years old I spanked her once, and I've never had the courage to touch her since."

Jerry continued: "When she stood brushing the sand off that damned Florida water I felt like groveling at her feet. Now I want to get to a saloon and get drunk for thirty days. Scovil, to-night I leave you."

The other groaned.

"But don't you see that it's useless to try to stir her up?" explained Aiken. "I know how you feel; you think that that glimmer in her eyes, now and then, may become the real fire of life. I feel the same way, sometimes, as if she were full of an explosive, and the right sort of a blow would make her explode.

"But we'll never learn the trick. Scovil, she's helpless and hopeless. When a mustang won't eat crushed barley you can take it for granted that he's a very sick horse. He'll die soon. When a white man takes water from a Chinaman, it doesn't need any prophet to tell you that he's ready for the junk pile. When a girl won't lift a hand to save her only jar of cold cream, and when she who has been used to having a houseful of servants submits without a word to dishwashing — she's lost beyond recovery. That's final. If a horse doesn't feel the whip and respond, there's no use putting it on the race track. Now, will you do me a favor?"

"Well?"

"Go back to the camp and leave me alone here. I've got to get hold of myself."

The financier obeyed without a word; he was too far crushed to make an answer. And Jerry sat down on a convenient rock to think — or rather, to keep himself from thinking. But in spite of his efforts, now and again he found his teeth set hard and gritting.

How long he had been there he had no way of telling when a muffled voice behind him said: "You!"

He looked around and saw Nancy Scovil.

"Yes, me," he answered, rising, and taking off his hat.

"You're like a villain on the stage," said the girl carelessly. "You're polite when we're alone and rude when you have an audience."

"Sit down, please. We need to talk."

"We do," she agreed. "I've quite a little to say."

And she took the place which he had abandoned and sat with one leg draped carelessly over the other. It was odd that she could be so unstudiedly graceful in every posture. He decided that it was because she was so perfectly without affectation or ruse of any kind. She acted as she felt, and such action is generally graceful.

"I suppose you want to begin," he suggested, "with my politeness off stage and my villainy on it? Of course that surprises you?"

But she replied to his astonishment. "Of course it doesn't. I know other men who have the same silly ideas. They're ashamed of acting like gentlemen when others are around. They show off when they're in company. They like to play the rough man, the caveman, the primitive creature."

She uttered this slowly, without heat. In fact, she was almost smiling up to him, in that dim way of hers. A great desire came to Jerry to turn her across his knees and spank her.

"You think I'm playing that part? The caveman?" he queried.

"Yes, and very badly. Like a small boy imitating the gruffness of an Indian chief. Well, you do it as well as could be expected."

"But not very close to nature."

"About as close to nature as the villain in a dime novel, I think."

He studied her like a picture. She was remarkably lovely, with the bandanna loosely girt around her neck and the shadow from the broad-brimmed sombrero falling across her face. And her eyes watched him steadily, with unemotional, critical understanding. It was a very hard pair of eyes to meet. She had settled back in the scoop of the big rock, her head resting against the rim of it, quite at ease. And her quiescence made him, naturally enough, want to beat down her barrier with sheer force.

"Listen to me, girl," he said abruptly. "We're not balancing teacups on a tray in a drawing-room. We're in the mountains doing a trail."

"Well," she asked lazily, "if we're on a trail why does everything have to be done topsy-turvy? You got a horse for me who moves like a broken-down rocking-chair — all bumps and jerks. He almost rattles every step he takes."

"I know that isn't the finest horse in the world," nodded Jerry. "But cattle ponies, take them by and large, aren't beautiful pieces of horseflesh. Not at all. I got the best I could for you."

He watched her narrowly. He would have been satisfied if she had showed a certain amount of irritation, but she spoke as calmly as if they were talking about the weather. Then an idea came to him. No doubt if he had not been desperate he would never have thought of it, but being desperate he welcomed it as an inspiration. In short, if he could not stir her with annoyance, he made up his mind to make open, blatant love to her. He did not wait for the idea to grow cold.

"One would think, to hear you," she was saying, "that the whole trip was planned to make me comfortable."

He replied instantly. "And you'd laugh if I said that was exactly how it was planned."

"I might smile, at least," yawned the girl. She regarded him like a distant landmark. "For instance, bad cooking is bad cooking, but yours is torture."

Jerry swallowed hard.

"Admit that it's bad cooking, and that I'm the worst cook in the world —"

"I do admit it, without an argument," she nodded. "Well?"

It was a shrewd blow, even to the impetuosity of Jerry, but he nerved himself to go on. Indeed, now that he had committed himself to the new experiment, it was not altogether unpleasant. He studied the curve of her throat. It was quite small, perfectly rounded, and showed very white and soft against the flaming bandanna.

The line of the chin curved with delicate precision, an infinite promise of refinement. Just then the lowered brim of the sombrero shut out the rest of the face, and he caught himself craning his neck to peer at it. He felt his thoughts wander, swiftly, and he had to use an almost physical effort to bring himself back to his argument.

"If the horse is bad, if the cooking is bad, those are faults I can't help. The truth is, I'm trying my best for you."

"By breaking up my things, smashing jars and so forth? You've a rare way of trying."

"Do you think I'm a hard-handed bully?" he asked hotly.

"Aren't you? Is that just your stage part?"

"Girl!" he cried suddenly. "I'm through with all this palaver and nonsense. I'm going to talk straight from the shoulder to you — and you're going to listen!"

He could not see her eyes under the hat. It was well for Nancy that he could not. For the lids opened suddenly, and a light gleamed in them. It required a conscious effort for her to make them droop idly again. She looked up in his face and covered a yawn carefully.

"There's no way for me to escape from it. I suppose I have to listen."

"No way in the world for you to escape. You've got to hear."

"Very well, then, I'll listen."

She gestured him to go on, and he noted the hands as they flashed in the sun and then lay motionless. They were very slender, the fingers rounded and tapering delicately to pink-and-white nails. His glance, for comparison, rested on his own paws — hard, lean, brown, sinewy. One grip of them would crush her hands to shapelessness. And yet, he remembered the ease with which she had swung the heavy hatchet, the grace and tirelessness of her riding. Somewhere in her body there was a reserve of energy. He felt a thrill pass through him. It was not all acting now.

"Forget what I've done. You haven't understood. Now I'll tell you straight. I made up my mind when I first saw you to get you away from your old life and into a new life — my life. Understand? You've been housed. I've got you out into the open. Look around you. Everything is strong. Look at that bush. The hottest sun in the world can't kill it. Look at that mountain — see the way it jumps into the air. Doesn't it make you want to raise your head and shout?"

She glanced at it covertly.

"I'm able to restrain myself," she answered. But she dared not let him see her eyes.

"You are now," he rushed on, "but it's all soaking into you, whether you know it or not."

He began to walk up and down, working himself into a passion, and when his back was turned, the girl stole covert, wondering glances.

"You'll begin to want freedom and action. You'll have to have it. You can't breathe this air without having it change the quality of your blood."

"Really?" she drawled.

And her heart leaped.

"I don't care what you say or what you think — if you think at all. I'll do your thinking for you. That's why you're here."

"That's interesting."

"You'll find it interesting before I'm through with you."

He was behind her now, leaning close. She felt him lean as though she had eyes in the back of her head. And her pulse quickened in that surprising manner. With all her might she steeled herself against it, but she felt the change. It was like the stir of new, awakened life.

"You'll fight against it — in your own sleepy way. But you can't help yourself. Do you suppose I would have gone to all the trouble if I hadn't been sure of the result? Do you suppose I'd waste my time for nothing? Girl, this big country, these mountains, this air, these vast, starry nights, are all doing my work for me."

A ring came in his voice. "They're getting you ready."

She wanted to cry out, excited, "For what?" but she kept a firm grip on herself with greater and greater effort. She sat perfectly still, her hands clenched together.

"They're getting you ready for me! Some women can't stand it. They wither like hot-house flowers. But you can. The metal is in you. And I'm going to strike it and make a ringing go through your soul."

He gained confidence as he talked — perhaps because he was behind her. He leaned closer, his breath coming fast, and then he caught the sense of her, all the indefinable, sweet, keen thing, which is femininity.

"You can struggle against it, but everything works for me. The winds speak for me; the stars talk for me; they find you out like eyes. They tell me what you are. It's like a river. It picks you up. It carries you along. It sweeps you through the mountains and the plains. It carries you toward the ocean. Do you understand? It brings you down to love! It opens your heart, and you're conscious of love like a man when the ocean bursts on his eyes."

She prayed silently that the beating of her heart was not making her whole body tremble.

"Tell me," he commanded. "Do you think you can hold out against me? No, you don't have to answer. I want you; I'm going to have you — in spite of hell! Look at me, girl!"

And then she knew that he was leaning over to look into her face, and she knew that she dare not let him see her eyes. With a great effort she closed the lids, let her lips part naturally, and began breathing deeply, regularly.

And when Aiken looked, he found all the semblance of deep and perfect sleep.

He sprang to his feet and at the same time she opened her eyes and sat up, rubbing the sleep carefully away from them.

"You talk really very well," she said.

CHAPTER X

Jerry Starts

Which sufficiently explains why Jerry strode back to the camp with long steps and a down-bent head. He started the cavalcade going with sharp commands.

Scovil, grave with anxiety, reined his horse close.

"Aiken!" he pleaded, guarding his voice so that no one else could possibly hear.

Jerry slowly turned his head.

"What happened?"

"Nothing," Jerry laughed viciously. "Absolutely nothing. And to-night you can go on with your trip alone."

But as they rode across the sand-littered, naked hills, there was so much ready obedience in the girl that Jerry almost changed his mind. Not once did she loiter, and now and then she asked questions of Pete or Red with something approaching interest. Only when the sun reached its hottest did she begin to droop and drowse in the saddle, and to talk to her was to talk to an equestrian statue. At dusk they made a dry camp.

Jerry, usually bubbling with life and humor, was now silent, sullen; and merry John Scovil wore a thunderous frown as he lumbered about. The Runt and Red, however, were not still for an instant. They sang snatches of cowboy songs — weird songs to weird music; they called cheerily to each other; they even conversed with fluent good nature with the mules.

Jerry had no word for any one. He would not even harry Nancy Scovil in his customary fashion, but sullenly occupied himself in undoing the packs and distributing their contents. It was during this work that the catastrophe happened. Out of the pack he produced Nancy's traveling bag and tossed it toward her. It landed with a true aim upon the surface of a flat rock and there was a sharp sound of splintering glass. The last of the Florida water was gone, and the girl drew the shattered remnants from the bag. Every inch of the bottle was broken and every drop of the stuff gone.

Jerry stood as if he had been struck fairly in the face. He regarded not the evil scowls of Runt and Mack, but he stared as if fascinated squarely at Nancy Scovil. She turned on him and flipped the neck of the bottle to his feet.

"A souvenir," she said calmly, "for an awkward man. You ought to work in a china shop, Mr. Aiken."

"Nancy," said Aiken suddenly, "I want to tell you that — that —"

"Jerry!" cut in Scovil.

Aiken started, raised his head, and, like one aroused from a trance, moved away. He did not speak for a long time, but seemed to brood in his silence. Once he met the dark, meaningless eyes of the girl, and he turned away with a shudder.

To shut out the thought of her he began to talk with Red Mack.

"Sort of an empty desert, Red," he remarked.

The latter grunted.

"We seem to be in the middle of nothing," continued Jerry.

"That's the way the range seems most generally to a tenderfoot," answered Mack. " 'S a matter of fact, Number Ten ain't so far away across the hills."

As he waved in that direction, Jerry moved thoughtfully away. He began to care for his horse and, after hobbling it, slapped it heavily on the hip. The animal moved slowly up the ravine away from the camp. So hobbled, even if it worked away in a straight line and did not wander, it could not move more than half a mile from camp before morning. Now it wound off among the hills and was soon out of sight.

The finest efforts of Red Mack and the Runt, in the meantime, went to the cooking of supper, a masterpiece to which Nancy Scovil did such ample justice that the two beamed upon her. But Scovil and Aiken ate in silence, and shortly after the meal the whole party was wrapped in their blankets. It was the first time during the entire trail that Nancy Scovil had not had to lift her hand when work was in progress.

Jerry lay wide awake, listening to the breathing of the others and waiting for the absolute dark. And as he lay there, he began to think and remember. At first he had planned simply to slip away, as he had threatened Scovil, but lying there in that utter silence he remembered those dark, expressionless eyes of Nancy. Yes, they would haunt him many and many a day thereafter.

If he could rouse one spark of life in them, one human flicker of interest, he might be able to resign them to oblivion — they and their owner with them. Otherwise, she would remain an enigma, calling him back to her like a voice. In truth, he had spoken something more than pretty lies to her that afternoon. What could, for instance, make her smile?

And then the great idea came to him. It

was so foolish that he flushed even in the darkness; but he knew that he would carry it through.

It was not destined to be a dull night, for as the reds and yellows of sunset melted away to a deep purple, the moon floated up and rolled a thin, golden edge across the lower hills. It lifted and lifted, to the eyes of Jerry Aiken, still apparently retaining the spinning motion with which it had seemed to wheel up out of the sunset. Now it lost the red tinted gold and faded to yellow, and at last to a metallic white like burnished steel.

It changed the rolling desert to an astonishingly lifelike semblance of the ocean with frozen waves. For the moon glittered on the summit of each swell of ground and deep shadows filled the troughs between. To Jerry Aiken, lying upon his elbow, it would not have been surprising if the desert had slid into fluid motion.

There was no use waiting for darkness which would not come. By the breathing he could tell that the party slept.

Presently he slipped cautiously from his blankets and picked up his saddle. He paused, then, and surveyed the sleepers once more, but not a head raised to watch him. So he stepped off into the night, walking cautiously, lest his foot dislodge a pebble and send it rattling down a slope.

His horse was even closer to the camp than he had hoped, but at such a distance that it would not neigh to the other horses when he rode away. He saddled quickly, swung into his place, and then jogged slowly across the hills. In a few minutes he was safely beyond all hearing from the camp, so he touched the nag with his spurs and galloped swiftly for Number Ten.

No one knew the why or wherefore of Number Ten. As a town it was an anomaly — its like was not, even in the mountain desert where so many anomalies thrive. Lumber, cattle, railroad, mines, health resorts — none of these were the bases around which the life of the town grouped itself. On either side the tall, naked hills skidded down to a narrow plain — a mere gully of sand — and in the center of this gully stood Number Ten.

If it did not thrive, neither did it fail. It was, in fact, one of those points where the myriad loose-flung lines of desert trails crossed, for no good reason. And if cattle, lumber, mines, health resorts and railroads gave no visible support to its existence, yet they all contributed. They all existed on the edge of the circle of which Number Ten was the center, and consequently travelers continually came to and fro and stayed in Number Ten only long enough to eat, drink, sleep, curse, and pass on.

Sometimes, in boom days, five hundred people were known to have flooded its flimsy shacks. Sometimes the population dwindled to a paltry dozen — storekeeper, blacksmith, hotel proprietor, gambler, *et cetera.* Women were not in Number Ten, for women only go where a population can strike root, and the roots of Number Ten could only slide trough three feet of unprofitable, waterless sand before they struck solid rock. To be sure, sometimes worn females, with hard hands and souls still harder, drifted into Number Ten, but they soon drifted out again.

Yet Number Ten persisted. It would not die.

It gained its name in a way typical of the mountain desert. There is a saying, concerning desolate places, that they are only ten steps from hell, and some one passing through the little village said that this was the tenth step; hell was just around the corner or all signs failed. A remark so poignant could not be allowed to die. It was taken up by word of mouth, and then it was made immortal on the sign in front of the hotel:

NUMBER TEN.

There was at least one feature Number Ten of which it was justly proud, and that was its marshal. To be sure, that was not altogether unique. Many a town could boast of having seen a Federal marshal at work, but there were few, indeed, who could claim a United States marshal as their sole and peculiar property. Yet this was the case with the huddle of shacks called Number Ten.

Those rapid travelers who paused in Number Ten very often had a reason for traveling across the waste of desert which stretched on all sides of the town; and very often steel flashed in Number Ten, and guns spoke when the travelers met and clashed.

In this center of trouble there was one point where danger concentrated. As the marshal often said, "If this town is the last step toward hell, then hell itself must be in Grogan's place."

Grogan's place was the saloon and gaming hall. And Grogan did not mind at all what the marshal said. He had seen too many marshals. Their average life in Number Ten was eight months. And so Grogan paid no heed to the remarks of such creatures of a day.

This marshal, Bud Levine, had already persisted in Number Ten for a full six months, which meant that his time of life was not long; and some license must be allowed to men about to die. Marshal Bud Levine himself was as fully aware as any one that his time was about overstayed, but he was one of those half-resolute, half-laughing fellows who take things as they come and work instead of worry. He never cast a suspicious eye of surveillance upon new arrivals in Number Ten. He waited for trouble instead of hunting for it; and he never waited through very long intervals.

Sometimes it was a gunman fleeing from a ranch who reached Number Ten a hair's breadth before his pursuit and took and gave toll in the single, sandy street. Sometimes a card sharp from the mining town carried his wares across the desert and thumbed the card-boards at Grogan's until a keen eye detected a cheat and a smoking gun gave witness of the detection in a short, sharp voice. Sometimes lone riders, silent, gentle men, reached Number Ten and were driven amuck by red-eye or ennui.

But every little while death came grinning through the street of Number Ten and knocked at the door of the marshal, and he got up and answered the call and came back alive, knowing that each time he had used up one more chance of life — had gone one step nearer to his own doom.

Into this town Jerry Aiken rode in search of — Florida water!

He went, of course, to the only place where it could possibly be found, the general merchandise store. It was a roomy shed, unpainted, the roof beginning low at the front and sloping up gradually toward the back, so that the structure looked like the beginning of some more pretentious building.

It was not many years old, but sand storms and pelting hail in winter had already riddled it, and the keen sun of the mountain desert had warped and bulged the boards until it looked as if there were some fluid mass inside the place, taxing its strength to the utmost. Every post and every angle of the walls leaned back and back. Some day that store would collapse like a house of cards.

It was for the sign, "General Merchandise" that Jerry looked as he swung down the last pitch from the hills and entered the single street of the town. Entering the level, he eased his horse to a walk.

It was all very quiet and very dark. The moon had blown behind a thick drift of cloud, so that even this illumination failed him, and Jerry squinted carefully at every shack, for fear he might override his mark. But there was not the twinkle of so much as a match in any of the places he passed.

The little shacks crouched away in the darkness as though they were conscious of their own squalor. No sign of life reached Jerry, except the reek of his sweating horse, and the steady, rhythmic creaking of the straining saddle leather. For the rest, he caught the sharp, alkali scent of the desert, as keen as if he were a thousand miles away from any human habitation. Nothing to greet him! Not that unspeakably cheerful perfume of frying bacon; not the wail of a child, with all its comfortable suggestions of feminine tenderness and feminine comfort; not the full-throated laugh of a man; not the sharp, quick voices of gossiping women, not even the whine or howl of a dog.

All was silent; all was hushed and waiting until he had passed half the length of the street, and then he came upon one spot of light, which shone through the open door of the general merchandise store. No mistaking its identity even in that first glance into the interior. He swung from his horse with a sigh of relief, tossed the reins over the animal's head, and entered.

He found the usual array within. There on one side were the groceries, heaped on the floor and piled upon shelves, sacks of flour and of meal, and a bright host of canned goods. Just opposite were the leather goods, saddles, bridles, harness of several kinds, whips, *et cetera,* and on tables between were heaped shirts and overalls and hats. Somewhere in those dark corners to the rear, he knew, there were firearms; and other nooks and crannies might yield an unbelievably varied stock.

The general merchandise man gathers his wares from a thousand sources. Sales agents, traveling peddlers and others of their ilk supply part of the stock, and other parts are pawned goods, and a great deal, in this particular store, consisted of the goods of people who had left Number Ten suddenly, in far too much haste to gather their effects before they departed. These things old "Baldy Matt" was usually able to purchase from the hotel or the marshal for a song.

Baldy himself tilted his chair forward with a bang when Jerry entered. His baldness began at his forehead and stretched back in a smooth and shining red to the nape of his neck, broken only by a tuft of stiff white hair, which stood up in the exact center of the baldness, like the scalp lock of an Indian. From the sides of this scalped head the ears thrust out sharply, round as the ears of a bear, and lobeless. And between the ears was a round, red face, with little keen eyes and a shapeless nose squatted in the center.

Long sitting and much eating had altered the once slender form of Baldy. Beginning with his shoulders his body rippled out to a heavy paunch; and when he stood up, his long, thin legs gave him the seeming of a short, fat old man walking upon stilts. He smoked a black pipe with the stem bitten away almost to the bowl.

" 'Evening," Jerry nodded to this grotesque.

" 'Evening," answered a husky voice.

Baldy made no effort to rise and ask the wishes of his presumptive customer.

"You have a pretty quiet town here," went on Jerry.

"In spots it's quiet, and in spots it's noisy," stated the husky throat of Baldy.

"Not even a dog in the street when I came through just now," pursued Jerry amiably, and he leaned an elbow on a pile of overalls.

Baldy turned his head with some effort on the short, thick neck and observed carefully that there was no palming of one of those suits of overalls. Stranger things than that had happened in his store. He took note now that the stranger wore no gun. This was odd.

"No," he answered at length, "which it ain't particular a healthy town for dogs."

"Any news, partner?"

"Nothin' particular. Old Jenkins died last week."

"Yeh? How old?"

"Ten years younger'n me," said the antique.

"How'd he die?"

"Shot."

"Is that so? Did they get the fellow who did the shooting?"

"Right over there."

"Eh?"

"You're standing on the spot."

Jerry looked down to a broad, ragged-edged stain on the floor. He stepped cautiously away, like a cat coming out of water.

"Bud got him," pursued Baldy. "Took two shots. Only winged him the first time and had to shoot ag'in to finish him. Bud is slowin' up considerable with his gun."

"H'm!" murmured Jerry. "Any other news?"

"Nothin' much. Two gents was bumped off week before last."

"Here?" grinned Jerry.

"Nope," answered the unperturbed old man. "On the verandy."

He nodded.

"I could see 'em drop right from this here chair without even gettin' up."

"H'm!" murmured Jerry again. "Any other news?"

"Not recent," answered Baldy. "Things is pretty slow around here lately."

Jerry drew a long breath and expelled it with a low whistle.

"I'd like to be around for a week or two when things are really booming," he remarked. "Where's everybody to-night?"

"Where they always are," answered Baldy. "Up the other end of town in Grogan's."

"I'll be getting on, then. But, first, have you any perfume in your store?"

CHAPTER XI

The Battle

If he had rolled a bomb with fizzing fuse toward Baldy he could not have created a greater disturbance. The little eyes bulged; a puff of white smoke arose from the bowl of the pipe.

"Which you might be speakin' to me?" asked the dazed Baldy.

"Yep. Have you any perfume? Florida water is what I want."

Baldy rose from his chair and removed his pipe, a sign of emotion which no shooting scrape he had ever witnessed could elicit from him.

"Florida water!" he gasped.

"Right. Or if you haven't that — any sort of sweet-smelling stuff might do. Even a jar of cold cream would be welcome to me."

"Cold cream!" groaned Baldy. He put his hand to his forehead after the manner of one who has received a heavy blow.

"They was a woman in town once," he said. "She went out sort of hurried and I got a pile of her junk. Maybe —"

He led the way to the darkest corner of the store and held up his lantern to illumine a dusty shelf. There stood a short array of bottles. He peered close and read the titles aloud:

"Hair tonic; corn cure; Brilliantine —"

He stopped in his reading and faced Jerry with a sudden understanding on his face.

"If it's drinkin' stuff you're lookin' for, sort of abbreviated redeye," he said, "I c'n tell you this ain't the right stuff. I've tried 'em all."

"No," answered Jerry. "Not drinking stuff. Go on."

"Henna," continued the storekeeper, "Florida water —"

"Here!" cried Jerry gayly. "Fork it over, partner."

"How much of it?"

"Have you more than one bottle?"

"Two of 'em."

"One will do me."

Baldy straightened, and brushed the cobwebs off the bottle.

"How much?" asked Jerry.

"I dunno. Looks like pretty old stuff, don't it?"

He peered at it closely, squinting his eyes.

"They ain't no date or gov'ment stamp on it," he mused, "but it ought to be ten years old. I've had it five. A dollar a year. Five dollars too much, stranger?"

"Steep, but not too much. Give it to me."

He slipped a bill into the storekeeper's hand, and hurried out into the night. He was very happy now. He waved adieu to Baldy, who stood with stunned face at the door watching the departure of his guest, and trotted his horse up the street.

"He looks like a man," muttered Baldy. "He talks like a man; he rides like a man; but he ain't got a gun and he uses — Florida water!"

He shook his head.

"Things is changed a pile in Number Ten," sighed Baldy. "Pretty soon they'll be havin' women and babies in here and they won't be no peace."

But in the meantime Jerry went singing up the street. He had in mind the face of the girl when she should receive the Florida water. If she were feminine — if she were even human — that face must register some emotion when that happened. And he felt that there might, after all, be some reward for his labors. But first there was a long ride back across the hills, and he wished to fortify himself against the trip.

The noise of Grogan's came out to meet him on the way and usher him in, so to speak. It consisted of a deep, humming undertone, split here and there by a sharp curse, a single, loud laugh, and once by the tinkling crash of broken glass.

As he jogged closer to the splotch of yellow light which sprawled across the street from Grogan's door, he made out a cluster of horses ranged on either side, and even placed across the road. With the latter he left his own mount and strolled carelessly into Grogan's with the weight of the Florida-water bottle tugging at his right hip pocket and a light conscience buoying up his heart.

Grogan's consisted of one low, long, rectangular room with a bar stretching along one side, a round stove in the middle, and chairs and tables scattered throughout the remainder. A roulette wheel winked and hummed in one corner; and another table was set apart for chuck-a-luck. The other tables were given over chiefly to dice and poker.

At Jerry's entrance there were few indeed at the tables, for a sandy-haired man had made big winnings at the roulette wheel and was correspondingly filled with good will to the world. He had already enjoyed more than his portion of redeye, and now he stood at the middle of the bar, slapping both hands upon it, one of them jammed full of greenbacks.

"Let her run, Grogan," he bellowed to the big man behind the bar, who was now spinning glasses down the board with uncanny dexterity, so that each whirled into place directly before its destined user. "Let her run. Fill 'em up as many times as they can belly up to the bar. Hey, you!"

He had seen Jerry enter the room and stand a moment to take stock of his surroundings.

"Step up, stranger, and liquor."

Jerry obeyed with a willing grin, a glass spun before him, a tall, black bottle came to a halt beside it, with the contents awash within. He stood next to the man who was standing treat.

"Up with her, boys," called the sandy-haired man, "and then down to the bottom."

A score of glasses flashed; a score of glasses tilted; a score of glasses glittered empty and clattered down against the bar.

"Fill 'em up ag'in," roared Sandy. "To-night, gents, I aim to irrigate Number Ten and get her wet from her toes to her eyebrows. What d'ye say, partner?"

He emptied a whisky bottle above his glass, and whirled it around his head.

"More booze, Grogan. Me and my frien' ain't hardly got a drop. Have we, partner?"

With the empty bottle he playfully slapped Jerry across the hip, at that portion of his body where the heavy bottle was surest not to hurt him. But under the blow there was a very definite, distinct crash and crunch of glass.

"Blast me!" groaned Sandy in dismay. "Did

I bust a flask for you, frien'? Don't take no care of that! I'll get you a new one — and a quart at that. Grogan, a quart for this gent!"

Jerry, cursing softly to himself, tossed the broken fragments from his hip pocket and shook off, as well as he could, the liquid which flowed down his leg.

"Hard luck," went on Sandy. "Hope it wasn't no special old brand of your —"

He stopped; he gaped; he drew in his breath with a prodigious sniff. And then he drew back a long pace from Jerry. If the latter had been changed into a rattlesnake he could not have affected Sandy so vitally.

"Gents," gasped Sandy, and could say no more.

"What's the matter, Sandy?" asked Grogan.

"Him!" wheezed big Sandy.

"What's wrong with you?" Jerry asked angrily.

And he thought of the five spot which the other bottle of Florida water would cost him.

"Smell him!" choked Sandy.

There was a general inhaling of breath; the air was thick with the fumes of the Florida water.

"Why," shouted Sandy, his voice returning to him, "it ain't a man at all. It's a female. Perfume!"

Every breath they drew backed up Sandy's

words. Perfume! On a man! In Number Ten!

It was a lasting disgrace to the town; it was a thing unprecedented.

"What kind are you?" snarled Sandy. "Man or woman?" And a roar of laughter echoed through the big room.

"Throw him out!" shouted one. "Rope him!" yelled another. "Perfume, ha, ha, ha!"

They swirled in a thickening group, with Jerry as the vortex. Sandy reached across the bar and caught up a brimming glass of whisky.

"Here's something to sweeten you, ma'am," he called, and dashed the contents full in Jerry's face.

What followed is writ large in the memories of the good citizens of Number Ten. Jerry was not a big man, but his arms were long and his shoulders were thick, and his weight was compacted and placed at the critical places. Luckily, he had blinked while the liquid was in the air, and so he got none of the stinging whisky in his eyes; but if it had been liquid fire it could not have maddened him more.

He made one swift step toward Sandy, who was leaning back, bellowing with laughter, and drove a clenched fist squarely into Sandy's stomach. It doubled Sandy like a closing knife when the spring is strong. His middle body struck the bar behind him; his head and heels landed on the floor at almost the same moment. And then Sandy flopped upon his side and began kicking and clawing in the vain effort to recover his breath. But Jerry was just beginning.

Pressing close upon him, crowding him, two faces leered into his own. He snapped two uppercuts into those faces — uppercuts which borrowed power from his rise to his toes, from the straightening of his legs, from the convulsive jerk of his shoulders — and the two faces disappeared. That gave Jerry room and he began to fight.

Not that it was an easy crowd to handle. Those first three blows cleared their minds effectually from the fumes of the whisky they had drunk, and they went at Jerry with a rush. They had bulk; they had brawn; they had fighting heart; and against them there was only a brain which knew how to direct its fists. Besides, a frenzy had fallen upon the single man.

When those two faces disappeared, he leaped back against the bar to give himself still more room, his head went back, and he emitted a yell. There was no rage or hate in it; it was all concentrated joy. Half a dozen men were rushing straight at him, elbowing, jamming, crowding each other in their eagerness to get at the perfumed stranger. Jerry leaned forward and sprang in football fashion at their knees. He caught two pairs in his strong arms, and two heavy bodies catapulted over his back and crashed against the bar with a force that brought a yell from Grogan.

Then Jerry rose in the midst of a confused circle of foemen. He hooked his right in one face; he buried his left to the elbow in the paunch of a fat man. They rolled away into the crowd, pressing back others, and when the wave of fighting men swept back at him, Jerry had room to hit with full-arm punches. He hit straight, with the speed of a striking snake and the force of a riveter. Always at the face; and the *spat, spat, spat* of his blows sounded with the regular rhythm of the paddles of a stern-wheeler going at full speed. And always he fought with cunning eyes, never wasting blows on the less vital points, but aiming at the mouth or the eye or the nose or the chin.

A stocky, red-headed man leaped through the air to bring down the enemy. Jerry met him with an overhand punch that turned his mouth to a red smear and dropped him on the floor.

"Hey!" yelled Jerry, and stepped on the face of the red-haired man as he whipped a full-arm drive against the chin of the next in order.

If the blood he drew with every cracking,

cutting punch had been wine in the stomach of a starving man, it could not have had a greater effect on Jerry. He seemed half drunk with the joy of the battle.

A burly fellow came at him, down-headed, with the lunge of a charging bull, and drove Jerry back against the bar, only to be dropped senseless by a short, clubbed blow that landed accurately behind his ear.

Then the next wave of the fighters came at him. Some of the first down were on their feet again by this time with the red marks upon their faces. Split lips, swollen eyes, cut cheeks, bruised chins, they lowered their heads and rushed. They came raggedly, without order, each man fighting with a silent lust for blood.

If they had fought in order, and come on in a steady semicircle, Jerry, for all his wrestling and boxing skill, could not have stood against them for half a minute; but they were lost to reason. A single man was baffling them all, and the thought maddened them; they strove to crush him by stupid mass attack, and Jerry was not to be crushed. He slipped from place to place. To get a handhold on him was like trying to clutch an oiled surface. He literally slid and oozed through their tearing fingers, and sent them reeling with spatting, hammer-driven blows.

Here and there he sprang as if his muscles were watch springs. They dived low, after his own fashion, came in under his arms, and hurled him back against the wall, and he rebounded like a rubber ball and was slipping and springing here and there. He was like a wolf fighting a pack of dogs, never pausing for a death grapple, but slashing and darting on.

Then Sandy, his breath returned, rose to his feet, and stood on the edge of the circle watching the fight. He had misjudged this man, this laughing, shouting, taunting, yelling demon who carried perfume like a woman and fought with the strength and venom of a pitching mustang and the intelligence of seven devils — sadly he had misjudged the stranger. But Sandy's stomach was sore; he had been felled to the floor and now the stranger must pay. So Sandy waited until a rift showed in the crowd — a rift which led straight to the dancing, fighting figure, and then Sandy bellowed like a bull and rushed on his man.

A full-arm trip-hammer right whacked against Sandy's chin, but two hundred and twenty pounds of hard muscle and bone were driving Sandy on, and he merely shook his head at the blow, and closed on Jerry with a snarl. His clutching arms crushed the smaller man to his chest; the impetus of the rush hurled them both to the floor, and they rolled over and over among a forest of stumbling legs.

How it happened Sandy could never tell thereafter. He only knew that both the arms of the stranger here within his bear hug; he only knew that a roar echoed in his ears as the crowd yelled, "He's down! Sandy has him! Kill him, Sandy! Gimme a chance at him! Break his back!"

Such was the chorus which shrilled above Sandy, and he locked his hold more firmly. And then — it was very mysterious. One of those helpless arms slipped, snakelike, from his grip. A strong palm caught him under the chin and jerked his head back; the other arm was instantly free. Sandy whirled, then, to rise to his feet and get a new hold. But he kept on rising. He was held somehow by shoulder and hip. He was swung up in the air, whirled around; his flying hands struck one man in the face; his flying heels knocked down another; and then Sandy crashed with stunning force against the floor and all memory left him.

Over his body the fight raged like the battle of the Greeks for the corpse of Patroclus. Jerry's sharp tongue whipped on his foes to the battle; his darting fists hurled them back again. His shrill yell echoed in their ears from one side one instant; the next a hammerlike blow felled them from the opposite direction. He danced among them like a will-o'-the-wisp; and almost as impalpable a target to strike. They struck him — aye, a thousand times — but that flitting target offered no solid resistance to their blows, and their desperate, whirling fists glanced away from swaying shoulders, rolling head, or swiftly blocking forearms.

Then Grogan entered the fight. He, too, like Sandy, had seen and admired from the distance; but Grogan admired more intelligently, for he knew something about the fistic art; and he chuckled as he saw hooks jolt home, and uppercuts whip true to their mark, and overhand punches cut faces, and straight drives carry men before them like foam on the crest of a wave. These things Grogan saw and stirred not. Let them fight it out. At least, as long as no one pulled a gun, and no one *would* pull a gun till the stranger set the example. There is too much chivalry for that in the mountain desert.

But when Jerry Aiken caught a rushing fighter up into a flying mare and heaved the man through the air, and when the floundering body struck the roulette table and sent the only roulette wheel in Number Ten whirling across the floor, it was plain to Grogan that he must bring his burly shoulders and some of the boxing lessons of yore into play.

He slapped one hand upon the top of the bar, and then he vaulted lightly — in spite of his bulk — to the other side.

That spring brought him face to face with Jerry. The crowd was at the end of an ebbing wave, leaving Jerry for an instant comparatively alone in the middle of the floor. And Grogan bellowed at them, "Leave him to me. Stand back. Gimme room!"

Then he leaped for Jerry. As for the crowd, it was rather glad to pause to collect its battered and scattered wits; so it stopped, panting, and wiped off the blood, and watched with none-too-good will the attack of Grogan.

He came in well enough, Jerry was armweary — too weary to strike with his usual bullet speed. Also, he was accustomed for the past few seconds to striking at faces which knew nothing of rolling or ducking in the approved manner. But when he shot a hook at the onrushing Grogan, the big man partly blocked the force of the punch and let his head sway with the rest of it. He was not even jarred by that hook, and as he plunged he whanged a hard right into Jerry's ribs, and caught him with a terrible lifting left in the same midsection. The blow literally carried Jerry off his feet and sent him smashing back against the wall. There he tottered, and Grogan steadied himself for the finishing punch, leaned far back; and then whipped across his right in a perfect shift for the final knock-out blow. But the wavering figure staggering, leaned, and the knock-out punch shot hissing past Jerry's shoulder. Grogan stumbled forward with the force of his spent punch, and then whirled with catlike swiftness, cursing, in time to see the smaller man start a long, low left swing for his body.

Grogan's guard dropped. But the blow did not flash home, did not even touch his blocking forearms. Instead, it stopped in mid-air. The feet of Aiken did a dancing step at the same instant, so that he seemed to blow on the wind closer, his right hand shot up, over, the clenched fist twisted — and then the roof dropped upon Grogan's head.

CHAPTER XII

The Last Scotch

It must be said in justice to Grogan that he was far from the type of whining bully which runs for help when he is licked. But his brain was sick and dizzy — and the roof had fallen brutally upon his head.

He saw the knotted tangle of the fighters, he saw a table toppled over and crash upon its side, and then, with the instinct to preserve his property uppermost in his numbed brain, Grogan started for Marshal Bud Levine.

He staggered into the marshal's house, after banging once at the door — an unceremonious manner of entrance which brought the marshal to his feet from behind his newspaper with nervous fingers and thoughtful eyes. Then he saw Grogan stumble into the room. A great purple welt stood out on his chin; from his nose — where the treacherous floor had so needlessly smitten him — a trickle of blood ran down over his shirt front, drop by drop.

"Well, Grogan," snapped the marshal,

"what the devil is behind this?"

"Murder!" gasped Grogan, and collapsed into a chair.

"Where?" said the marshal, and his thin lips grew taut, with a line of white edging them. Death had knocked at his door again, and this time — perhaps —

"In my place, Levine."

"Who's there?"

"A gang."

"I've heard no shots."

"They're using clubs."

The marshal stood at the door with his revolver in his hand.

"Any dead?"

"The floor's covered with 'em."

"And me in the town when it happened!" said the marshal through his teeth. "I'm done for!"

And he started at a run for Grogan's place.

The marshal went for the fighting, tangled gang, his gun leveled, barking orders like a watchdog, and they split and gave back before him. They staggered away and leaned against walls, and upon their bruised faces Levine read an expression which seemed to say that they were glad of his coming. But the stranger?

"One more!" he yelled, and leaped at Levine.

Just in time he checked his rush. A man

more hasty and rash than Levine would have sent the fatal bullet on its way at the first threat, but he held his fire, amazed by the spectacle of a naked-handed man attacking a .45. And Jerry came to a halt with the mouth of the gun fairly pressed against his chest. But Levine noted from the corner of his eyes that the last of the prone figures on the floor was staggering to his feet.

"Put up your gun," said Jerry joyously. "Have a drink, and join the party!"

"What does this mean?" queried Levine, finding it rather hard to meet the bright eye of the madman.

"It means a party," Jerry grinned. "The boys are showing me a good time."

"Bud," said Sandy, reeling toward the marshal, "you got the wrong tip. This ain't no gun play. It ain't no more'n a frolic. Jest close your eyes and beat it. We got something more to say to this here gent."

"Leave him be," pleaded the rest of the crowd, and they thronged closer. "We ain't near done with him."

"Keep off!" commanded Levine sharply, and his gun described a little arc. As though a stream of icy water had gushed from it, the crowd fell away from that magic gesture.

"And you," went on Levine, puzzled, for he could see no others on the side of the stranger, "come with me. You been disturbin' the peace!"

"I'll see you in hell first," remarked the genial stranger. "This party is just getting on its first legs."

"Shut up — quick — and hold out your hands," commanded Levine.

Jerry grew suddenly sober.

"If that's the way of it," he nodded, "there's nothing for it but to go with you."

He held out his wrists and Levine, deftly, with one hand, snapped on the manacles.

Jerry turned toward the crowd.

"Of all the rotten burgs, cheap jay towns, and bogus villages," he announced, "Number Ten is the worst."

A growl answered him, soft and deep as the rumble of distant thunder.

"And of all the ham- and cow-punchers, near-men, has-beens, also-rans, and yellow gangsters, you fellows are my choice of the lot."

The growl rose to a snarl.

"Bud," pleaded Sandy, with tears in his voice, "for my sake leave us at him — jest once more!"

"Will you shut up and come away?" snapped Levine to his prisoner. "Or d'you want to be pushin' daisies in about five minutes more of yapping like this?"

But Jerry was laughing in the faces of the crowd.

"Let you at me?" he ran on merrily. "Why, I'd eat a whole cityful of guys like you. I'd beat up a town like Number Ten and not get an appetite for breakfast. Why, you birds are so cheap that a Chinaman could go through you like a knife through a pile of cheese."

A yell came from the badgered inhabitants of Number Ten. Levine tugged his captive with desperate haste toward the door.

"You're so cheap," concluded Jerry as he was dragged through the door, "that a Jew couldn't make a living in Number Ten, and even a Scotchman would starve."

And as he disappeared he waved a final and supreme insult toward them.

In the dark of the street Levine whirled with outstretched gun, as a roar of rushing feet rose within Grogan's place, and then a dozen pursuers tumbled through the door.

"Keep off!" commanded Levine. "Boys, you know me, and if you try to take this crazy gent, this locoed nut, away from me, I'll drill some of you before you get at him. I ask you, is he worth the price?"

The crowd, after a moment of growling, ebbed back.

"Now walk on," commanded Levine. "And keep away from me. Phew! Man, you stink!"

Then Levine prodded his captive into a quickstep by jabbing the gun into the small of his back. They went straight to the marshal's shack, for the back room of this house was the jail. Even the reckless population of Number Ten had discovered that they needed a secure place in which to incarcerate their criminals until they could be taken away to the county jail; so that they joined their efforts, gathered rock in volunteered wagons, quarried off the irregular edges with their own unaccustomed hands, and built a room with four stone walls and a stone roof, and a floor of two-by-six planks. They fastened the door with a pound of padlock and intrusted the key to the marshal — the third before Bud Levine. But before Bud locked up his prisoner, he sat him down in his own room and looked over the fighter.

He was neither drunk nor sullen. Two things only were remarkable about the stranger. The first was his dancing eyes; the second was a light, sweet aroma which clung about him. He stood without embarrassment, humming a tune.

"You," said the marshal, lowering his eyes from the scrutiny and dragging open a long, well-filled ledger, "what's your name?"

"Smith," said Jerry promptly, "Jeremiah Jonah Smith."

The marshal squinted dubiously at his man and then reluctantly indited the long name.

"And what in hell have you been up to," Jeremiah?" he asked.

"Enjoying a little party the men of Number Ten staged for me," replied the dauntless Jeremiah.

"Jeremiah," said the marshal, "I got an idea you're one of the largest-sized liars that ever dropped in on me."

"Thanks," nodded Aiken, not a whit abashed. "Anyway, I'd rank among the first ten. Some of 'em have it on me for distance, but I get an edge for number."

"Wash your face over there at that bucket," commanded the marshal.

Aiken obeyed, still humming, and when he turned and mopped his dripping features with the stained towel, the marshal observed with much interest that there was not a scratch on the skin. Here and there were little red splotches which might grow blue or purplish in time, but they were no more than a youngster might collect wrestling half an hour in the school yard.

Moreover, his clothes were torn to shreds, but where the skin of the body showed through it was unmarked. The marshal squinted his eyes again thoughtfully, and recalled the disarranged features of big Sandy, and the marred nose of Grogan, the Redoubtable. He sighed, and then something very close akin to a smile began with twitchings at the corners of his lips. He favored his prisoner with another close scrutiny; as far as he could see the man was simply a boy in the skin of a man.

"Who started that fight?" he demanded suddenly.

"I don't know," chuckled Jerry. "Like Topsy, it just grew."

"Who was with you when you tackled that crowd?"

"I was with myself."

"H'm!" murmured the marshal. He cast another dubious glance toward Jerry and then rose slowly, and wandered to a corner of the room. A little hidden door opened, and displayed a small hutch in the wall with two tall, gleaming bottles therein. He drew one of them forth and a pair of tall glasses. And he placed them on the table. Then, without a word, he unlocked the manacles which bound Jerry — and turned his back while he poured the drinks.

To be sure, Jerry started involuntarily toward the door as soon as the irons fell away, but he checked himself with a start. He raised the glass which the marshal pushed toward him, inhaled a certain fragrance — and then lowered it with a jerk.

"You haven't, by any chance," he said wistfully, "a dash of seltzer?"

The marshal grinned broadly, and still in silence returned to the hutch and brought forth the second bottle. It was a siphon of soda.

"Here's how," said Jerry.

"How!" grunted Levine.

The only pair of Scotch highballs on the mountain desert flowed, slowly, smoothly, evenly, into cavernous mouths.

There was not a motion in the camp for some moments after Jerry Aiken rode away that evening; then the broad shoulders of Pete the Runt heaved slowly up and peered into the deceitful dimness of the moonlight.

"Mack!" he whispered.

Red was instantly upon one elbow.

"I think Aiken has beat it."

"But he'll be back again."

They waited.

"Nope, he's gone out for a walk, Mack. Now's our time!"

"What if he comes back before we're started?"

"Knock him on the head and gag the houn' dog. Now start for the hosses. Nothin' will wake old Scovil; listen to him snorin' like a hog. Funny how a man like him could have a daughter like that, eh?"

"They ain't no telling how heredity will work out."

"No, they ain't. Your dad was a good-lookin' man, Red."

Even Red's snort was measured so as not to endanger the sleep of Scovil. Then the two started quickly out of their blankets, caught the horses at a little distance, and saddled the three quickly. When they returned for Nancy Scovil, however, she was sound asleep. Red Mack kneeled and touched her shoulder.

"Nancy!" he whispered.

No response.

"Wake up!" Louder, but not a sign of life.

"Hey, Nancy!" Not a stir.

In desperation, not daring to speak more loudly for fear of rousing John Scovil, the Runt slipped an arm under the shoulder of the girl and raised her to a sitting posture. But her head fell partially back, and her figure slumped limp against the side of the Runt.

"The champeen sleeper of the world," groaned Red Mack. He caught the girl's shoulder in a strong grip, and squeezed and shook at the same time. At length they caught the glimmer of her eyes as the lids raised — slowly.

"We're ready," whispered the Runt.

"For what?" She yawned carefully.

"To start. Are you?"

"Start where? I'm just asleep!"

The Runt groaned.

"Are you going to ride with us to-night?"

"Oh," she said, "can't we wait a while? I'm — fairly aching with sleep!"

"Lift her up," muttered the Runt. "We'll help her to wake up."

So they raised her up between them and the motion fully wakened her. She set about pulling on her riding boots, yawning prodigiously as she worked, while the two men waited with one nervous eye upon the recumbent form of John Scovil, and the other turned in the direction in which Aiken had disappeared.

Finally she was ready. They took her, floundering between them, through the soft, deep sand, to where the horses stood around the corner of the hill. Even now they were lost if Aiken returned and spied them. Scovil groaned behind them. But it was only a nightmare that troubled him. In an instant they had lifted the girl to her saddle — an inert weight — swung into their own places, and the horses jogged off, with only the swishing of the sand about their hoofs to give notice of their departure.

Still they maintained a cautious pace for

some distance from the camp, with many a nervous glance behind them, until they were safely beyond earshot. It would have been hard to trail them in any other way, for when they were wakening Nancy, the moon had slid into a thick cloud, and now the darkness of almost full night was veiling them; and once they were beyond earshot they were safe from pursuit.

At the same time they passed from the soft sand onto firm, hard going. The shod hoofs of the horses came down with a sharp, ringing clink on the surface of the ground, and they trotted on more swiftly.

It was at about this time that Nancy Scovil began to awaken in earnest.

Up to this moment sleep had hung like a curtain both before her eyes and over her mind. She only knew that she was doing what others directed her to do — as she had done all her life. To be sure, she remembered dimly that a vast time before she had planned some such escape from the cruel surveillance of terrible Jerry Aiken; but all that was dim and in the past.

The only vivid thing of the present was that two wills were imposing themselves upon hers and forcing her to do as they wished her to do. That was so familiar a thing that it could not rouse her to full wakefulness. But now the horses struck the firm going, and the trot shook the sleep away from her brain, and for the first time that night she began to think and feel.

It did not come to her all at once. But by degrees she sensed something new. Always her life, her days, every moment of her time had been planned for by others. Now, strangely, she was independent. She was riding by night, at her own wish and in her own direction. She sensed it slowly, tasted it gradually, listened to it, almost, like a distant sound of ravishing music.

Freedom! But was she free? That could be easily seen. She halted her horse.

"That gait is tiresome," she murmured. "Let's walk a ways."

The two men changed their pace obediently.

"Sure," growled the Runt. "Why didn't you think of that, Mack? Ain't you got no sense but to ride a lady at a trot on ground like this?"

"Don't lay all the blame on me," snarled Red Mack. "Who was ridin' in the lead?"

Yes, they rode by her direction and at her will. How had this come? From the French girl whose patient finger had first pointed out and whose patient lips had so many times repeated, *"Je suis, tu es, il est,"* to the tutor who monotonously drummed dates and facts into her mind, to the groom who had taught her to ride, to the dapper little man who had taught her to dance, all and every one of them had merely been parts and portions of the great supervising will against which it was useless to contend.

"Miss, your father wills it." "Alas, ma'm'selle, it is the desire of monsieur." "Ma'am, it ain't me that keeps you at it, it's the master, Lor' luv you!" These were the things they had said.

From her earliest recollection, her existence, her future, was not according to her own will. The shadow of her father lay before her, and in that shadow she must inevitably walk. Yes, even the youths who met her had only one eye for her; the other was fixed steadfastly on the great man and his millions. After a while she had learned that if it was useless to resist him, it was at least possible to refuse to swim with the current.

So she had learned to lay back against it, and the will of her father must both carry her along and support her. If she could not think of herself, it was at least some satisfaction not to think the thoughts of others. And she finally had reached a point approaching the Hindu Nirvana; Nancy did not think at all. Her life passed in a haze, which even the deep voice of her father could not shatter. The keen insistence of Jerry Aiken, indeed, almost drew away the veil, but at length she had found the way to baffle even him; and even if she could not baffle she could escape him.

But now?

She looked up to the dark forms on either side of her. The lean, ugly features of Red Mack were etched sharply against the shadow of the night, except when the broad brim of his sombrero flapped far down over his forehead. He rode lightly, his long body swaying to the gait of his horse. And that horse, like the master of it, was long and lean, catlike in agility.

Far different was Pete the Runt on the other side. His broad-shouldered horse stamped along, shaking the earth and tossing his head under a giant burden which set the saddle leather creaking and groaning. The man himself bulked huge and stable, unshakable as a rock. He seemed fixed in his place, defying time and the weathering of the elements. And yet they both rode with their heads turned a little toward her. If she trotted her horse they also trotted; if she walked, they walked. Their whole attitude breathed a yielding to her will.

Imagine a man held in irons in the dark hold of a ship whose very home port and destiny he does not know. Think of that man taken suddenly out of the hold, his irons struck off, his hands placed on the wheel which guides the ship, the stars before him, and the stalwart shapes of the crew obedient to his slightest will — and then you will have some inkling of the emotion which surged and grew, like a mounting and growing tidal wave, in the heart of Nancy Scovil. She was free; strength was hers to command.

Not that it all came to her at once. She felt her way toward the new position by degrees. Her body and her mind were numb with the lifelong sleep. And the thrill of the happiness was so novel that she actually shrank from it. But she whose every thought and act had been guarded and directed — she was now riding alone, in the desert, destination unknown, with two men who were almost strangers. The consciousness of it broke wave by wave upon the sleep-charmed beach of her mind.

Now they climbed up a long slope, at a walk. And as they reached the crest of the hill, a wind, keen and sweet and chill with the night, blew upon her face. The same wind brushed the cloud from the face of the moon, and all the rolling landscape changed — the hollows were poured full with trembling blue shadows, and silver covered all the high places.

And then something snapped in Nancy Scovil, like the breaking of a violin string.

CHAPTER XIII

Awakening

It was like a great burst of music sounding within her — that instant of breaking from her past — and the sound welled up and overflowed, and set her heart thundering, and made her lips part, and set a new light in her eyes. The unexpected strength of all her sleepy life now quivered in every muscle of her body. And a great store of electric energy flooded her, tingling. Her head tilted back a little, and when the wind blew up and curled the brim of her sombrero the two men saw her face, saw her smile, saw the gleam of her eyes.

She stretched out her arms — flung them out, rather — and raised her slender hands and cried: "Isn't it — glorious?"

What a voice! All the softness of old was in it, but there was the new thing, the mystery which some call fiber and some call soul. Whatever it may be named, it was in the new voice of the new Nancy Scovil.

"Gosh!" gasped Red Mack.

And the voice of the Runt, small and singularly strained, queried: "What!"

"The whole wide world!" she cried. "I love it all! Let's ride into it!"

The thrust of her spurs sent the broncho pitching straight into the air, and he came down stiff-legged. It would have thrown the old Nancy Scovil, familiar as she was with the saddle, to the ground like a limp, half-filled sack, but the new Nancy Scovil clung easily, and snatched off her hat, and with it slapped the mustang on the flank.

That was enough. The mustang stretched out his head and began to run in earnest, and the Runt and Red Mack urged their horses in pursuit. They were alarmed at first, but now they noted that as she rode she shouted back to them gayly, and each of them remembered the light which had been in her eyes. They wanted to see it again, so they rode desperately to catch up.

They could never have succeeded had they not been far better mounted than the girl, for she rode in a straight line, heedless of rough or smooth. The wind twisted out the braids of her hair and set the long, night-dark stream of hair blowing behind her, and the moon gleamed upon it.

Straight over the hills they headed, and topping the last rise, they saw at length the few, uncertain lights of Number Ten. No pause for that sight. The girl spurred again, and raced down the steep last slope, her broncho pitching with every leap. The shrill of her tingling cries sent queer, creepy threads of emotion chasing through the bodies of the two men, and when they entered the main street of Number Ten, the three were yelling in chorus like three demoniac spirits turned loose from the nether regions for a debauch on earth.

It was that chorus which burst upon the ears of the marshal and Jerry Aiken as they lowered their glasses slowly, rather mournfully, from that Scotch highball. The marshal listened and frowned. It was not the first time he had heard such sounds. Jerry heard it and grinned; it was not the first time he had listened to such sounds.

But the yelling fell away suddenly, or rather, over it rose a sweet, clear, ringing voice. It was not heavy, but there was a piercing beauty in it, and as if in recognition of that quality, the wild shouting died away, and the song went on by itself. It swung closer — with the marshal and Jerry Aiken standing frozen with astonishment — and then, in a rattle of racing hoofs the song and the singer swept by, and only the crash of the running feet came back to them.

The marshal mopped his forehead; he

turned toward the door suddenly; then he turned back and faced Jerry with a rather shamefaced smile.

"In the name of the devil," he said thoughtfully, "what is a woman doing in Number Ten?"

"Don't you ever have 'em here?"

"Not that kind."

"How do you know?"

"I could read it — you could see her face in her voice."

"If her face is like her voice," stated Jerry, "this jail won't hold me, marshal."

The latter grew serious at once.

"None of that, Smith!" he cautioned. "I'm a good fellow — and you seem square to me. I suppose you haven't broken very much of the law to-night, but all Number Ten knows I brought you here, and" — here his jaw thrust out a significant trifle — "and here you are going to stay!"

"Well," murmured the prisoner, "it looks as if you have the drop on me just now."

The marshal laughed.

"I'm as touchy as a hoss with sore feet to-night," he said. "I think I know you, Smith. I'd like to let you camp here to-night without irons on — without even locking you in the jail room."

"Jail?"

"A little beaut. Couldn't wish for better. Just open that door."

Jerry obeyed. He turned toward the marshal again with a shrug of the shoulders.

"A bit damp," he remarked.

"You're not going to sleep in there," said the marshal hastily. "All you have to do is give me your word to stay put." His eyes narrowed again as he studied the open face of Jerry Aiken. "Your bare promise will be jail enough for you, Smith, or I'm a tenderfoot."

"Thanks," nodded Jerry. "I'll certainly appreciate a sleep in a man-sized bed. You have my —"

He stopped short. His eyes widened; his head canted a trifle to one side. And then an indescribable expression changed his face.

It came very thin and far away, no louder than the drone of a mosquito on a thick, warm, spring evening. That was the volume of it, but it pierced through distance and walls — the singing of the girl again!

"Levine," said Jerry with a sigh, "I'm afraid I can't give you my word."

The marshal frowned.

"Listen to me, lad," he cautioned. "I know you're game and all that, but you're a nut if you show yourself to the Number Ten gang for a day or two. Give 'em time to cool off. If you go out now, some one will pull a gun and plug you — sure!"

"Wrong," smiled Jerry, "I've ridden the ranges quite a while, and I've never seen a skunk who would pull a six-gun on a fellow who wasn't armed."

"That's up to you," said the marshal with decision. "But now — I'm in a hurry. Will you or will you not give me your word to stick here to-night?"

"No."

"Why not?"

"For the same reason, partner, that you're in such a hurry just now."

To be sure, Bud Levine flushed, but he remained serious.

"Business is business," he said. "You give me your word, or you bunk in that jail to-night. Why, if you were to show yourself to-night, my reputation would go smash."

"If you put me in there," said Jerry calmly, "I'll bust your jail and your reputation, too, marshal."

"What's the matter with you, Smith?"

"The girl — the voice, Levine. It reminds me of some one I've heard before, and I'm going to find out for sure."

"In you go, then, Smith. And shake it up."

Jerry turned reluctantly into the stone cell, and the heavy door closed with a jar behind him. At once darkness swept around him like a tangible thing — a moist, disagreeable darkness.

First, from the outside, he heard the grind and click of the lock which sealed his imprisonment; then the humming of the marshal as the latter stepped swiftly around his room making preparations. Then the slam of the front door which announced that Bud Levine was starting out to go the way of all Number Ten this night of nights.

Jerry Aiken stood perfectly still in the center of his cell and began to think. Far off, still like the humming of a fly, but infinitely sweet and stirring as wine, he could hear the pulse of the girl's song.

In the little combination entrance hall and office of Gray's hotel, Jim Gray himself dropped his boots from their perch on the edge of his desk and sat up to listen. The three other men who lounged about the place imitated his example, and all were perfectly moveless while the chorus of yells swept up the street, changed to one sweet, high-voiced, ringing song, and stopped abruptly before the hotel entrance.

"Hollerin'," observed old Jim Gray calmly, "most generally means booze, but singin' means anything from booze to a blood-trail. Gents, I'll ask you to stand clean of the door."

The loiterer at the door hastily side-stepped,

thrust away, so to speak, by the hard, narrowing glance which came in the eyes of Jim Gray; and at the same instant the door was pushed open, and a youth stood in the entrance, laughing. The strangest boy they had ever seen. He might be anywhere from fifteen to twenty — slender, rounded, ridiculously small of foot and hand and wrist.

His sombrero brim furled up in front, blown to that position by hard riding, the open shirt exposed a gleam of white, soft throat, which the bitter sun of the mountain desert had surely never touched. He stood with his hands on his hips at the door, and his legs braced easily, to survey the room; and his eyes and his smile went from face to face with a sort of gay, challenging insolence. Such eyes! It was the light in them, at once merry and dangerous. In fact, the whole poise of the youth was one of fearlessness.

"And where did you drop from?" grunted Jim Gray, leaning back in his chair with a sigh of relief.

"I just blew in," remarked the stranger, "to wake up this sleepy old burg."

"You did, eh?" chuckled Jim Gray. "And might that have been you singing up the street? Or was it your pet canary?"

"Pull the wool out of your ears, Father Time," said the stranger, "and come alive."

A heavy step sounded on the veranda behind the stranger.

"And what," said Jim Gray grimly, "d'ye mean by that?"

Behind the slender youth, half framed against the darkness and half lost in it, appeared two gigantic forms, head and shoulders above their companion. One was lean, with a savage, hungered look about him; and the other of himself nearly filled the doorway.

"Nix," said this last individual, pushing past the youth and stepping into the room. "Jest lay offn that line of chatter, my frien'."

And he approached Jim Gray.

"Woman," he whispered to the proprietor.

The jaw of Jim Gray dropped to his chest with an almost audible jar.

"Woman?" he whispered back.

The sibilant murmur stole about the room; the other three men grew stiff, with widening eyes. They were like old Indians who glimpse the smoke of hostile camp fires. Woman! In Number Ten!

"The best room you got," went on the Runt.

"Which of you is with — the lady?" queried Jim Gray.

The Runt grew very red.

"She's alone," he said. "We're jest travelin' with her."

His voice was carefully modulated so as to escape the notice of the girl. She, indeed, was now occupied in sauntering down the length of the wall, looking carelessly at the bright calendars which served in lieu of pictures for adornment; but the other men in the room were leaning at acute angles toward the conversation of the Runt and Jim Gray. And they heard.

They straightened; they exchanged swift, eloquent glances. The girl in Number Ten was unmarried! One removed his sombrero and quickly brushed its rim; another fumbled covertly at his bandanna. And on every face came a strange softening; they seemed to be preparing their mouths for smiling. And that far-away look? Each one was vigorously combing the past to remember some attractive thing which he or some friend of his had once said to a girl like —

In the meantime Jim Gray was rising to show them to their rooms in the second story, for Gray's hotel — built in boom days when there seemed a likelihood that Number Ten might grow into the proportions of a real town — boasted two stories.

With Jim Gray in the lead, the four climbed the winding stairs to the second floor, their varying weights attested by the different pitch of each squeak; and so they came to Jim Gray's sanctuary — the front room. It boasted the only wall paper in Number Ten, warped here and there into puffs and wrinkles, dyed by time here to a deep brown and there faded by sunlight to a dirty white — once it had been a pleasant yellow. There was, moreover, the only iron bed in Number Ten in a corner of the room, a washstand near it, a chest of drawers on the farther side, and a rectangular mirror above it.

To be sure, all these articles of furniture were more or less marred. Most of the white enamel had peeled from the bed, and what was left of it was wrinkled and brittle as a thick coat of overdried whitewash. The pitcher on the washstand lacked a lip, and the rag rug near the bed was worn quite through in the center. As for the mirror — but Jim Gray, by way of conversation, explained the mirror. It was quite useless, for a thousand cracks issued from a little hole in the exact center of the glass.

"Ma'am," said Jim Gray, "you'd of laughed to of seen how that mirror come to be busted like that. Old Conway was in town on a big drunk three year hack. He was up most of the night puttin' away the redeye, and when he got up the next mornin' he seen himself in the glass, and bein' sort of upset, he was so plumb scared by that face in the mirror that he pulled his six and plunked a chunk o' lead right through it."

And Jim Gray burst into merry, deep-throated laughter.

"Partner," cut in the Runt, "is this the best you got?"

"Ain't it good enough?" asked Jim sharply.

"It's perfect," broke in the girl from the window. "If it gets hot I can put a chair out here on the roof and sit there until it's cool enough to go to bed."

For the second story was not as large as the first, and the roof jutted down from the base of it, extending past the front of the building and stretching on into a wide, low canopy, where the horses of day visitors found shade at noon.

"And," continued the girl, turning with a smile from the window, "I thank you for giving me your very best, sir."

Jim Gray pushed back the hat which never left his head and grinned back at her.

"If it ain't right I'll make it right," he assured her. "Now, rooms for you two gents —"

"We'll fix that later," said the Runt. "S'long."

The proprietor took a slow and reluctant leave, and his last sight of Nancy Scovil was the picture of her sitting on the edge of the bed and smiling to him over the hat of Red Mack.

"Now," said the Runt, "I'm sure sorry this is all he's got. Is they anything else you want?"

"Lots," said the girl, "but I haven't a cent to pay for anything," she added.

"Nancy," proffered Red Mack eagerly, "seein' that we might call ourselves partners, it's sure goin' to make me some happy to give you any coin you need."

"Jest name what you want," said the Runt, "and I'll bring it to you if it's in Number Ten. Maybe you're kind of tired now. We'll fix you up when you get up in the morning."

"Morning?" she echoed. "Why, the night is just beginning!"

They cast sharp glances at each other. Where had she left the sleepy creature they had known? That shell was far away; and now a new being, filled with electric energy, set them thrilling with every touch of her eyes.

"I won't take a gift, but if I can borrow from you —"

"You sure can!"

"Then let's go shopping. I want to get out of these men's clothes."

And before they could turn around she was out of the door and running down the stairs.

CHAPTER XIV

Action

Her hair, already loosened by the hard riding, was pouring over her shoulders and rippling far below her waist by the time she whirled down to the foot of the stairs, with the heavy boots of Red Mack and Pete the Runt thundering after her. Jim Gray cast a wild glance after her as she slipped through the door, waved back to him, and was gone into the night.

Up the street, before Baldy's, she left Red Mack and the Runt to await the result of her purchases, and with their combined rolls grasped in her hand, she entered the store. It was doubtless of more moment than anything which happened on this strange night that Baldy the moveless actually rose from his chair unbidden when Nancy Scovil entered his shop. Still staring mutely he led the way to the back of the store and dragged from under a shelf a box literally buried under a mass of dust and cobwebs. But when the lid was raised a heap of white things showed within.

And, furthermore, at her bidding, Baldy brought a second lantern and hung it before a piece of cracked glass in the storeroom. Then he went wonderingly back to his chair; for a freak of fate had brought that box of woman's apparel into his keeping, and to Baldy the fact that it was to be used was stranger than the accident which had first made it his.

After several moments he recalled his senses with a start. There was a terribly strong taste of sulphur in his mouth, and he discovered that he had been lighting match after match and wasting them on an empty pipe. Old Baldy cast sheepish glances in all directions, but having made out that no one was within eyeshot, he stuffed the pipe into a hip pocket and rose again from his chair.

Very gingerly he stretched first one leg and then the other. Next he straightened, shook back his shoulders, puffed out his chest, and drew in — a little — his stomach. Finally he tightened his belt, hitched his trousers, and brushed several streaks of ashes from his flannel shirt.

"Well," muttered Baldy as if to an unseen listener, "who said I was so old?"

A light, quick step cut short his reflections; the very sound of that step quickened one's heartbeat in the strangest manner. And there she came around the corner of a pile of boxes, walking swiftly and jauntily and swinging the lantern at her side as she stepped. She was all in white, shoes — there had been only one pair in the box and by a miracle they fitted her — stockings just tinged with the pink skin beneath, skirt not overlong, a loose blouse, whose sleeves were cut off at the elbow and the neck open to show a deep triangle of white, with a splash of crimson where a big ribbon ended the triangle — and on her head was a crushable white hat. It would have been the despair of another woman, but on Nancy it was perfect.

"What's the verdict?" called this cool, clean vision. "And what's the price?"

"It's a gift," said Baldy.

"No gift."

"An exchange, then, ma'am."

"For what?"

"For the ten years you've made me younger, lady!"

"Pete! Mack!" called the girl. And two giants loomed instantly at the door with faces savagely prepared for trouble.

"Make him take his money for these clothes."

But Pete the Runt gave back half a pace and fumbled for support. At the same time the groping arm of Red Mack found that of the Runt, and they leaned together as if for mutual support.

"Don't you like the outfit?" said Nancy with a shade of trouble in her eyes. "Look!"

She stretched out her arms, rose upon her toes, and swung slowly around. On one toe she pivoted, and the other pushed her around, but there are no words to describe the motion — the lightness of it. It was as if the air had suddenly caught her up from the earth and were turning her in a faint wind; and her cheeks were flushed and her eyes starry as if from a high, cold wind, when she faced them again.

"Nancy," said the Runt in a hoarse voice, "you'll knock 'em dead. But I don't feel, somehow, like it's the same girl we come to town with."

"It isn't," she assured him instantly. And she turned on Baldy. "What can one do in this town at night?"

"They ain't much to do," said Baldy, scratching his head, "savin' Grogan's. And that ain't no place for a lady."

"But is it fun?"

"Ma'am, it's a gamblin' hell," said Baldy solemnly.

"Ah!"

"And saloon combined — full of rough men, lady."

"I like the rough men," said Nancy Scovil. "I love 'em rough. Pete, will you take me to Grogan's?"

Pete cast a single glance of triumph at Red Mack.

"I sure will," said Pete, and offered his arm.

"Jest one minute, ma'am," suggested Baldy, his little ancient eyes twinkling like lighted windows through a heavy fog. "These here gents don't know the town, maybe? Then it'd be a good idea for me to show you around."

"But who'll keep the store?"

"Hang the store!" exclaimed Baldy with deft motions, straightening his hat and pulling his bandanna taut. "And if you want to take a chance with Grogan's, jest leave it to me to see that you don't find no trouble there. 'Scuse me, partner."

The old man brushed between the astonished Runt and Nancy, and took her off upon his arm. Out they went into the night, the door of the store slamming, unlocked, behind them. She was singing softly, and dancing rather than walking beside old Baldy. And with a crippled hitch he strove to accommodate his gait to that wind-free pace of the girl.

Behind them Red Mack and Pete the Runt communed as they walked.

"What's up?" grunted Mack.

"Keep quiet, step soft, and have your gun

handy, Mack," replied the Runt. "Mack, all hell is sure goin' to bust loose when that girl hits Grogan's. Before mornin' we're going to have to fight — and fight to kill. Look at her now! She's loadin' that old fool with dynamite."

Just as she reached the door of Grogan's, the big gasoline lamp in front of the hotel up the street was lighted, and the whole street was illumined by the sudden flare. Nan paused to watch it, and Red Mack regained her side at once.

"Nancy," he muttered at her ear, "if you was to ask me for some good advice, I'd tell you not to go into Grogan's. It ain't cut out for ladies. It's got that name."

She whirled and laughed up into his face, so that Red Mack straightened and fell back a little.

"I'm not asking for advice," she answered. "I want action, action, action! If you two don't want to come in, I'm sure my friend will take care of me."

She slipped her hand back in the crook of Baldy's arm. His chest puffed like that of a pouter pigeon.

"If Number Ten can't show you action," he said, "they ain't no town on the range that can."

They turned aside and stepped into the door

of Grogan's place. The Runt and Red Mack followed helplessly. Inside they found that Grogan and his helpers had repaired the disorder and some of the actual damage of the mass fight against Jerry Aiken. The roulette wheel, unbroken by its fall, once more sat on its table. Here and there a chair leaned awry, but on the whole there were no signs of the conflict worth noticing.

No signs on the furniture, at least, but the tale of battle was written in plain language on the faces of the men. Big Grogan himself, with a lopsided, blue-stained jaw, stood behind the bar serving a man with one purple eye. Another approached the bar with a noticeable limp. In the groups around the card tables and the circle at the roulette wheel, Nancy saw lumps upon cheek and forehead and jaw, and here and there strips of sticking plaster stood out white or black against the bronzed faces. Jerry Aiken had left his mark with every dart of his hard fists.

Not that all the men were bruised in this manner, but there was a sufficient sprinking of the injured to make the whole crowd look as if it had just come in from a hard campaign. A whisper rose as Nan stepped into the door, and then there was a stir of faces toward her. If the sun had risen in the middle of night, Number Ten could have hardly been more astonished than it was to see this cool vision in white.

She smiled back at them with such dancing eyes that the smile seemed to dwell particularly on each face; just as the muzzle of a six-shooter leveled on a crowd seems to pick out every man and center upon him. So Number Ten whispered, moved, and then each man drew himself a little more erect, and brushed off dust, and straightened his sombrero, and shook himself to make sure that he was fit, like so many athletes making ready to toe the mark in a race.

These small signs did not escape the shrewd eye of Red Mack without comment. He muttered to the Runt, half groan and half whisper, "Hell is gettin' ready to pop, Runt. Keep your eyes open now."

"What is there to do first?" Nan was saying to Baldy.

"Anything you want, lady," responded the veteran.

"What's that wheel that shines so down there?"

"Roulette? I'd say they wasn't no faster way of makin' money or gettin' rid of it than roulette. But that there wheel is the most unluckiest one I ever see. Nobody never come out a winner on an evenin's play agin' that wheel, ma'am."

"But speed, partner, is what we want," answered Nancy, leading the way to the roulette wheel.

There were particular reasons why no one ever beat the roulette wheel at Grogan's for a large sum. Behind it stood "Dago Lew." He got his nickname from his swarthy complexion and his small, dark eyes. In reality Dago was born no farther east than Second Street and Third Avenue, Manhattan. For reasons best known to himself and the New York police, Dago long ago drifted out of the big city carrying with him an armor-plated conscience, deft fingers, and a bag of tricks.

In time he reached Number Ten, and in Number Ten he showed Grogan a single specimen out of his bag. It was a very cunning brake which could be applied to a roulette wheel and defy all chance of detection. Grogan accepted the trick and installed Dago behind the wheel. Not that Grogan was by nature a crook, but he reasoned in a philosophic vein that the men who came to Number Ten usually came to get rid of their money, and it was hardly a crime to make the process smooth and fast.

With Dago Lew behind it, his roulette wheel left little to be desired along these lines. Just between the feet of Dago Lew one of the boards of the floor was a little loose, and by pressing on a certain portion of this board the weight touched a button concealed below the floor, and the button in turn operated the brake.

To be sure, the appalling frequency of losses at the wheel made men look askance at Dago Lew, but he was never detected touching even the table while the wheel spun, and the losses were simply ascribed to amazing luck. So Grogan prospered.

Straight to the roulette wheel Nancy Scovil went. Before her the circle of gamblers opened by a sort of mutual consent, and behind her came in the wake first the guard — Pete and Red — and then the other men, from the bar, from the card tables. They swayed in toward the center and wandered idly toward the roulette wheel.

Big Grogan, having nothing to do behind the bar for the moment, followed suit. A red, round-faced man from the mines pushed back his hat and surveyed Nan with sweat-dimmed eyes. He had been losing heavily.

"Lady," he said, "you're takin' the hardest chance in the house. Ask Dago Lew himself."

The Dago was staring at the girl with his little eyes widened to almost twice their ordinary size. Now he passed his sleeve rapidly across his forehead and blinked. It was actually real, not a phantom woman in white.

"A chance is a chance," he said emphatically, and he smiled on Nancy by way of encouragement.

The muscular contraction which produces a smile was rare indeed on the face of Dago Lew, and what his thin lips produced now was closer to a sneer than to any semblance of mirth. But Nancy Scovil did not shrink from the beady brightness of the gambler's eyes. Her smile dwelt frankly, joyously, on him. All dreams of treachery and cheat were a thousand miles from her mind. The whole world was filled with gayety and honesty, as far as she was concerned, and she asked: "How is the game played?"

"Playin' colors red or black," began the Dago, singsonging his explanation, "pays a dollar for a dollar, and playin' odd or even pays a dollar for a dollar, and playin' single numbers pays thirty-six for one, and seventy-two for one if you let her lie. Playin' groups —"

His explanation rattled on swiftly, a lean, grimy forefinger pointing out the bets on the board beside the wheel as he talked. Before he was ended a twenty-dollar bill fluttered from the hand of Nancy and lay on the board. Dago Lew stared and frowned. It was high play for a woman and very high indeed for a woman who didn't know the game. Moreover, even the hard soul of the Dago had caught some of the infectious chivalry of the mountain desert. He didn't like to skin a woman — with a brake on the wheel.

But as he spun the wheel and the spokes glittered with a dangerous brightness, the old instinct rose strong in the soul of Dago Lew. Easily, skillfully, as the wheel spun back, he applied the brake. It stopped. Lew gathered in the crisply rustling bill with his usual expressionless face. He was surprised by a growl, almost inaudible.

As a rule the men of the mountain desert lose their money gracefully, and complaints are rare around a game of chance. But when Lew glanced up he saw a set of scowling faces, and just on each side and behind the girl there stood a swarthy giant and a red-haired one with danger in their eyes. Lew shrugged his shoulders. He was not to be intimidated.

"Take a whirl at the cards. They's a poker game jest over here," pleaded Red Mack. "Roulette ain't no game for a beginner. It goes to the head, that wheel does. The whirlin' of it sort of gets a man drunk."

"I'll say it does," cut in Dago Lew, his East Side slang and whining nasal contrasted sharply with the language of the men around him. "Lay off on the roulette, lady. You ain't got a look in here."

He cast a furtive glance toward Grogan, but the latter nodded approvingly. There was enough plunder among the men without fleecing a girl.

But she was laughing again. "I'll try this group. Four to one?"

"Pays four to one," Dago Lew nodded encouragingly.

"A chance is a chance," laughed Nancy, and placed another twenty.

The wheel spun, almost blinding her with the sharp sparkle of the whirling spokes. Then she felt another thing drawing her glance up, and met the steady gaze of Dago Lew.

He was intent upon her face, and this time, when she smiled openly up to him, a stain of red dyed his cheeks, and he looked abruptly away.

Slowly the wheel's motion grew slower and slower. By chance Nancy looked down and saw one of Dago's feet move in a peculiar fashion, as if he were fumbling for something, hesitate, and then move away. Untouched by the brake, the roulette wheel came to a stop. She had won. A growl of applause and relief came from the little crowd around her, and Dago mechanically began to count out her winnings. Nan laughed joyously.

"Who's thirsty?" she called. "Where's Mr. Grogan?"

"Here, lady."

"Drinks all around for the crowd, Mr. Grogan."

There was a moment of stunned silence. It took a flush man to treat that crowd at Number Ten prices; but then there began a rapid dissolving of the host around the roulette wheel and a swifter gathering at the bar.

CHAPTER XV

Story of Jeremiah

Number Ten spoke its mind while it gathered at Grogan's bar.

"Is she a sport? She is!"

"What part of the country turns out girls like that?"

"Where'd she come from? Who brung her to town?"

"Them two gents over there."

"But how'd Baldy get her?"

"I dunno. Ain't she a whirlwind, Mike? Look at her now, cool as ice, fresh as the mornin', happy as a bird. What's she drinkin'? Mike, is that redeye she's got?"

"Nope. It's ginger ale. She's a lady, you fool!"

Grogan summoned an assistant with a gesture to serve the crowd, and he cornered Dago Lew, who never left his post behind the wheel.

"What happened, Lew?" he asked anxiously. "Did your foot slip?"

Dago Lew eyed him without wincing.

"I didn't use it," he returned calmly.

"You mean to say," said Grogan hotly, "that you let her walk off with them eighty bucks without tryin' to stop her?"

Lew maintained sullen silence, which was usually a sign of danger, but Grogan was too angry to pay any heed.

"Is this a charity dump?" he asked furiously.

"Take it from me, bo," sneered Dago, "it ain't no charity dive."

"Dago," demanded Grogan, more soberly, "what's it mean?"

"It means this," snapped Dago. "Bring on all the men you want, and I'll do the dirty work for you. But when the women come in, they's got to be a change. The game's square as soon as a piece of calico plays the wheel. Did you watch her? Take most girls, and they go nuts when they drop a five; but she flipped a twenty and never batted a lamp. She's game; that's all. And she gets a straight deal while I'm behind the wheel."

His lower jaw thrust out viciously, and he leaned close to the proprietor.

"If you don't like the way I'm runnin' the game," he hissed, "take your own turn at it."

"You got me where you want me to-night, Dago," answered Grogan. "I can't run the wheel, and you know it. To-morrow we'll talk this over again."

"Cheese it!" whispered Dago Lew softly.

"Here's the dick lookin' for trouble."

The common danger made them forget their enmity of the instant before; for in the door stood no less a person than Marshal Bud Levine.

The marshal, however, did not wear his usual expression of rather drawn concern. He stood erect, one hand dangling from his hip, a glint of light in his eyes, and in all respects ten years younger than he had seemed when he last entered Grogan's place that night. For the marshal came in search of the source of the song which he had heard floating down the street, and accordingly he had come to the source of all things, good and ill, in Number Ten — Grogan's. He paused only a moment at the door, and then he saw the spot of white and smiled.

At that instant she was drinking with John Rapp, a broad, middle-aged fellow with a scarred face. Those scars had a story behind them. One of them dug deep into the cheek just beside the mouth, pulling the lips back in a continual grim and mirthless smile; another twisted like dim lightning down from his forehead, slipping past his eye.

It was generally thought that the scars came from a hand-to-hand conflict with a big puma; in reality they were scars gathered at *schlagerfests* in his student days, when Johann Rapp had been the gayest and noisiest fellow in Heidelberg. That was twenty years before, and a great many things had happened in between, but to-night the old days drew suddenly back to the duelist. His scarred face, his ugly smile, his surly temper, had made every girl he had met in the last decade glance with a shudder away from him, but this lovely creature in white had smiled on him in a way that nearly stopped his heart.

"*Fraulein,*" he said, "will you drink with Johann Rapp?"

"Surely."

"As comrades, then?"

"As comrades," she nodded.

So he had slipped his arm through hers and now they drank in the old student fashion, their elbows interlocked. She sipped her ginger ale, but Rapp downed his drink at a gulp and then dashed his glass into a thousand fragments on the floor. That had been the custom in the old days when the students drank a certain silent toast. Some one shouldered in front of Rapp, and he submitted tamely, for his heart was full.

"You come into town singin'," said the intruder between them. "Now, ain't you goin' to sing for us ag'in, lady?"

And a moment later a little semicircle cleared like magic before her, and with her back to the tall bar she began to sing. It was an old Hungarian folk song, with a rhythm as broken as ragtime. No one understood the words, but her eyes and her gestures told the story.

They stood mute about her, their hands tightening around their glasses, their eyes fixed on the pulse and throb of her throat, their ears filled with the dancing rhythm of the song, their hearts carried away by the purity of the voice. She sang without effort, but the sound filled the room. She sang for the joy of singing; and to each man it seemed that she was singing straight to him. For her eyes were never still, and a smile played about the corners of her lips. The song stopped abruptly, and Nan curtsied. There was a breathless pause, and then a roar that jarred the rafters over Grogan's place.

Followed a time of confusion in which some pleaded for another song and others banged the bar for a second drink. In this interval, the marshal found his way through the crowd to Nancy Scovil. She recognized him as a power in Number Ten by the way the others gave place to him. The marshal doffed his sombrero rather awkwardly. It was a year or so since he had tipped it last.

"I'm Bud Levine," he said. "I heard you singin', and I had to come and tell you I ain't heard nothin' like it yet."

"Thanks," nodded Nancy, "I'm Nancy Scovil, and — I'm glad to know you, Mr. Levine."

They were shaking hands when a change came over the face of Nancy Scovil. She raised her head; she sniffed; then she looked oddly at the marshal. For when Bud Levine took Aiken from Grogan's place, the trousers of the captive, soaked with Florida water, had rubbed against the captor and left him fragrant indeed. To Nancy it was like finding a field of spring wild flowers in the midst of the sands of the desert. She sniffed again.

"Florida water!" burst out Nancy Scovil.

To her astonishment the marshal started and cast a glance of alarm over his shoulder. He sighed with relief when he saw no danger approaching.

"I thought," he explained to her, "that he'd busted close when you said that."

"I couldn't help it," chuckled Nancy, "I didn't know that Westerners used perfumes."

"Miss Scovil," answered the marshal, very red and earnest, "no more do we. This smell come from a nut that I locked up a while ago. Me bein' the marshal, you see?"

"Florida water?" she echoed.

"Don't seem nacheral, does it?"

"I like a little of it," said Nan, "but, marshal,

you're as fragrant as the rose room in a greenhouse."

"Lady," he pleaded, "don't rub it in. It ain't my fault if the stuff is catchin'. This queer gent near busted up Number Ten because he lost a bottle of the stuff."

"Really? Tell me about it!"

"Hey, marshal," called a voice in the crowd which gathered thicker and thicker around them, "are you makin' an arrest? Has the lady busted the law?"

"She ain't," growled the marshal, "but you'll get your face busted, Steve, if you don't watch sharp and keep it shut."

He turned to the girl.

"I didn't see how it started, but I was told," he went on. "This funny gent come into town and bought a bottle of Florida water and got it busted in his hip pocket here in the saloon. The minute the boys smelled it they allowed he was a nut, and they started to manhandle him. But they didn't more'n get started, and he done the finishin'. Look at old Grogan's jaw; and Steve's eye. Yes, he went right through 'em. Wasn't a big man, either, but he sure wrecked the party here in Grogan's. They kept hittin' where he wasn't, and he kept landin' 'em where they live.

"Pretty soon big Grogan come for me and told me there was a riot, so I come over. You wouldn't believe it, but he near ran into my gun with his bare hands. He was like a wild cat, lady, but all the time he was laughin' fit to bust and havin' a fine party out of that fight. So I put him away to cool down, but I rubbed up agin' him and got this stuff all over me. I dunno how to get it out."

The eyes of Nancy sparkled with interest.

"What sort of man is he?" she asked.

"Nothin' much. Sort of broad. Medium tall. Always laughin'."

"What's his name?"

"Jeremiah Smith."

She shook her head, puzzled and a little disappointed.

"At least, that's the name he give me," said the marshal.

"I don't suppose I could see him?" asked Nan.

"Nothin' easier," nodded Levine. "The jail is jest across the street."

It was not easy to break away from the crowd, however. They thronged between the marshal and the door, big men, rough men, angry men. They had heard her sing, they had seen her laugh; it was like taking a toy from a child to deprive them of Nancy Scovil. Chief of all, Red Mack and Pete the Runt reached her side and elbowed between her and the marshal.

The Runt laid his great hand on the shoulder of Levine and growled in his ear: "Listen to me, partner, and go slow. This lady is here with us, and she ain't gallivantin' around with nobody we don't know."

The marshal glared.

"Thanks," he gritted. "Why, you big ham head, if I need advice I'll —"

"Please!" cried Nancy, slipping between them. "I *asked* him to take me, Pete. Besides I'm my own boss. Are we going?"

This last to the marshal, who paused to send a sinister glance at Pete before he swung about and took her arm. A moment later they were out on the street with the crowd behind them.

If a vote had been taken then on the most unpopular, obnoxious public nuisance in Number Ten, Marshal Bud Levine would certainly have stood first on the ballot. Nancy knew it, and he knew she knew it. Indeed, she seemed bent on making amends by being particularly pleasant to Bud. Not that she sympathized with him to the exclusion of the men within the gambling hall; for she felt in Grogan's place as if a little intangible thread bound all those strong, rough men to her.

And along each thread ran an electric current that set her tingling. Indeed, there had been times, in Grogan's, such as the moments when she was singing to them, when she felt as if they were all gathered in the palm of her hand, and she had only to close her fingers in order to see them wriggle.

It was all very new to Nancy. In the dull oblivion of her past life men had been merely meaningless landmarks, hardly more vital than hills and not half so pleasant as green trees. Now they were different, amazingly different. They were vast powers which tugged at her oddly. She liked them all. It was pleasant to be near them. The ugliest, roughest face in Grogan's thrilled Nancy because she sensed infinite strength, determination, danger.

Out of Grogan's, she felt as if a thousand impalpable hands which had been touching her had fallen away. The keener air of the night was in her face; above her the stars burned low and yellow in a vast arch, like yellow diamonds bedded in rich velvet. And here was a single man walking beside her. He had had the power to take her away from Grogan's in spite of opposition. He was the strongest, and Nancy wanted to pay him some tribute.

"A lot of long-horned mavericks!" the marshal was muttering savagely to himself. "Wild men — man-eaters — some day I'll be doin' harm to 'em!"

"Why, marshal," said the girl eagerly, "they're a fine lot. I never saw such men before!"

"Lady," said Levine solemnly, "you can take this from me; they's a difference between them and other men like the difference between wild mustangs and tame hosses."

But Nancy stopped short in the middle of the street, and faced the marshal; the glow from the gasoline lamp of the hotel flickered strangely across her face and lighted her smile.

"But, Marshal Levine," she cried, "you're just like the rest of them — only stronger — that's why I like you so much!"

She walked on with him toward the jail.

The marshal's head was reeling. It was not so much what she had said as it was the way she had said it. Convention chains up a woman most of the time and dims the light in her eyes, and controls her smile, and gives gravity and monotony to her voice, but when Nancy faced the marshal her femininity flamed in her eyes, and made her voice rich, and quivered about her lips.

The marshal drew one deep, gulping breath, and it was like strong wine of Samos and set a humming in his brain. He could not know that all the power which was quivering in Nan was the pent-up energy of years now bursting forth in one riotous night. And she would have talked to any man as she had talked to him. She would have walked as close beside any one. She would have hummed in the same manner beneath her breath.

But as they went toward the jail the rest of the way the marshal was adding up swift columns of figures. He was wondering if he could support such a wife comfortably on his income. And as he opened the door of the place he was deciding that he must give up this hard life. When he had some one to live for —

"Where is he?" cut in the voice of the girl.

Still walking in a trance, the marshal unlocked the door of the cell.

"Hey, you!" he called. "Come out of it!"

And Jerry Aiken, alias Jeremiah Smith, stood leaning against the door, in the full glow of the lamp which the marshal had lighted the moment before.

"You!" cried Nancy Scovil, and burst into a peal of laughter that filled the room with music. "You!"

"Right-o!" nodded Jerry, not the least abashed.

"D'you know this gent?" queried the marshal.

She paid no attention to him, but approached the prisoner.

"Whew!" sniffed Nan as she came close. "Have you been trying to turn yourself into a rose?"

"Sweet as a song, eh?" Jerry grinned.

"A song in a jail," echoed Nan. "In for breaking the peace? I never knew that Florida water went to the head."

"Fifteen per cent alcohol," nodded Jerry. "Not bad in a pinch. Try it some time."

She sat down and tilted herself back in a chair, still chuckling.

The marshal looked from one to the other of them in full amazement.

"But they've messed you up, Jerry."

He fingered the shredded remnants of his shirt.

"Yep," he smiled, "they spoiled everything except my perfume."

"Keep away!" she cried, waving her hand. "Jerry, you're going to *my* head."

"Of course. Give me time, girl; I'm just making a beginning."

"When do you expect to get out?"

"When I'm through resting," he answered, and favored the marshal with a grin. "What's happened to you, Nan? You're awake!"

He stood brimming with curiosity, eagerness, fairly on tiptoe with surprise and alertness. And Nancy, for her part, saw him with new eyes. In front of the rather ordinary bulk of Jerry the phantoms of the men of Grogan's passed before her, huge men, rough-handed, keen-eyed. Men, in all seeming, who could crush this fellow without exertion. And then she remembered the swollen jaw of Grogan himself, and the bruised features of many of the rest. Jerry Aiken had done it all. He had wrecked Grogan's. How?

She squinted at him, puzzled. Perhaps it was the spirit which made him mock her now, unabashed in his rags and tatters; the spirit which glittered in his eyes. There was hardly a bruise on his face; not a mark of the battle he had passed through.

"Jerry," she broke out, "I never knew you before."

"Nancy," he answered, with the same ring in his voice, "I never knew *you* before."

He had approached close to her, and the marshal watched their lighted faces with a growing unrest. For some reason or other he was no longer figuring the details of his income.

"Keep back, there!" he commanded harshly.

"Sure," nodded Jerry Aiken.

A muffled sound reached them from Grogan's across the way. Nancy listened to it with her head canted a little to one side.

"We've got to get back to our party," she announced, rising and nodding to the marshal.

"Into the cell with you," said Bud Levine gruffly.

"Party!" echoed Jerry.

"The boys and I," replied Nancy.

"Good-by, then!"

She took his outstretched hand, and he held it with a strong pressure. His eyes were glittering against hers, burning into her like an acid, and from his grip a tingle of strength meeting strength went shivering up her arm.

And then he said, "Nancy, before morning there'll be the devil to pay in Number Ten. Don't forget me."

And he retreated into his cell. The last she saw as the darkness swallowed him was the glitter of his eyes. Then the marshal closed the door and locked it.

"But can't you let him loose?" pleaded Nancy as the latter turned toward her.

"Why?" asked Bud Levine sullenly.

"He'd be a bully one to have at the party."

"Let him keep on restin'!" scowled Levine. "The kind of fun he makes keeps me workin' overtime."

She shrugged her shoulders. By the time they were outside the door she was singing softly again to herself as she had done before. But there was a great difference to the marshal. He felt as if he were a thousand miles away. He walked by her side, crossing the street back to Grogan's, but he knew that he was not in her thoughts, and furthermore, he knew that her thoughts were walking by the side of some other man.

If Levine had been asked to name the man, he could have made a very shrewd guess.

CHAPTER XVI

The Ouija Board

They welcomed her back to Grogan's with a shout, and a great happiness came singing back in Nancy as she stood at the door. They turned toward her from the bar, from the gaming tables. They threw up their hands and roared a greeting to her. What a crowd they were! What color! What variety!

They were no sooner inside the door than a swirl of men rolled toward her from the bar, pleading for another song, and swept her back with them. The marshal left her, downcast, thoughtful. He had a feeling, as soon as she was away from him, that he had been handling fire, delightful, but decidedly hot. He looked after her with a touch of amusement and a touch of concern.

She was having a wonderful time. His own heart leaped as he saw the brightness of her face, and she danced through the crowd, scattering smiles and words. In front of her all was expectancy, but the moment she had passed men began crowding after to get close again, elbowing each other aside, and exchanging bitter looks. Bitter looks, in Grogan's, do not come very long ahead of bitter deeds. And Marshal Bud Levine knew it very well.

For one thing at least he was thankful. Jerry was in the jail and safely retained there. The thought of him joining forces with this girl was like the thought of oil added to fire. The marshal shivered a little.

As the crowd gathered up Nancy again, much in the manner that a wave licks up the beach and sweeps down to the ocean a bit of driftwood, Pete the Runt used his massive shoulders to get close to her, and Red Mack came closely in his wake.

"Nancy," said Red Mack, lowering his voice so that it might not be heard by any save the girl, "it's time we was out of here."

"Why?" she asked, and looked up to him with a frown.

She was beginning to feel that both Red Mack and the Runt were a weight which she was dragging after her as a ship drags a sea anchor. They spoiled her party with their serious faces and their warnings. A sudden desire to get rid of them swept over her.

"Why?" echoed the Runt gravely. "Because this ain't no place for a lady. I been here long enough to see that."

"Pete," she said sharply, "I'll decide what places are fit for me." She turned toward Red Mack. "Won't I, Mack?" she appealed.

"Of course she will," said Red Mack, rather illogically. "Don't she know her own mind?"

The crowd bore Nancy away; but Pete and Red were facing each other, glaring.

"Who called for any lip from you?" queried the Runt savagely.

"It don't need no call to keep a gent from makin' a fool of himself," declared Red Mack. "Don't you know better'n to talk to a lady like that?"

"Mack," said the Runt, "I've bore a lot from you. If you was born ignor'nt, it ain't no call for you to show it all the time."

Over the heads of the crowd he saw Nancy. She had turned back toward him, smiling, and the Runt took the smile as a warrant to go forward; but Red Mack had seen the same smile and received it as a special encouragement.

"They ain't no doubt that we ought to get her out of Grogan's," continued Mack; "but you ain't goin' to get her out by insultin' her — nor insultin' me."

The Runt turned a dark and angry red.

"Why," he exclaimed, "you red-headed scarecrow, you walkin' skeleton, since when have you been readin' the minds of ladies?"

"Hell!" hissed Red Mack, and smote the Runt upon the root of the nose. For a moment the Runt was too astonished to make any rejoinder. Then he leaned back, rested his weight securely on his right foot, and swept forward his right hand with force enough to have knocked Red through the wall, had it landed. But before it came near him, Red Mack ducked under that terrible blow and came up close to the Runt whaling away with both fists at close range. Pete the Runt received the stunning blow upon one side of the jaw, and then his face was knocked straight by an equally hard punch on the opposite side; and an instant later Red's lean fists sank to the wrist in Pete's stomach.

Any one of these strokes would have laid up a lesser man for repairs, but the Runt merely grunted, and brushed Red away to full-arm distance with a backhand sweep. Then he smashed Red on the ribs with bruising force. It doubled Red over like a closing jack-knife, but as he stooped he launched an over-hand swing, doubly strong with the pain of his contracting muscles. It landed squarely upon the Runt's already damaged nose and brought out a spout of blood. At that point the battle really began, for the Runt went mad with the sight of his own blood, and Red Mack fought like a demon to plant another blow on the same point.

Marshal Levine was by no means idle in the meantime. He was struggling desperately to get to the two combatants, but around them had gathered with uncanny speed every man in Grogan's. A good many of them had already felt the bruising of fists earlier in the evening, and now they danced with glee to see the damage the two giants worked.

For it was veritably an engagement of giants. The Runt struck with thrice the power that Mack could possibly put into his lean arms, but on the other hand Mack hit with thrice the speed. His flashing hands whacked the Runt on head and face and body like the play of a trip hammer, but the Runt, grunting at every stroke, stuck by his guns.

Somewhere in the distance he heard the voice of Levine yelling that the fight must stop, threatening the jail for any one who kept him away from the combatants. Before going to jail the Runt wanted to get home one finishing wallop which would square all accounts and leave a considerable sum in his favor.

He commenced to press in. Blows glanced from his forehead, cracked on his jaw, thudded on his chest and ribs, and still he shook his head and came in doggedly waiting for an opening. If Mack had had room he might have kept away, but the circle about them grew smaller and smaller as the audience, in its growing enthusiasm, pressed in to watch every blow. So eventually, when Mack leaped back, his retreat was stopped by a wall of flesh, and the next instant the massive fist of the Runt whacked against his jaw, and Mack struck the man behind and literally rebounded to the floor.

He was hurt rather than stunned, however, and just as the Runt stepped back to wipe the blood from his face and survey the conquered, Mack leaped to his feet again and charged like a wild cat. They clinched, struggled a moment, and then rolled under the feet of the crowd in an inextricable, cursing tangle.

All of this Nancy had watched from the outskirts of the mass. She had known when she left the two that there was apt to be trouble between them, but she could think of no better way of getting rid of them than by playing one against the other. She had felt like the marksman with his finger pressing the trigger, but when the rush began to watch the fight, she floated to the edge of the circle.

From this point she could see the heads of Runt and Mack rising aloft above the surrounders, and she saw the fists dart out and land, and saw the heads bob and sway under the impact of the blows. Once, twice, and again she strove to slip into the mass of spectators and get to the combatants to separate them, but every time the hustling backs crowded closer together and shut her out. There was nothing to do but stand and watch.

She was sorry for the fight; she would have given a good deal to stop it; but she would not have been the new Nancy if she had not felt something more than regret. She was the cause for which they fought, and the strength behind every punch was a tribute to her power. This was some of that danger she had sensed in the very air over Grogan's. What if the whole place should break into turmoil, with her the center of it all?

There was a shouting from the center of the crowd: "They're down!"

Then, as the group scattered, she saw the two writhing, twisting fighters on the floor; the next moment Marshal Bud Levine, his hat off, his bandanna torn from his throat by the struggle to get through the crowd, leaned over the two and placed a hand on either shoulder. They were under arrest.

The hand of the law had a remarkably sobering effect upon both the Runt and Red Mack. They rose, much bedraggled, bloodstained, glaring at one another, but decidedly amenable to reason; for Bud Levine carried that in his eyes which usually cleared the minds of even the most violent.

"Jest face that door and start marchin'," said the marshal. "And don't march too fast. If you do, I'm apt to halt you, and when I halt you, you may stand still a long time."

He did not show a gun, but there was a certain nervousness about his right hand which said many things to the eye of the initiated. Number Ten had watched Marshal Bud Levine at work long before this. And now Number Ten stood aside as meekly as a shorn lamb and did not even bleat. Only Nancy dared to interfere. She stepped to Levine.

"Marshal," she said, "are you really going to arrest them?"

"Miss Scovil," answered the marshal, "it sure looks like I am."

"But what harm have they done to any one except themselves?"

The marshal looked at the bloody face and the red-stained shirt of the Runt and then grinned.

"They ain't been no murder here, ma'am, and I aim to keep it away. But they was a killin' jest next door to us. These gents can rest up in the coop."

She turned to them, her eyes soft with pity. One hand received the brawny fist of the Runt; the other hand took the hard, lean fingers of Red Mack.

"I'm sorry," she murmured. "So sorry!"

"Don't think nothin' about it," said Mack reassuringly. "He had this comin' to him for a long time. He never knowed nothin' about how to talk to a lady."

The Runt wiped the blood from his face with his free hand. With the other he squeezed the fingers of Nancy.

"I'll finish him later," he said. "He was always in your way, lady."

"Forward!" commanded the marshal, and the procession wound out through the door.

It was no sooner gone than it was forgotten. The card games at the tables began again; the roulette once more spun; the glasses flashed and tinkled across the bar; and a considerable group waited with an eye upon Nancy. Number Ten had been diverted, but now it resumed the serious business of spending money.

"Noisy pair of gents, them two that come to town with you," remarked Baldy, hobbling to the side of Nancy. "Mostly Number Ten is uncommon quiet till strangers blows in. You foller me the rest of the evening, lady, and you won't be havin' no fights around you. They ain't been so much noise in Number Ten since the night old Wendell made his strike and hung the weejee over yonder on the wall."

Here the great Grogan himself approached

the girl with a request for a song, and a clamor rose to back him, but Nancy had caught a spark of interest in Baldy's remarks.

"Tell me about old Wendell," she said.

"He was a queer old nut," said Baldy, "and he come here and sat over yonder at that table with a big piece of paper spread in front of him and a piece of board with a pencil at one end of it. He put his hand on the board, and the pencil began writing — leastwise, old Wendell said it was writing, but we couldn't make much out of it. Jest a big scrawl. But old Wendell got pretty excited. He called the thing a 'ouija' and he said the ouija had told him where there was a big lead of gold up in the hills."

"Was he crazy?" asked the girl.

"Sounds like it, ma'am," nodded Baldy, "but old Wendell hit off through the hills where nobody never thought of ever lookin' for a smell of gold, and three months later he come back through Number Ten loaded with dust, and he kept Number Ten drunk for two days and hung up his ouija on the wall, yonder. Since then they ain't been so much noise ag'in, askin' your pardon, miss — until you come to town."

On the wall in the corner, hanging from a nail by a bit of string, Nancy saw a little triangular piece of thin wood. When she asked to see it more closely, Baldy brought it and she noted it in detail. It was a perfectly plain bit of wood cheaply varnished. It was rudely heart-shaped, and from the top showed nothing except a hole through which the pencil passed. Underneath, at the broad end of the triangle, were two more or less wabbly little wheels. They made two points of support, and the third was at the apex of the triangle, being the tip of the pencil thrust through the hole in the board.

The device was very plain. When it was placed upon paper on a smooth surface, the wabbly wheels stirred here and there under the slightest pressure, and the pencil tip was bound to move irregularly up and down and to and fro, carrying on a scrawling line which might and might not look like writing.

Having come so far in her examination of the ouija board, Nancy was about to hand it back to Baldy when she saw something like letters on the under side of the board. She blew off the dust, and then she found, written in pencil which had dug into the soft wood the following: "The hand which writes with me shall describe the past, the future, and the hearts of men." Nancy read it aloud, laughing up to Baldy.

"Do you believe in it?" she asked.

"I dunno," muttered Baldy, scratching his

head. "It ain't the sort of thing I like to fool with. It brung gold to old Wendell. Maybe it'd bring somethin' else to the next man that handled it. No, I don't believe in it; and I don't disbelieve; I'm sort of betwixt and between."

But Nancy wished to try out the ouija board, so Grogan himself brought out a stray roll of wall paper. The under side of it presented a broad, smooth, white surface, ideal for the clumsy scrawl which would result from the pencil of the board. A chair was drawn up for Nancy to the table on which the paper and the board were placed, and a curious group stood around to watch.

"As I remember," suggested Grogan, "old Wendell jest rested his finger tips real light on it, and the thing writ right off. I couldn't make out what it said, but old Wendell he seen through it right away. He made words, but it looked to me like a baby's scribblin'."

"You try," said Nancy, and pushed the board toward Grogan.

He took it, grinning sheepishly.

"It ain't that I believe in it," he assured the smiling crowd. "But they's something queer in it. Seemed to sort of hit off the right thing for old Wendell, boys. But they's got to be a question asked before it'll write. Old Wendell he kept mutterin' a question, and then the thing would scribble. What are you askin', gents?"

A wit immediately bawled from back of the circle: "What sort of a gent is Grogan?"

"Well," grinned Grogan, "we'll see what it says to that."

He laid his big fingers on the little board. At first there was not the slightest motion.

"Fake," grunted a bystander. "They ain't nothin' goin' to happen. Must have all been drunk, includin' Wendell, when it writ last time."

But he had no sooner finished speaking than the board stirred. Perhaps it was because Grogan had shifted the position of his hand a little. The clumsy wheels wabbled a little, and the pencil trailed out several dots and dashes, and then a long, scrawling line. Grogan lifted the board, and a cluster of heads crowded above the table to read the verdict.

"N-o," spelled Nancy. "It says they weren't drunk when it wrote last. Now try again, Mr. Grogan: 'What sort of a gent is Grogan?' "

There was less laughter now. Grogan, with a look of dull wonder which seemed perilously close to apprehension, rested his hand on the board again. This time, without the slightest hesitation, it started wabbling across the paper, trailing the pencil line swiftly out. It stopped; Grogan raised the little instrument, and once more there was the swift shadowing as heads crowded above the paper.

"C-r-o-o-k," spelled Nancy. "Crook!"

The shadowing heads suddenly removed themselves.

"Ha, ha, ha, ha!" roared some one. "Grogan's a crook. He says so himself!"

"Who was laughin' there?" shouted Grogan, balling his hand into a huge fist. "What empty nutshell that calls itself a brain started laughin' at that?"

He searched the crowd in vain for a challenging face, and growled as he found none.

"It's a fool idee," proclaimed Grogan, glaring around in dumb desire to find some object on which to wreak his vengeance. "It's a fool game and no sense to it."

And he stamped off toward the bar, followed by a soft, controlled murmur that might have been low laughter or might have been a thoughtful whisper.

"You try it now," suggested Nancy to Baldy, and she pushed it toward him.

But Baldy shook his head in instant decision.

"That ouija don't do no good. It's finished diggin' gold, and most like it's started to raise somethin' else. I don't want to use it none, ma'am."

"Maybe it's got some pet names for you,

Baldy," said one of the men; and the laugh began again.

"You, then," said Nancy to the last speaker.

But he snatched his hands away and held them behind him like a boy.

"Not me, ma'am. Which I got no hankerin' particular to use it."

Another laugh, for McIntosh was a known man.

"You try it," they urged Nancy, and she obediently rested her slender fingers upon the little board.

CHAPTER XVII

Prophecies

A tension had grown up in Grogan's since the little board was first placed on the paper. A whisper of it had reached the poker tables, and thinned the group at chuck-a-luck, and drawn many from the roulette; and even those who still played their games, or idled at the bar, kept an eye open for the ouija board and its pronouncements.

Nancy tried her hand upon the board; it wabbled oddly to the touch, but she found that it was possible to control the shaking, give it direction, and, without apparent effort on her part, make the pencil write at her will — a sufficiently unimportant discovery, but it thrilled Nancy Scovil.

These men about her were gathered from a hundred quarters of the globe — strong men seeking action — and in her hand was an instrument that could control them all. She watched them, smiling from face to face, and under her eyes they lifted their glances for an instant, but on the whole the air was charged with an uneasy, superstitious distrust. They looked at one another, and they stared at Nancy's white hand upon the board.

"Questions?" she asked.

"Nothin' about gents in particular," said one man hastily. "Let's get somethin' by and large — something about the whole room —"

He stopped short, for though Nancy was still looking in his face, the ouija board was moving under her hand, and it scrawled a long line across the paper, and it was writing still when it reached the edge of the paper. Such fluent writing roused a hum of interest, and they commenced to spell out the words:

"In this room there is a cattle thief and —"

"And what?" grunted a score of voices.

A cattle thief? Among all the men in Number Ten there were few indeed who had not occasionally rustled a stray, but one of these innocents — because he had followed the mines from boyhood — spread out his feet and growled: "Let's get the name of the damned crook! Go ahead, lady, and see if the board will get his name?"

A stir came from the group about the questioner.

"Are we a sheriff's posse?"

"Let the marshal get the rustler. That ain't our business."

"You ask too many questions, partner."

"And what? Put her back on the paper, lady!"

So Nancy obediently lifted the ouija and started it again. Bobbing, swaying, staggering as if the spirit of an imp controlled it, the little heart-shaped board moved along the paper, and the hand of Nancy rested so carelessly on it that it seemed to be dragging her unwilling arm after it.

This time it completed the sentence:

"And the silent man with the long spurs is on his trail."

Another stir, but this time less open. Each man surveyed his neighbors with covert glances, and found many a silent man, and at least two out of five wore very long spurs.

The change which came about in Grogan's was accomplished in the twinkling of an eye. Just an instant before all had been hail fellow well met, but now the noise was blanketed. Men began to look toward the door. They attained a comfortable distance from the rest; the compact little crowd sifted apart until a man could have worked his way in any direction through the mass.

Jaws set hard; eyes with a cold glint in them moved with restless glances here and there; hands became extremely nervous; and each man grew a little irritated because there were others behind him. Scratch the surface of a dog, and you're very apt to find a wolf. Nancy had scratched the surface of Number Ten, and now teeth were beginning to show.

"It ain't no point talkin' about men," put in another member of the crowd. "What I'd like to know is why the roulette here ain't never been beat much?"

"This here ain't no mind reader," replied his companion scornfully. "What d' you expect from it?"

But Nancy was remembering how the foot of Dago Lew had fumbled as though reaching for something, and then withdrawn. She was suddenly very angry. She, in fact, had escaped without a great loss, but if the wheel were indeed crooked it was a crime beneath contempt to cheat these big, strong, careless spendthrifts.

Even as they were, money slipped like water through their fingers, but to lead them into an ambuscade to wheedle away what might almost be had for the asking was a depth of villainy that made Nancy cold inside. And she felt toward the men of Number Ten, in a peculiar mixture, sisterhood and impish desire to torment them.

Now, under the cunning pressure of her fingers, the ouija began to write the reply to the last question.

"Look under the floor behind the wheel."

This was what the clustering heads around Nancy read trailing across the paper behind the board.

"A brake, by the Eternal!" rumbled a voice of low thunder at Nancy's very ear. "And I've dropped five hundred on that crooked frame-up if I've dropped a five. Boys, let's tear up the floor and see."

They melted away from around the ouija board; even Nancy was forgotten as they poured toward the roulette wheel. The first wave of their coming scattered the few who were already playing the game. The vanguard surrounded the wheel and Dago, while the more providential gathered hammers and axes to strip up the floor. Then they flooded back to do their work. There was no shouting, no cursing, but a little murmur much like the humming of angry bees — a sound which will make the strongest beast of prey in the world take to its heels.

They swept about Dago and carried him staggering back by the weight of their numbers. The first ax fell and splintered a board.

"Hey!" yelled Dago Lew. "Lay offn that stuff."

His voice was sharp and shrill and small as the voice of a small boy. He was almost sob-bing with rage as he shook off those who shouldered him. His words came squeaking out:

"Scatter, will you, you big dubs — you ham-and four-flushers!"

Grogan himself came with a rush on the opposite side, roaring: "What's up here? Where'd you get that ax, Pete? Damn you, you will, will you?"

For Pete raised the ax to gouge the floor again, and Grogan wrested the thing from him with ease.

"Now, you gents," he bellowed, "tell us what's gone wrong with you? Been chewin' loco weed?"

They fell back a little, partly because of the ax in the ample grasp of Grogan, partly because of the shrill fury of Dago Lew.

"We're goin' to get up part of this floor and see what's under it," stated Pete, who elected himself spokesman. "We don't mean to harm you, Grogan — not less'n we find something wrong. But they's always been something kind of queer about this wheel."

"Rip up my floor?" thundered Grogan, his eyes contracting to points of dangerous light. "Drop that wedge, Shorty, or I'll bean your blockhead."

Shorty was lately from the mines; and he had dropped most of his stake at this same roulette wheel. He dropped the wedge obediently, and the hammer as well; but as he stood up his right hand was resting significantly on his hip.

"You get this straight, Grogan," he said quietly. "We're going to look into this. Don't make no fool of yourself. If we spoil some of the floor I'll stand good for it."

He snatched out a number of gold coins and jingled them in the hollow of his left hand.

"I guess that'll be enough to cover the damages. We ain't sayin' they's anything wrong with you, Grogan, but they was always something different about Dago. He don't belong in these here parts."

It afforded a loophole of escape to Grogan, and being desperate he took it.

"Go as far as you like, boys," he said, "if you think they's something crooked with the wheel. Maybe Dago *has* doctored it."

"Doctored it? Me? You put it all on me?" screamed Dago Lew. "Why, you cheap lifter, wasn't you in on it? Lemme out of here; I'm done with it all!"

"But we ain't done with *you,*" said Shorty. "Hey, Pete, stop the little rat, will you?"

"Get back in the corner!" roared Pete. "Get back, or I'll squash you, Dago."

Dago had been trying to wriggle through the crowd, but now he went back to the corner in a single leap. As his shoulders struck against the wall a gun jumped into his hand. It was a short-barreled .45, a pudgy, ridiculous-looking gun, but it had about it the air of having been well worn, and in front of Dago Lew an empty circle appeared, widening every instant like a ripple around the stone which is dropped in a pool. For the face of Dago was colorless with something more than fear, and there was murder in his beady eyes. He shook from head to foot, not with terror, but with a frenzied desire to kill.

"Now you got me here," he said, whining the words shrilly through his nose, "what d' you want with me?"

"We'll tell you, in words of one syllable," announced Pete. There was a long .45 in his hand; a dozen other weapons gleamed. "Throw your gun on the floor, Dago," advised Shorty. "You ain't got a chance."

"You fool," cried Dago, "I'd go to hell happy if I could send some of youse guys there along with me."

No one spoke in answer to that — there was only one answer which could be given. Silence entered Grogan's place and stole about like a living thing. There was no chance to bluff, no chance to escape. Dago Lew had to die, but before his eyes closed, his bullets were bound to find flesh in the closely compacted crowd around him.

CHAPTER XVIII

Enter Scovil

Inside the outer room of the jail he made the pair stand against the wall while he unlocked the door to the inner chamber of stone and called out the prisoner. The latter came rubbing his eyes.

"Hate to wake you up," remarked the marshal, "but two have got the call over one. You bunk out here. These two gents get your place."

But Jerry had spied the two, and now he burst into ringing laughter. It lasted so long that he had to lean against the wall to steady himself.

"So," he said, when at last he could speak, "she's sent both of you up?"

The two big men glowered in silence upon him.

"How the devil," cried Levine, "do you know that the girl is behind this?"

"Because I read her mind," answered Jerry. "She's shaking them off; she's getting clear for a cruise of her own, and when she gets through with that cruise, marshal, you'll have your old jail packed like a tin of sardines."

"Smith," muttered the marshal, "they ain't any doubt that you got a brain. Raisin' hell comes as natural to her as buckin' comes to a mustang. Hey, you two gents, step inside that door. You got no guns, but you got your hands, and if you want to fight it out, go to it. Step lively."

"Marshal," snarled the Runt, "get a broom and a can ready. When I get through with Mack you'll need to do some cleanin' up of pieces."

"Five minutes alone with him is all I ask," answered Mack as they stepped through the door.

The marshal closed it and then turned toward Jerry with an expectant grin.

"I only wish," he said, "that I could watch that scrap."

"There won't be a fight," answered Jerry.

"Why not?"

"Because the girl isn't here to watch."

"By gum," chuckled the marshal, "I think you're right. I don't hear nothin' but talk. And even that's quietin' down."

"Sure," nodded Jerry. "In the morning they'll be sitting holding each other's hands like a couple of schoolgirls. Why, man, they're pals. Why don't you sit down and chin a while?

You'll need all the rest you can get before the night is done with."

"The girl?" queried the marshal.

"It's in her eyes," agreed Jerry. "Hell is popping in them."

"I'd give a hundred even," sighed the marshal, as he sat down, "if she was out of Number Ten. This town was always jest one step from hell, but that girl has taken the last step. We're right at the gates, Smith. Say, that was a fine pannin' she give you, comin' here to laugh at you."

Jerry gritted his teeth, but the next moment his eyes danced.

"It's nothing," he said, "to what I'm going to do to her when I get out."

"Speakin' of that," said the marshal, "if you're to stay in this room to-night I got to get your word not to try to escape."

"No parole," grinned Jerry.

"Then it's the irons for you, partner."

"Get 'em out. I'll take —"

Into his sentence ripped a sharp explosion, the short bark of a revolver.

"Grogan's!" cried the marshal, and bolted for the door.

He barely paused to lock it after him, and then raced for Grogan's down the street.

The rush of the men from the table where Nancy sat manufacturing prophecies to the roulette, the interference of Grogan, his betrayal of Dago Lew, and the cornering of the latter, were all episodes crowded into the briefest space. By the time Nancy had reached the semicircle which hemmed in Dago, she saw the gambler with his back to the wall, his chest heaving rapidly, his mouth twitching, the gun jerking ominously in his hand.

For the first time in her life Nancy found herself face to face with naked masculinity, all the droning monotony of custom and commonplace torn away, and the beast underneath staring into her eyes. The acid was about to strike the clear liquid and fill it with the precipitate of stormy action. And she rejoiced in it. Her heart raced. A berserker joy dimmed her eyes, and she wanted to tilt her head back and shout shrilly with delight in the battle. It was all her work. She had gathered those elements of strength in Grogan's, and poised them with consummate ease, and then dashed them together.

Then, tearing into her consciousness, lighting her mind like the lightning which rips the sky apart, a gun exploded. It was not an intentional or an aimed shot. One of the younger men, carried away by the tenseness of the moment, had allowed his forefinger to contract, and the lead ripped a long splinter from the floor and lodged in the wall.

It was the signal. A second later a dozen guns would belch, and Dago Lew, crushed and torn by the storm of lead, would lie writhing and screaming on the floor, and empty his gun at his murderers with the last of his strength of mind and body. Yet that vital second lay between the signal and the battle, and in that breathing space, even while Dago crouched, Nancy sprang through the crowd, whirled, and leaped back in front of the gambler, her arms thrown wide as if to welcome the deadly volley. A groan of horror burst from the men; she stood there before them, flushed with excitement, fearless, light-footed as the wind, eager as childhood.

Behind her she heard Dago Lew cursing softly with astonishment. At least, he had not cheated her, and for the sake of that square bit of play she would save him. The conscious power to do it welled up in her. She picked up face after face in the crowd with her dancing eyes.

"Partners," she said, "twenty to one is not man to man. If Dago has been crooked, a good many others have been crooked, too. Give him a running chance for his life. Will you?"

No one took it upon himself to answer as spokesman; but there was a general murmur of wonder.

"They *will* give you a fighting chance,

Dago," she said, without turning her head toward him. "Keep behind me. We're going straight for the front door."

As she advanced along the wall, the men before her gave way. The eagerness for the kill was still on them, but they could not meet her eye. They passed the danger line with a deadly silence in the room; they glided among the gaming tables; they reached the door.

"Lady," Dago was saying in a swift, trembling murmur as they proceeded, "if you ever need me, send for me. Bars won't keep me from comin'; walls won't keep me out; before I go to hell I'll pay you back!"

They were at the door when the marshal leaped through it, his face ashen gray, his weapon in his hand.

"What's up?" he gasped.

"Inside," said Nan instantly.

The marshal plunged through the entrance, and Dago Lew slid out and down the street as swiftly and silently as a racing cloud shadow. In ten minutes the desert would swallow him.

"What's up?" barked Bud Levine. "Grogan, what was that gun play?"

Big Grogan stood leaning weakly against the bar. His own face was as colorless as that of the marshal.

"I dunno," he muttered. "I dunno nothin'. Ask the girl."

There had been a general movement of restoring guns to holsters as soon as the familiar, lean face of the fighting marshal appeared at the door. Levine did not miss that movement. He turned and glared at Nancy.

"You!" he exclaimed. "What have you been up to now?"

"I've been acting as your deputy," answered the girl carelessly.

"Ma'am," said Levine angrily, "I mean it. What's happened here?"

"You're on a back trail, Bud," said Shorty. "Keep off the lady, Bud. Hadn't been for her, Dago Lew would be hungerin' for a place to push daisies, and you'd be here smellin' smoke and lookin' for a murder. Look here!"

He tore up, with his wedge, a board which had yielded suspiciously to his tread.

"Boys, gather around and slant an eye at this — a brake!"

The marshal hastily went to the spot. There was a growling chorus from the men.

"What about this, Grogan?" called Bud Levine.

The proprietor measured the distance to the door; and then he remembered Levine's speed with a gun and changed his mind. Legs cannot travel as fast as bullets.

"Crooked work, Bud," he answered. "I always had a hunch that Dago was a crook, but I never could get no dope on him."

"Damned funny business, Grogan. You must of come in for most of the gain on this brake."

Inspiration came to Grogan, and he heaved a great breath of relief.

"You're wrong, Bud," he said. "I only got a percentage, and I had to take Dago's word for what it was. I never could afford to put two men on the roulette. He handled the wheel and the coin all the time."

It was not the most water-tight explanation in the world, but the crowd had been close to one tragedy already that day, and they had exposed one thief. It had taken the edge from their appetite. A good many shrewd glances traveled toward Grogan, but in a matter of seconds they were drifting back to their old places. Except for Bud Levine, who approached the proprietor and, choosing a moment when no one else was near, murmured: "Once more, Grogan. You've got by again, but only by the skin of your teeth. Another time, and you'll eat lead as sure as hell."

"Now, how the devil," said Grogan, blustering, "can I keep my dealers from bein' crooks?"

"Shut up," answered the marshal in disgust.

"I know you, Grogan, but I ain't huntin' up trouble until it comes my way. If they had cleaned up on Dago to-night, they'd of gone ahead and finished up with you. Smoke that in your next cigarette, Grogan, and walk soft. You can't be lucky *all* your life. But say" — and he drew the big proprietor aside — "how can I get that girl out of Number Ten?"

"Tell me how," groaned Grogan, "and I'll do the work for you — crooked or straight. Who's this new gent?"

For in the entrance to Grogan's stood a perspiring man of middle age. Dust lay thick on his riding clothes, and a face pink with soft, fine living glowed with sweat. He was loosening his shirt at the throat and fanning himself with his hat, though it was a cool night. It was John Scovil, and exercise and worry had supplied the place of hot sunshine with him.

The neighing of his lonely horse, trying in vain to call back the wanderers, had wakened him not so long after Nancy and her two guides left the camp, and he sat up among his blankets with an echo of his last snore still ringing in his ears. And he had found himself alone.

At first his sleep-befogged brain refused to register the truth, but finally he realized that he was alone with two pack mules and a riding horse in the midst of an unknown desert. Still bewildered, he saddled the horse and let it take its head. In this manner he roamed blindly through the hills, followed by a thousand wild fears and spurred by horrible conjectures, until at length the horse brought him to Number Ten and to the open door of Grogan's Place.

The light had attracted him to dismount, and now the tinkle of glasses invited him in with no uncertain voice, but when he reached the door he looked about him on the crowd for a moment.

The house of amusement was running in full blast again, and he caught the gleam of dice, the sheen of gold, the flash of cards in the deal; but last his eye rested upon a pleasant spot of white. It was a girl, dressed — most amazing! — in the coolest and crispest of summer whites, with a soft, foolish little hat of the same color perched on her head. Around her the crowd drifted as around a center. Her back was toward him, but he saw the beauty of her face as if in a mirror through the expressions of the men who fronted her. They watched her as if fascinated and could not turn their eyes away.

She was shaking dice with four others, and even now she made her throw. She had lost, but she tossed up her head and laughed as she paid the debt. A wonderful laugh. It roused something like a forgotten spring in the blood of John Scovil, and yet there was a touch of familiarity in it. He drew closer, forgetting his thirst, forgetting his weariness and all the worries which beset him.

He came with a hungry look in his eyes, like the traveler who rides with an empty canteen through a wilderness, and in the evening comes upon the sweet music of running water.

"How much?" one of the partners of the girl was saying as he rattled the dice.

"Anything you want," she answered, "from a house and lot to a six-gun. You're on, partner!"

She turned; it was Nancy!

At first the mind of Scovil ceased to work. It stopped functioning just as the mind of big Grogan halted when Jerry Aiken struck the "button" of his jaw. Then, consciousness rushed back upon Scovil. It was real, perfectly real. The lights were not the lights of fairyland, the voices around him were not the sounds of a dream. The cursing from yonder corner as a man quit a poker game — broke — were too true to life.

It was Nancy; yes, there was no doubt of that; but what had become of the shell that formerly concealed her? Her old self compared with this was like the sky of December compared with that of June. Beautiful? Yes, she had always been that, but now she was intoxicating. She literally made his senses drunk. And there were a thousand little differences. The smile which never left them now made the whole curve of her lips new. And the eyes were all new, because they had new things to say. In a word, he had seen a blank slate when he last looked upon her. Now he found the slate filled with the words of a new and enchanting poem.

Suddenly he wanted to wave his arms, reach above his head, shout his happiness. For the miracle had been worked. Nancy Scovil was awake! No more days and weeks and months and years of a weight which dragged him down; but here was one to charm the wisest man he knew — a beauty greater than any he had ever known — a grace bewitching.

Now that he was himself again, he had a vague feeling that she had turned and faced him for a moment, and then moved away. She stood shaking the dice, her back to him once more, when he stepped forward and touched her shoulder.

She brushed his hand away and made her cast, and won. But those who lost to her were as good-humored about it as she had been. They seemed more happy to lose to her than to win from another. They laughed and jested as though the broad gold pieces and rustling greenbacks were so many idle, senseless baubles — toys of exchange. One of the men slapped his pockets and threw up his hands in token that he was broke, but Nancy leaned over swiftly, and before he could dodge away had poured a stream of heavy gold into his trouser pocket.

Scovil touched her again.

"Nancy!" he called.

She turned and cast a fleeting glance over her shoulder. There was not the slightest recognition in her eyes; they jarred against the stare of Scovil with a shock that made him gape. He was hardly sure that it was really his daughter.

"I say!" he continued with some irritation, and placed his hand again on her shoulder.

"Bill," said the girl, without turning, "this fellow is bothering me. He must be drunk. Take him away, will you, partner?"

Her "partner" was a stocky, middle-aged man, his face grizzled with a stubble of four days' growth. He walked with a lurching waddle that noted a lifetime spent in the saddle. Above the waist he was a reduced copy of Hercules. Below the waist he was a boy of twelve, his little, thin legs bowing out under the weight they had to carry. Now his arm shot out and struck away the hand of John

Scovil from the shoulder of Nan. He pushed in between and sent the taller man back a staggering pace.

"What's your line, stranger?" he asked aggressively. "Are you drunk or jest nacherally a nut? Or don't you know how to talk to a lady?"

"And who the devil commissioned you to quiz me?" asked Scovil hotly.

"That ain't the point," returned the other, hitching his belt around. "I asked you a question. Are you going to answer it?"

"I'll see you damned first. Nancy, come here!"

She did not stir, and when Scovil made a step forward he was caught much as a yearling is handled by the practiced, and sent crashing into the wall. It partly knocked the wind out of him; it partly enraged him like a bull when it sees the red cloak of the matador. He was about to rush on the other, when he observed that the hand of the man was closed over the butt of his gun.

"You fool!" thundered Scovil. "Don't you know the girl is my daughter?"

When he smashed against the wall he brought all eyes upon him; and now Marshal Bud Levine stepped between him and danger. Oddly enough, the marshal had no eyes for either Scovil or Bill. His gaze held with stern intentness upon the girl.

"Ma'am," he said angrily, "what's the meaning of all this? D'you set out to keep me busy all evenin'?"

At last she turned.

"What's wrong now?" she asked. "Why, marshal, you aren't angry with me, are you?"

The coldness of Bud Levine melted as ice melts on the first warm day in spring. He had to lay strong hold upon himself to keep from answering her smile.

"All I know," he managed to growl, "is that you got two men fightin' ag'in. What's up?"

"I'll tell you," she said.

She faced her father squarely, and to his unnerving astonishment not a flicker of recognition was in her eyes. Cold horror swept over him. Has she lost her mind? Was that the meaning of brightness in her eyes?

"That man," she was saying, "laid hands on me, and I asked my friend Bill to protect me."

"Huh!" snarled Bud Levine, and he whirled on his heel and looked through and through Scovil. "Is that the kind of a houn' dog you are? Ain't you old enough to act like a man? Listen to me, stranger, Number Ten has got ways of teachin' gents manners. It's got ways of its own, and what it teaches ain't forgot soon!"

A stern hum of assent breathed from the

men around; a thundercloud of frowns surrounded Scovil.

"Damn it!" cried the latter. "Haven't I a right to speak to my own daughter?"

"Eh?" grunted the bewildered marshal, turning back to Nancy. "Is that so?"

But she chuckled softly, musically.

"Why, marshal," she answered smoothly, "I never saw the fellow before."

"You never did?" echoed Bud Levine, facing Scovil again. "Look here, you damned, fat-faced blockhead, d'you think you can run a bluff like that on me?"

"Good heavens!" cried Scovil, and he raised his arms in desperation. "Are you mad, Nan? Is your mind gone? Don't you remember me? Or are you trying to work a practical joke? Marshal — if that's what you are — ask me questions — prove me — I'll show you that I'm her father!"

The marshal and the men around were impressed in spite of themselves by the downright energy of Scovil's statements. Many a hat was pushed back, and many a shaggy head was scratched in bewilderment.

But Nancy Scovil leaned against the table, laughing. She seemed to enjoy the scene.

"I leave it to you, Bill," she said with an appealing gesture. "Do I look like that — that —"

She paused; a roar of laughter supplied the missing word. It was the clinching word in the argument; the marshal saw his way clearly.

"Here, you," he said to Scovil, "you come with me. You don't get the girl, frien', but you get a night's lodgin' free."

"But," began Scovil, "God above, man, do you mean to say you're goin' to arrest me?"

"You shut your face," snarled Levine, "and thank Heaven you don't get what's comin' to you. No, I won't arrest you if you want to be turned over to them."

He waved his arm toward the angry crowd of men, who were pressing closer and closer. John Scovil turned pale.

"Marshal," broke in the pleasant voice of the new Nan Scovil, "don't you notice that wild look in his eyes? Ask him what he's been doing."

"Hey, you," snapped the marshal. "Don't you hear a lady speak to you? What have you been doing?"

"Riding to beat the devil half the night, trying to get back my runaway girl!" snorted Scovil. "And as for you, my fine marshal, I'll have you —"

"You see," cut in Nancy. "I knew it was that way. The poor old gentleman has been riding in the hot sun all day, and it's scattered his wits. These fat old fellows can't stand the heat, you know."

"Poor old gentleman? Fat? Sun?" stuttered Scovil. "Nan, I'll make you sweat for this prank! Marshal, I want to say —"

"Save it for the judge. Turn around and head for that door. Sun or no sun, you need watchin'. S'pose, gents, that he'd come on that poor girl when we wasn't by to protect her?"

A snarl from the crowd answered.

"But, marshal," pleaded Nancy, pressing to his side, "can't you put him in the hotel instead of the jail? He *looks* like a gentleman; and I'm sure I bear no grudge against him. He appears a little simple, too. I don't suppose he's ever had very good sense. If you'll lock him up in the hotel I'll pay for the room."

"Hell and furies!" roared Scovil.

"Shut your face," snapped the marshal. "Ain't you got even enough manners or sense to thank the lady for what she's done for you? Now get out of here before I kick you out!"

The eyes of the marshal carried their threat even through the mist of Scovil's rage, and he knew enough to turn on his heel and stamp toward the door.

CHAPTER XIX

Advice Gratis

The mention of the hotel to the marshal, and the fact that her father was being taken there for confinement, recalled to Nancy that she was tired — no aching weariness, in spite of the long, hard ride and all the action of the night, but a pleasant sense of fatigue. She took advantage of the diversion of attention which the exit of John Scovil and Bud Levine made, to slip out by a side entrance and hurry toward the hotel unnoticed. There, in her room, she lighted the lamp beside her bed and threw herself into a chair to dream over the day and the night before she went to sleep.

From the open window an air of coolness stirred and rustled the shade and played gently about her face, and up from the street she caught a score of light sounds, voices, and the clatter of hoofs as some one entered or left Number Ten. Then, with startling clearness, she heard the voices of Levine and her father just beneath her. She could not understand it at first, but presently she made out that the sound traveled up through the stovepipe that rose to her room through the ceiling of the room below. When she stood beside it she could hear them below with perfect plainness.

"You'll be feelin' better in the mornin', my frien'," the marshal was saying. "Now you jest rest up here and try to get hold on yourself."

"This infernal outrage —" began her father.

"They ain't nobody goin' to hurt you, stranger," said Bud Levine, "if you don't hurt yourself. The girl has begged off for you."

It was too much for Nancy. She burst into a short peal of laughter, checked swiftly when she remembered that she might he heard.

Even then it was too late. For Scovil bellowed furiously beneath her: "The vixen is laughing at me now."

"Maybe she is."

"I tell you, she's right above me, laughing her head off because I'm here."

There was a brief pause. Then the marshal's voice: "I guess she was right. It's a case of too much heat. Well, partner, you lie down there and take it easy. I'll come around in a few minutes and see how you're makin' out."

"But —" began Scovil.

The slamming of a door put a quick period to his speech, and then Nancy Scovil heard a deep-pitched rumble. It was composed of many words, linked together with fluent speed, and Nancy retired to her chair again and put her hands over her ears.

Another idea, however, brought her back to the stove. She found that it was comparatively simple to remove the joint of pipe which connected the stove with the main stem. With this gone she could speak directly down the shaft to the room below. She called guardedly:

"Mr. Scovil!"

The cursing ceased abruptly.

"Mr. Scovil!" she called again.

She heard footsteps draw closer; there was a rattling of the stove beneath.

"Mr. Scovil!" for the third time.

"Well?" boomed her father's voice up the chimney.

"Do you recognize my voice?"

"Nancy, you shall regret this, by Heaven!"

"I think not."

"What in the name of all that's wonderful is in you?"

"I was thinking what an excellent joke it would be considered back in New York. Think how the papers will play it up: 'Eminent financier locked up for claiming relationship with young lady. Sunstroke suspected.' How will that sound, dad, dear?"

A groan answered her.

Then: "At least, thank Heaven, they'll never know!"

"I've pen and ink here, and a two-cent stamp will do the mischief."

"Nancy, you would not?"

"I don't know. It's a temptation."

"Nancy, my dear child, it would be more than a joke; almost a scandal. You won't do it, Nan?"

"I'll think it over."

"How long is this infernal jest to continue?"

"Jest? Do you think Number Ten takes it for a jest?"

She chuckled softly.

"Nancy — confound it, girl — you seem to have influence with these barbarians. Tell them to stop this nonsense."

"It's gone too far. They wouldn't turn loose such a dangerous character even on my request."

Subdued curses rumbled from her father's throat.

"There's only one way out for you, dad."

"What's that?"

"When Levine comes back, pretend that you've just recovered; act like a man waking up from a delirium."

"Do you mean to say I'm to pretend that you're not my daughter?"

She paused to laugh again.

"I don't see any other way out for you."

"I'll never do it!"

"Then you'll go to jail and have to talk with the judge later on. Sorry, dad."

"What's in your mind, Nancy? What do you intend to do with this practical jest?"

"Get clear of every one I know. That's all."

"Eh?"

"Oh, I'm tired of all the old stuff. I wouldn't go back to New York now for a million dollars!"

"Where *will* you go?"

"I haven't the slightest idea in the world."

"But who'll go with you?"

"There are plenty of fine fellows in Number Ten who'll do anything I ask of them."

She heard him gasp.

"Nan, you are stark, staring mad."

"No. You're all wrong. For the first time in my life I'm perfectly sane and clear-headed."

"Do you mean to say you'd go away with one of these wild men?"

"Why not?"

"Why not? Girl, you'd be barred from all respectable society ever after!"

"Not at all. I'm perfectly safe in the hands of any of these men. They may be rough on the surface, but they're gentlemen underneath."

"That may be true, but how will New York understand?"

"Hang New York! I'm through with it."

There was another pause. Then she heard him mutter to himself: "It isn't possible. This is a dream, and I'll wake up pretty soon."

He said aloud: "Did you leave camp alone?"

"No — with Red and Pete."

"I thought so. The thieves! What's become of them?"

"They're in jail."

"Eh?"

"They grew troublesome; kept bothering me. So I had them put away for safe-keeping. They'll be turned loose after a day or so."

Another gasp from below.

Then: "Nancy, I'll have Jerry Aiken take your trail."

"You'll have to get him out of jail first."

"What?"

"It's true. Ask Levine, if you doubt me. In a word, dad, I want to get rid of every one I know. I want to cut away into a new line."

"Nancy, I've got to save you from yourself."

"You can't. You'll be doing your part if you save yourself."

"What do you mean?"

"If you can induce Levine to turn you loose, the best thing for you to do is to get a horse and ride away from Number Ten as fast as it'll carry you."

"Why? I'm a citizen; I have rights."

"You're an undesirable citizen here. The boys don't like you, dad, and they've ways of showing their dislikes out here. Sorry, but it can't be helped."

"I'll come back, then. Nancy, you'll regret this prank."

"You'll never find me, dad, till I'm ready to be found. You can lay to that."

"Girl —"

"Hush! What's that?"

Outside her room, from the street below, a mellow baritone voice rose in song.

Nancy called: "Good night, dad; I've a caller."

While Scovil shouted beneath, she replaced the joint in the pipe. A shower of soot whirred down the chimney, and the last she heard from her father was a spluttering series of curses, interrupted and finally quite subdued by snorts, coughs and sneezes. He must have been too close to the lower end of the pipe, and received a quantity of the choking soot in eyes and nose and throat.

In the meantime the song rose:

May thy sleep be as deep
As the depths of my love for thee;

May thy dream ever seem
Sweet remembrance of constancy.

For the first time in the history of Number Ten a serenade was heard in its dusty street!

CHAPTER XX

Lefty Harris

No sooner did Scovil exit from Grogan's, with the redoubtable marshal behind him, than the crowd turned to Nancy again — and behold! she was gone. They looked about them like children deprived of a rare and amusing toy, and in another moment a hunt would have begun, combing every inch of Number Ten, had not an event occurred which thrilled even the war-worn nerves of Number Ten.

The marshal and his prisoner were not well out of sight past the shadowy doorway of Grogan's, when another man stepped into view. In the door he did not pause an instant, as though he disliked the illumination there, but he glided with a swift side-step into a gloomier place along the wall.

He was a remarkable fellow in a way. He was well above the average in height, and he had the broad shoulders and thick chest tapering down to a slender, sinewy waist which characterizes most versatile athletes. There was both strength and alertness in the man, but more than this was his impressiveness.

He stepped into Grogan's and slid into an obscure shadow, but at once, like the star on the stage, he dwarfed all the others in the place.

For he was one of those few men who are lords of their presence, and thereby rulers over a kingdom. He could have stepped with equal assurance and poise upon a Broadway stage. Dignitaries in the social and political world would have respected him; for he had the air of importance — an importance of which he was not vain, but simply conscious.

He was not a particularly beautiful form to behold. His neck, for instance, was thick with cords which stood out when he turned his head, and the head itself was too long and angular to be good-looking. A pale yellow mustache, faded and bleached by a life of exposure to wind and bitter sun, drooped on either side of his mouth, halfway to the chin. Above this mustache rose a thin, hooked nose that gave him a touch of fierce aggressiveness. But this characteristic of his face was at once denied by the eyes. They were a pale, misty blue, and behind the mist, when the man grew excited, little lights flickered and glowed and went out in an amazing fashion.

There were other noteworthy features about him. For instance, his six-gun hung high on his right hip, drawn well around to the front — the position for a left-handed man. And that left hand was brown as a berry — a sufficient proof that no glove was ever worn upon it.

While he stood there surveying the crowd a murmur began among those nearest him and spread in a varying whisper indicative of fear, surprise, wonder, anger: " 'Lefty' Harris! Lefty Harris is in town! What's up now?"

The name was explanation enough for the sensation and the whispers, for Lefty Harris had a reputation which extended across the mountain desert from mountains of the east to mountains of the west and far north and far south. There are varieties of rough men in that region, men with crimes on their shoulders and with notches on their guns, but far and wide there are few, indeed, who are real killers.

Usually the manslayer begins his career of crime in some drunken fury, runs amuck, and in twenty-four hours he is sowed with a seed of lead from the mouths of .45s, and twenty-four hours later he is part of a legend which grows and changes, until within a year the terror of a single day is reputed to have spent a long life in crime and excess.

However, at long intervals men appear who have both a peculiar talent and a peculiar taste for the destruction of life. Gifted by nature with a cool eye and a steady hand, they cultivate their gifts until they use a gun with the accuracy of a surveyor's instrument and the speed of a snapping whiplash. And when they have achieved this position, they are comparatively safe from the law, for they can wait until their victim, taunted or stung into action, has made the first movement toward fighting before they draw and shoot him down in "self-defense."

Sometimes they stretch out a long life in this manner. Now and again they serve short prison terms, but they return always to the mountain desert and to a career too fascinating to be surrendered for any other pursuit. In the end they are hunted down by numbers, or some Federal or State officer takes the desperate chance and brings down his man. But always, always they die with their boots on.

This is the sketch of the true killer; and Lefty Harris was a killer. He was somewhere between thirty and forty, and for ten years his name and fame had grown along the ranges. Twice he had been jailed, and twice his sentence had been shortened for "good behavior," though that good behavior was generally thought to have taken the form of a bribe to the warden. And now he roamed at large. The law had no claim upon him, but all men's hands were against him, and his hand was against the world. Odds which Lefty Harris accepted and enjoyed. It made the game worth while.

Yet, Lefty Harris was no snake. Among the terrible legends of blood and death which were gathering around him there was a scattering of other stories of help rendered in the midst of the desert to the lost wanderer, protection for the defenseless, charity to the starving. Indeed, it was said that Lefty knew only two motions: one was the throwing of gold pieces; the other was the throwing of his gun. Around him clung an atmosphere of the heroic. He was dignified by the very danger which he courted all his days.

That whisper buzzed and went out as Lefty walked to the bar and called for his drink. And it was noted that standing at the bar he kept his shoulders braced against the corner wall.

In this position it was impossible to attack him from the rear. The bartender was under observation from the corner of his eye, and his face was turned directly toward the rest of the crowd.

When his drink arrived they did not fail to notice, also, that he used his right hand for everything; that redoubtable left remained free for emergencies and hovered always near the holster. With his right hand he poured his drink — a small one. With his right hand he raised the glass, surveyed the crowd as if to make sure that no one was in the attitude of making a suspicious motion, and then tossed off his drink with a single short gesture.

There was reason for that remarkable haste in drinking. Other men, leisurely downing a glass of redeye, had been shot through the back or belly; and Lefty Harris was known as one who took no chances when he believed danger was near.

The drink disposed of, he walked on — keeping always close to the wall — and secured a corner chair from which he could keep the entire room under his observation. How could he tell? There might be a dozen personal enemies in Grogan's place, friends or even relatives of men who had fallen by his hand.

A stern, quiet smile of understanding passed from eye to eye in the crowd. One man gritted his teeth, glared, and then turned on his heel and hurriedly left Grogan's. He dared not stay there and face the murderous temptation.

But the rest of the crowd stayed quiet, pretending to occupy themselves with the games. In reality they were waiting for the return of Marshal Bud Levine. They had seen Bud in action; they knew him and his worth; but they wanted to see how he would act in the face of one so much greater than he himself could ever be — one who could plant three bullets in him before Bud could get his six-gun clear of the holster.

They had not long to remain in suspense. Bud Levine came swinging through the door, met the volley of curious glances, and halted in the midst of a stride, as a dog checks itself in the middle of a spring. One glance swept the room, and then his eyes rested steadily upon Lefty Harris. The latter sat perfectly at ease, rolling a cigarette with his right hand alone. Indeed, Lefty always acted as if his left hand and arm were paralyzed. That limb remained sacred to one use only. He received the concentrated attention of the marshal with detached calm, meanwhile lighting his cigarette.

Bud Levine hesitated a moment, and then crossed the room, making on a line straight as an arrow for the gunman. When he came before the latter he halted and, with every eye fixed upon him, stretched out his hand. The other accepted the sign of mutual good feeling.

"Lefty," said the marshal, "I know you, and you know me. Eh?"

"I ain't forgettin' the fordin' of that river, Bud," replied the killer quietly. "Glad to see you."

"I ain't glad to see you, Lefty," said the marshal, his tone as quiet as that of the other. "Jest now we're havin' our share of hell raised in Number Ten by a girl without you edgin' in for your own margin. But I'll tell you straight, Lefty. I ain't lookin' for trouble. I let trouble come and find me."

Lefty studied the face of the other with a glimmer of interest.

"That sounds fair enough to me," he nodded.

"All right," said Bud. "We'll let it ride that way. I'm with you, Harris, till you bust loose. S'long."

Passing the hotel Bud thought of Nancy Scovil and the man who claimed to be her father. A great wish rose in the heart of the marshal that he had taken the fellow at his word, and, right or wrong, sent her off with him. If she stayed much longer in Number Ten the village would explode. Perhaps even now it was not too late to undo the work. Bud entered the hotel and unlocked the door of Scovil's room. The other rose from the bed where he had been sitting and glowered at the marshal.

"Well, partner," queried the marshal, "I've come back to have a little chat with you. I'd like to hear what proofs you have to offer that the girl is your daughter."

But Scovil passed his hand across his forehead and blinked at Bud Levine in the manner of one awakened from a long sleep.

"Where am I?" he gasped.

"In Number Ten, of course," said the marshal, "I've come —"

"Why am I in Number Ten?"

"Looking for your daughter, I s'pose. Now, look here. I'm open to reason. Give me some proof that she's your daughter —"

"Daughter?" echoed Scovil, remembering the lesson which Nancy had given him from the room above. "I've never had a daughter!"

"Oh, hell!" groaned Bud Levine. "You never had one?"

"Not guilty," said Scovil instantly, and he watched the scowling face of Levine eagerly. "What am I doing here, my friend? The last thing I remember I was riding about midday and my head was very hot, and —"

"Hell!" repeated Bud Levine unsympathetically. "She ain't your daughter then? You give up all claim on her?"

"On who?" echoed Scovil, cunningly. Then, with a rising interest, "Has some woman been pretending that I'm her father? Sir, I have no daughter."

The marshal surveyed the other with bitter interest.

"Sunstroke," he said coldly. He sighed.

"Well, how are you now?"

"I feel as if I'd had a long sleep. I'm much better, sir," answered Scovil.

"Well," mused Bud Levine, "if you got your bean workin' ag'in, they ain't no particular cause for keepin' you locked up here."

"Have I been locked up?" inquired the big man calmly. "Well, well! Think of that!"

"Huh!" grunted Levine. "Yep, you've pulled a bonehead play, partner. Want to be on your way?"

"Of course."

"Well, the door's open. But take a tip from me. Don't be lingerin' around Number Ten."

"Sir," said Scovil heartily, "there is no place on earth where I have less desire to be."

"All right. Then get out and make your start. And don't let the boys get their eyes on you. They've got a sort of grudge agin' you."

"Really?" murmured Scovil. "I suppose my mind has been wandering then."

"It sure has. Now start."

Which was why John Scovil slipped stealthily from the hotel and wended his way cautiously down the street. In front of Grogan's he found his horse where he had left it, mounted, and spurred wildly down the road and out over the hills — anywhere so long as he was headed away from Number Ten.

CHAPTER XXI

Escape

Once left alone in the outer room of the jail — the room, in fact, where the marshal lived, Jerry Aiken took a careful survey of his surroundings. He knew not how long a time he might be left there before Bud Levine returned to fulfill his threat and place the handcuffs upon him. In the meantime he was surrounded by walls of wood, and wooden barriers were far different from the impregnable stone of the real jail room.

There were two windows, and toward these natural exits Jerry first turned his attention. But there were two things against such a mode of egress. In the first place the windows had been made purposely so narrow that a man's body could scarcely wriggle through them, were he ever so thin; in the second place, strong iron bars were affixed to the wall just outside the windows. He tried these bars with his full strength, but they did not yield enough to even emit a groan.

Next he tried the door. It was a heavy piece

of wood, securely locked. In the room, to be sure, there was a stoutly made table which might serve in lieu of a battering ram, but the racket he was sure to make while knocking down the door was equally certain to attract attention. So he looked up to the ceiling. It was composed of undressed four-inch boards, and from their width he guessed shrewdly that they were two inches at least in thickness. And by the rows of nails he saw that the rafters stretched above in thick, parallel rows. In time he might be able to cut this way through, but time he did not have.

There remained the floor, though it was some moments before he even looked down to it. One does not naturally think of getting out through the floor, partly because there is usually nothing but solid earth beneath it, and partly because a man's instinct is to break out or up; there is little of the mole's nature in the average man.

But Jerry was desperate, for in his ears there still rang the song of the girl riding down the street; and in his eyes lingered the picture of the new Nancy Scovil, the transformed Nancy. If he could get out he had one thing to do, and then he would find Nancy, if he had to break through walls of brick to get to her. He got down on his knees and examined the floor in detail.

It was made of broad planks, nailed so loosely and carelessly that here and there were large cracks. And in one place near the wall the board had warped up so that a space of well over an inch extended between the two edges. All that he needed to raise the plank was a lever small enough to insert and strong enough to stand the strain.

Such a lever he found ready made to his hand in the rifle which leaned against the wall in the corner. He took it and managed to jam the muzzle through the crack, then, at the first strong, downward pressure on the stock, the plank squeaked, groaned, and then yielded with a loud, ripping sound. It left an aperture a foot across, and the smell of the earth came through to Jerry.

So he lay on his belly and craned his head down. At first all was blackness, but looking to one side, he caught a faint lessening of the darkness. It was as he had hoped: the house rested upon short posts, raising it a little from the ground in lieu of a foundation. An instant later, Jerry had torn away the neighboring board and was on his stomach, wriggling toward the light. It was a close squeeze to work through between the dirt and the floor beam of the house, but presently he managed it, and stood erect, stretching his legs and arms. He was free.

He looked down the street.

During the last part of his work he had noted an uproar not far away, and now he saw a knotted crowd gradually dispersing from in front of the hotel. These were to be avoided, so Jerry slipped back, and skirted rapidly around the back of the jail. So doing, however, he passed first the corner of the house where the light from the hotel's gasoline lamp struck with the most force. He knew it not, but across the street, at that moment, no less a person than old Baldy himself saw the refugee darting and disappearing in the shadows in back of the jail. And Baldy turned on his heel and hurried back to Grogan's to give the alarm.

All unconscious of this, however, Jerry stole down the row of shanties until he came opposite the store, and he reached this with a swift run across the street. The door stood open, inviting him in, and within, he found the lamp burning as it had been when he first entered the place on this historic night.

There was time enough now, he figured, for even if the marshal returned to the jail immediately and discovered the prisoner gone, he would never dream of searching at once in Baldy's store. So Jerry strolled leisurely to the back of the big room and into the corner from which the proprietor had produced the fatal bottle of Florida water.

It was hard to find its mate, for the light glimmered faintly in this obscure recess, and there were a number of bottles which he had to hold up one by one and examine the seals before he found the right one. But at last he had it, and rising from his knees, he slipped the prize into his hip pocket, stretched his arms above his head, and laughed softly. Now he was ready for the difficult part of his night's work — to find Nancy.

Into his contented chuckle, however, a sound cut the faint squeak and jar of the closing screen door, and then a quiet but commanding voice, "Start your laughin' when the bets is collected, partner; the game ain't done yet. Stick up them hands!"

And turning he found himself looking into the steady gun of Marshal Bud Levine. Beside him stood the bulky form of Grogan, and crowding through the door behind were half a dozen faces of those who had come to join the hunt. Not the least was the grin of old Baldy himself as he peered at the looter.

"All right, gents," said Bud Levine, "we don't need you no more. Step right out, Smith. I got them irons I was talkin' to you about."

Smiling with content at the strange instinct which had made him come first to Baldy's store, the marshal beckoned the refugee out with a motion of his revolver. But it is ill to be overconfident even in the presence of an unarmed man. The moment Jerry saw that gun deflected from its true aim, his right arm darted behind him, seized a random bottle from the shelf, and hurled it directly at the lamp.

At the same moment he dropped to the floor, barely in time; for the instant the bottle flashed, the marshal jerked up his gun and fired; the bullet sang evilly just over Jerry's head as he fell. But after that he had a fighting chance, for the bottle struck the lamp fair and square, smashed it to a thousand fragments, and darkness flooded through the store.

"At him, gents!" shrilled the marshal furiously. "Go after him. No gun play. He ain't armed; and I want him alive."

A roar came from the doorway, and then a thunder of feet as the crowd rushed for Jerry. Hemmed into the corner, he had not a chance in a thousand of slipping through the cordon of the assailants. Once more he fell back upon stratagem.

Near him he remembered a small box, and this he picked up and hurled across the room; it landed with a crash against a table on the other side.

"This way!" yelled the marshal. "Go for the back door. He's trying to get out that way! Speed up, boys! Who's got a light, for

Heaven's sake!"

The rush of the pursuit flowed with a rumble of running feet in the direction of the place where Jerry's box had smashed. He himself ran straight for the door in front.

All chances favored his escape at that point had it not been that there was, in the crowd, one brain as cool as his own. For old Baldy had seen many a scene of violence in his day, and he knew perfectly well that darkness favors the man who fights against odds.

So the instant that the lamp was smashed he ran to a corner, snatched up a candle, and lighted it. Just as Jerry reached the middle of the floor the match spurted in the hand of Baldy, and then a thin tongue of yellow flame lighted the big room, or rather, made its shadows wildly visible.

"Here!" screamed Baldy. "He's goin' out the front door. Ten bucks to the gent that nails him!"

A wild yell rose from the eluded crowd. They turned and poured once again toward Jerry; but his start was too great. He would surely have reached the door and whipped down the street ahead of them had not Baldy again come to the rescue of the upholders of the law. He reached out his long leg and kicked over a deal table that landed with a whack on its side, directly in the path of Jerry. And over it he tumbled flat.

Before he could regain his feet the men were on him, but their very number were in their way. A dozen hands reached for him; and a dozen hands got in the way of each other. Up in their midst Jerry rose.

By that candlelight he made out his targets, and his fists whacked home with desperation now to give them added power. Half a dozen blows sent the nearest reeling back, and before they could close on him again he had turned, taken the table at a single leap, and was through the door and into the middle of the street.

Weak with laughter after she had watched the wild brawl in the street from the window, Nancy Scovil had dropped back into a chair to recuperate before she at last went to bed. There was a warm feeling of content in Nancy, like the feeling of the laboring man at the end of the day when his tired muscles assure him that he has earned his bread.

She was sitting with her hands clasped behind her head, remembering the wild, unshaved faces, when she heard, for the second time this night, the bark of a revolver far down the street.

Instantly she was at the window, but at first she saw nothing. There was a vague uproar, far away, but that was all. And then — it was like a shadow pouring out of a shadow. The light of the gasoline lamp reached in a dim flicker down to Baldy's store, and now, from this building, a figure darted, instantly followed by a flood of others. The single figure turned up the street, racing toward her, but before it could get under way, the crowd overtook and swallowed it.

It was still the most obscure of pictures to Nancy, but as she squinted and narrowed her eyes, she made out what seemed an irruption under the fluid mass of the throng. Legs and arms thrust up, heads bobbed, and then again a single form once more detached itself from the mass and raced up the street. But it was like the effort of a fly to crawl when its feet are sticky from the fly paper. Before the fugitive could get under way some of the rearward members of the pursuers swept upon him.

This time the group was close enough for her to see some of the details. The refugee was a bare-headed fellow, his shirt ripped to fragments, and the light glinting on the bare skin here and there. He fled until something told him that the pursuit was once more up with him. Then he wheeled with astonishing suddenness and struck right and left into the faces of his followers.

It was like watching a long black wave slide

up the sandy beach smoothly, and then, licking in vain against a jutting rock, recoil. Even so did the mass of the little crowd surge after the single man, and check in the very midst of their rush.

As they swayed back those in front holding back the vehemence of the men in the rear who urged forward, the refugee whirled again and bolted down the street.

This time he gained a running start before the crowd resumed its pursuit, and with such an advantage he increased it with every step, until he fairly seemed to fly down the street, leaving the crowd farther and farther behind. But in his haste, or his terror, he overlooked his best chance. In front of Grogan's stood several saddled horses, but — perhaps because he thought he could not get into the saddle and start the horse in time to outstrip those who ran behind him, the fugitive fled past Grogan's without pause.

His mistake, however, was at once noted by the pursuers. A hoarse, breathless shout of triumph rose from their throats. As they rushed by every saddle was occupied by a vaulting form, and at once half a dozen cattle ponies, starting with their usual speed, raced down the street and beat up the echoes.

The refugee cast a single glance behind him when he heard this sound, and then leaned a little more forward and fairly redoubled his speed. She could see him quite clearly now. He ran like a winged Mercury, his toe tips barely dusting the ground, his head erect, the tatters of his rent shirt fluttering behind him, his hair blown back by the speed of his running into the wind. The heart of Nancy beat and leaped. She would have given nameless things to have had a horse to place at the side of the man; a matchless horse which would outrun the ponies as far as the man himself had outrun his pursuers.

But the struggle was manifestly over. The cattle ponies had now reached full speed, their scrawny necks stretched out, their noses barely inches from the dust of the street, and their bellies hardly higher in the middle of the stride. At every leap they gained fearfully on the runner, and behind them streamed the rest of the crowd, yelling, eager to be in on the kill.

Once more the fugitive glanced behind him. He was nearly at the hotel now, and the horses rushed only a few yards behind him. The effort had been a gallant one, but it was over now.

And then —

It happened with such astonishing suddenness that Nancy could hardly believe her eyes. One instant the runner fled in the very center of the street. The next, he had darted to one side, sprung upon the watering troughs, and from these onto the awning, and then, while a roar of baffled rage came thundering up from the street, he turned and shook his fist at the horsemen who swept by just out of reach below him. The next second he whirled again, leaped through Nancy's window — and Jerry Aiken stood in the room beside her.

"You!" she gasped.

"You!" panted Jerry.

"What in the name of Heaven has happened? Have you killed some one?"

"Worse; I've stolen this for you!"

And he drew from his hip pocket the bottle of Florida water. Nancy gaped as she took it in a numb hand.

"You!" she breathed again.

"My wind's no good!" panted the man. "By the Lord, Nan, it was a lark!"

Feet thundered on the stairs before Nancy came to life. She sprang to the door, slammed and locked it. Almost at once fists beat upon it.

"Open up!" they shouted outside. "Open up, or we'll smash the door in! Lady, are you safe?"

"For Heaven's sake go back from the door!" screamed Nancy. "He's armed, and he's going to fire through the door."

There was a yell of terror from half a dozen throats in the hall, and then a sound of cursing and scraping and falls as they tumbled back in their haste to get away from the point of danger.

Nancy, doubling up with silent laughter, collapsed in a chair and held her sides.

"Spread a circle around the hotel!" shouted the voice of the marshal from the street just below the window.

"He's got a gun," yelled some one from the lower part of the hotel.

"Hell's afire!" groaned the marshal. "Get to cover, boys!"

"But it's serious," stammered Nancy, recovering from her laughter.

"It is," grinned Jerry, who was recovering his breath in great gasps as he sat on the bed.

"You're scented like a country belle!" laughed Nancy.

She waved him away, wrinkling her nose.

"Haloo, Smith!" called the marshal from below.

"That's me," translated Jerry.

"Come down and give yourself up. The game's played out."

"What in the world will you do?" stammered Nancy.

"Haven't the slightest idea," replied Jerry,

making himself comfortable on the pillows of the bed.

"Aren't you going to do a thing?"

"It's not up to me."

"For Heaven's sake, Jerry, this is apt to be serious even if it sounds foolish."

"Yes?"

"It is. These fellows below haven't much sense of humor. They'll go the limit."

"Very apt to," he replied, rearranging the cushion under his head.

"You're mad!" gasped Nancy.

"No, only resting."

"And you haven't even a gun?"

"Can't do much with one even if I had it."

"But aren't you worried?"

"Why should I be? You got me into this, and now it's up to you to get me out."

"*I* got you into this?"

She stared at him.

"Don't do that, please," observed Jerry; "it makes you look foolish. Certainly you got me into this — you and your Florida water. Now it's up to you."

"Jerry Aiken, you're the wildest person in the mountains!"

"Except yourself," grinned Jerry. "Now, go to it. Here am I inside. There's the crowd outside. They're loaded for bear, and I'm the bear. Go to it. Get me out. I've punched twenty heads in the last twenty minutes, and every one of them is aching to get at me."

"But aren't you going to raise a hand for yourself?"

"Certainly."

He raised his fists, bedabbled with blood.

"I'm going to clean up."

And he sauntered serenely over to the wash-stand and began to hum lightly to himself as he poured the bowl full of water.

CHAPTER XXII

Liberty's Chance

"Jerry," said the girl suddenly, "you're about a hundred-per-cent man. Shake on it!"

"Thanks!" drawled Jerry Aiken. "Get me out of this mess, and we'll save the congratulations."

"Smith!" roared Marshal Bud Levine. "I give you one more chance to come out and give yourself up. Don't be a fool. You've got nothing much against you now except breakin' the peace, but if you resist arrest you'll get soaked for the limit."

"He gets a couple of soaks from me, besides," added a voice.

"When the law gets through with you," added another, "I've got my turn comin', Smith."

But all the shouts died away when a white figure suddenly issued from the window on which all eyes were centered, and Nancy Scovil stood brightly illumined by the flare of the gasoline lamp.

"Come down," they pleaded. "Come down

now that you're clear."

But she stepped to the edge of the sloping roof and stood smiling cheerily down on them.

"Marshal Levine," she called, "will you talk with me?"

"Are you dickering for him?" asked the marshal, stepping into view.

"I am, marshal. All this trouble has been on account of me."

"I knew it," said the marshal between his teeth. "I had an idea all along that you had to be behind all this."

"The man you want is a friend of mine. Marshal, he came to town to get something for me."

"Florida water!" exploded Bud Levine.

"And the trouble that followed wasn't started by him."

"But he done a pile of finishin'!" exclaimed Levine.

"He has broken no laws," she insisted.

"But he's busted a lot of heads," remarked some one.

A groan rewarded the wit.

"Gentlemen," cried Nancy, "I want to make a gambling proposition to you."

"Shoot, lady."

"This man you want is in here, desperate and armed. If you try to take him by force it will cost more than money can ever repay."

"It ain't a nice job," agreed the marshal, "but it's got to be done. What's your game?"

"I'll toss dollars with you, marshal, and if you win two out of three he'll come down and surrender himself without lifting a hand against any one. But if you lose, he goes free."

The marshal scratched his head thoughtfully.

"It ain't legal," he objected.

"No," she answered instantly, "but it's a fair and square sporting chance." She raised her voice so that the rest could hear. "Boys, do you take me?"

And the answer came in an instant roar:

"We sure do! Flip the coins, lady!"

For the spectacular element appealed to them.

She drew out some money.

"Here we are. Three silver dollars. I'll spin 'em in the air so they'll drop on the ground down there. You fellows can call the throws; or else the marshal can do it for you. Are you ready, Number Ten?"

"We are!" they shouted.

"What'll you have, Marshal Levine?"

But there are ways of throwing coins so that they come down at the will and pleasure of the one who throws them. The marshal was determined not to be trapped so simply.

"Toss it up," he answered, falling into the

spirit of the occasion, and after all he had no great desire to attack an armed and desperate man in hiding, "I'll call her while she's in the air."

"Here you are then!"

With a wave of her arm and a snap of her thumb she tossed the dollar high in the air, and it spun and winked like a firefly whirling down.

"Heads!" called the marshal as the coin rose to the top of its curve.

"Heads for you," answered the girl.

Down flashed the coin and landed with a light *chug* in the dirt, a sound audible in the dead silence of the suspense.

Instantly a little crowd leaned over it, and then shouted, "Heads! Heads it is. Bud wins."

And then, "Here's your dollar, lady."

"Finders keepers," laughed Nancy. "Once more, marshal."

Again a dollar whirled high, snapping up from her hand.

"Tails!" called the marshal.

Down it swept, gleaming, and once more the crowd gathered around it.

"Heads again," they called. "The lady wins. Heads for you, ma'am."

"One apiece, marshal," called the girl. "Are you ready?"

"But how do I know," complained the marshal, "that he'll pay the bet when he loses? How do I know that he'll come down and give himself up if I win?"

"How does he know," she countered, "that if he wins you'll pay *your* side of the bet?"

"I'll tell you why," called Jerry Aiken suddenly from the window behind her, "it's because I trust the honor of Number Ten. And Number Ten will take its chance that I'm a square shooter."

"Good for you, partner," roared Number Ten. "You take a chance with us and we'll take a chance with you. Let her go, Bud!"

"All right," said the marshal, "it ain't right; it ain't law; but I'll stick to my part of it. Common law wasn't tailored to fit Number Ten. Toss the coin."

"Here you are," answered Nancy, juggling the last of the three dollars. "If you win, he goes down to you and gives himself up. If you lose, he goes scot-free. How about it, boys? And every one of you who has a grudge against him buries the grudge. Is that square?"

"Call it square," answered Grogan. "I got a sore jaw, and they's a lot more that's got worse. But he fought like a man and he gets a man's chance. I'm for him, for one. Shoot, lady."

The coin soared, whirling, higher than ever into the air. It passed beyond the immediate circle of the glow of the gasoline lamp, lost itself in the darkness above, whirred down again, flashed through the bright circle, and the marshal called for the second time, "Tails!"

The coin plumped in the dust.

"Head's ag'in!" cried the crowd in astonishment. "Heads three times runnin'!"

"Look on the other side of the coin," growled the marshal. "I don't think them dollars *has* a tails side."

"Nope, marshal, this is all O. K. And the gent goes free."

"Marshal," called the girl from above, "you're a good winner, but you lose hard."

The marshal rose to the occasion. He whipped off his hat and bowed low.

"Lady," he said, "this ain't the first time to-night that you've give me trouble, and I got an idea it ain't goin' to be the last. But this Smith gent goes free."

He turned to the crowd.

"You hit the high spots and get to sleep," he advised. "They's been enough happened in Number Ten to-night."

They dispersed willingly enough, but each man as he went kept an eye open for a man behind him — a silent man who wore long spurs.

Nancy turned back to the window and entered the room again.

Sleep fell over Number Ten, a sleep broken by rumblings here and there, as if the little town rested uneasily after the most hectic night in its history; but in Grogan's place a light still burned over the bar. For as long as there was business the eyes of Grogan's resolutely stayed open. Only that lamp above the bar burned. The rest of the big room lay drenched in shadow. The roulette wheel lay in its bowl, a dim glimmer amid the darkness, and the tables and chairs took on fantastic shapes as the flicker and flare of the smoking lamp illumined them faintly, and then waved them back into obscurity.

Business had drawn down to one customer, but that one customer was no less a person than Lefty Harris. Of all the men of Number Ten he alone had refused to leave his chair when the others poured out to hear the serenading, and again when the tumult swept once more down the street at the heels of Jerry Aiken. Now he sat close to the bar, silent. He drank very little, and he talked less, but his misted eye rested contentedly on his surroundings.

There was a reason for that content. Three days before Lefty Harris had shot down a man. It was not a mortal wound, but there had been no excuse for the shooting — not even self-defense — not even the well-worn excuse of the "hip-pocket movement." A reasonless passion had swept Lefty away, and before his passion left him an offending man had lain prostrate, clutching at the dust with his hands. And then the posse took the trail of Harris.

It was not the first time that he had been followed in his career, but in other times the law had had little or nothing on him. Moreover, there was a small, unhappy voice in Lefty, an insistent voice of doom; and he knew that the end of his trail was not far away. Not that he had any definite reason for expecting this adventure to turn out badly, but he sensed trouble as an animal senses a change in the weather. He had escaped too many times before. He was due for a reverse.

Moreover, a sense of guilt followed him since that shooting. A fine piece of horseflesh urged by a relentless spur had carried him far beyond the pursuers and not even the tale of his crime could possibly be known in Number Ten; but before the morning broke that story might run the rounds.

Then he would be an exile indeed. Then would begin another of those long vigils in the desert, days of hiding, nights of flight, terror behind him, ambush before him, uncertainty propping his weary eyes open, and distrust of every fellow man dogging him. Perhaps he now sat in the haunt of other men for the last time in many months. So the sight was grateful to the eyes of Lefty Harris. He smiled in a dim, unaccustomed manner as he looked around upon the empty chairs. He conjured up the crowded scene which he had noticed earlier in the evening, and smiled again. It was very pleasant; before three hours passed he would be in the heart of the desert.

Grogan watched him intently, studying his face. For though Grogan had seen many notables in his day, he had never known quite so famous and dreaded a man as Harris. He would have been pleased had the outlaw drank more and talked more; but Lefty drank hardly at all, sipping the redeye as if it were wine, and talking not at all.

And then Marshal Bud Levine entered.

The night was already ending. A weary gray, hardly noticeable, crawled across the windows, and across the street the cold forms of other houses, half rescued from the night, loomed clumsily, like things in a dream. Grogan felt a sudden exhaustion, such as comes to the merrymakers and dancers who have rioted all night, when the dawn surprises them and makes them chilly with a sense of guilt, and sets an ache in every muscle, and the brain is sick and sore.

That was how Grogan felt as he looked at

Bud Levine. The face of the marshal was as gray as the early morning light. Pouches showed beneath his eyes, and heavy lines were in beside the corners of his mouth — deep lines, as if cut by a chisel. His shoulders drooped and his knees sagged with unutterable weariness; for a moment he stood staring about him with a sort of sad defiance, and then, with a great sigh of relief, sank into a chair.

He looked upon the burly form of Grogan; he smiled into the misty eyes of the killer.

"Thank God," groaned Bud Levine, "I'm among friends at last!" He added, letting himself relax still more: "Redeye, Grogan!"

Grogan brought a bottle and glass, and then retired behind his bar again. He was curious to watch the man of the law and the man who broke the law sitting together as happily as bunkies. The marshal finished his drink in a single gulp. Grogan smiled, for much redeye means much talk.

"Have another, Bud," he urged. "This is on the house."

Bud reached for the glass, but even after his hand was set about it he released it slowly, very slowly, as if he had to make a special effort of the will to bring every finger free of the sticky glass. Then he shook his head sadly.

"Nope," he said. "No booze for me; not

while she's in town."

Lefty did not, or could not, hear aright. "Who's he? Who's the hell-raiser you're worried about, Bud?"

Lefty was anxious to conciliate the marshal. In the days immediately to come it might not be unwise to have a friend among the ranks of the men of law.

"Not he. It's a her, Lefty."

"A woman? You been fallin' for calico, Bud?" murmured Harris in his soft voice.

"Not me," protested Bud Levine. "I got almost roped at first, but after that she kept me so busy that it busted the spell. I didn't fall for her, but the rest of Number Ten did. And what's the result? Listen!"

He held up a hand for silence; far away there was first a rumble of deep-voiced cursing, and then the shrill, barking voices of men about to fight.

"Let 'em go," snarled Bud Levine. "Let 'em bust their fool heads. I won't stir till I hear gun talk."

Lefty made no comment; he watched the marshal shrewdly.

"It's all her, Lefty," sighed Levine. "She's done more to Number Ten than a hurricane could do. That's straight. First come a gent named Smith and started the wreckin'. He was a sort of advance agent. Then come the girl herself. In two days she'll have Number Ten burned to the ground. They're fightin' all over the town. And when tomorrow begins they'll start fightin' ag'in. Before tomorrow night they will be a feud."

"How does she do it?" ventured the other curiously.

"With her eyes, Lefty," answered Bud sadly. "You ought to of seen her in here pickin' up men with her eyes. One look and one smile, and a gent had an idea that she was some strong for him. You get fifty gents in love with the same girl, and you begin to get an idea how Number Ten is fixed now."

He shivered.

"I've looked death in the face twenty times since she come to town!"

"Why don't you get rid of her?"

"How can I touch her when she ain't busted any law? Even if she had, I could not lift a hand without havin' the whole town on my back. They watch her like a wolf watchin' its young. They show their teeth every time you frown at her."

"These here gents need some teachin'," smilingly remarked Lefty Harris.

"They've had their teachin'," nodded Bud Levine. "This Smith gent has gone through 'em like a five-year-old maverick through a herd of yearlin's. But still they come back for more."

He sighed again.

"And she don't mean nothin' wrong," he went on. "You can see that. The whole trouble, Lefty, is that she's too pretty."

"Huh?" grunted Harris.

"Girls goes in three classes," philosophized the marshal. "They's the common or garden girl. She don't look like much, and you don't never notice her much. But she's the kind that settles down and makes a home for a man and raises kids. She's the kind my mother was — God bless her! — and most likely she's the kind your mother was. She gets calluses on her hands, mostly, but her heart keeps tender. That's the first kind. They ain't nothin' to rave about on first sight, but they're the soil that things worth while grows in."

He paused, thoughtful.

"Then they's the second kind," went on Bud Levine. "They got plenty of looks. They're pretty. They catch your eye. Gents turn around on the street and look after 'em. And dream about 'em later on. If you go to a dance they's always about one of them there. And the gents keep a little circle around 'em.

"After the dance they's always a couple of fights, because somebody figures that he's been cut out of a dance, or something like that. And they's always a little trouble floatin' around a girl in that class like a cloud on the edge of the sky promisin' a norther. S'pose a girl like that marries. She's had a lot of men to pick from, and to the end of her days she keeps regrettin' that she got tied down to one gent. And after the kids come along, and she begins to get sallow and wrinkled, then she starts hatin' her husband and blamin' him."

The marshal paused again and gathered strength for his conclusion.

"Is that the kind of girl this one is?" asked Lefty, yawning.

"She ain't," said Bud sharply. "She's in a class by herself. She ain't pretty; she's beautiful. When she looks at a man it's like an electric spark was jumpin' from wire to wire. She turns you warm and cold all in a minute. They's nothin' calculatin' about her. She's strong, but she don't know her strength. She's like a hoss that's never been loaded with as much as it could pull. She's out lookin' for action like a man, and she don't care what happens so long as she's busy."

"Action?" repeated Lefty softly.

"Action all the time," nodded Bud. "They's two men in jail, one gone nutty, and the rest of Number Ten tryin' to cut each other's throat, all because of that one Nancy."

"It's a kind of pleasant-soundin' name,"

murmured Lefty.

"That ain't all that's pleasant about her. They's her eyes and her hair and her hands and her voice. What a voice, partner!"

Lefty stirred.

"She's the picture you been dreamin' about, come to life. She's the end of the trail, with nothin' lyin' beyond. But her smile turns a man's heart into gunpowder, and her eyes is the spark that sets it off. She tears you right in two. And yet — I'd give a thousand dollars to see her clear of Number Ten."

"What's she doin' here?"

"Lookin' for action, partner."

"Where's she goin'?"

"Lookin' for action. Anywhere."

"Who's goin' with her?"

"Nobody. Nobody could keep pace with her, Lefty."

"H'm!" murmured the killer.

"Unless," said the marshal, by way of an afterthought, "it's this gent Smith."

"What's become of him?"

"He's got a room in the hotel near the girl's."

"Is she thick with him?"

"She saved him from the crowd by as pretty a piece of nerve as I ever see."

Lefty Harris leaned across the table and touched the marshal's arm.

"Bud," he whispered, and now all the mist was gone from his eyes, "come outside. I got something to say to you."

"What's the matter, Lefty? You look loaded for bear."

"Come out," insisted Lefty. "You'll maybe be glad to hear what I got to say."

The marshal, bewildered, rose obediently, and the two stepped out of Grogan's and into the dim, chill street.

CHAPTER XXIII

The Killer

"S'pose," said Lefty, as soon as they were safely beyond earshot of Grogan's, "that some one was to take this girl and bring her out of Number Ten whether she wanted to go or not?"

"Eh?"

"Jest s'posin'," murmured Lefty.

"Lefty!" gasped Bud Levine. "D'you mean —"

"It wouldn't hurt your feelin's none, would it?" asked Harris.

"Lefty, I'd be your friend for life. But how could she be taken out of the hotel — without raisin' the whole bunch ag'in?"

"They's ways of doin' things a pile harder than that. Besides, how d'you know that she won't be glad to come along? Look here, Bud, this girl wants action, and I allow I can show her about as much as the next gent. She ain't fixed steady here. Neither am I. She don't know where she's bound. Neither do I. She wants to hit the long trail. So do I. Well, Bud, don't that look like a partnership? I'm askin' you?"

The marshal grew suddenly thoughtful.

"Lefty," he muttered, "you don't mean —"

"I don't mean nothin'," nodded Lefty. "She's safe with me. I wouldn't harm her — no way. But the trail gets kind of lonesome, ridin' it alone. And maybe she would not find it so bad comin' along with me. I know the ranges like a book, and maybe she'd be kind of glad to have me read it to her. Anyway, let me take her out of Number Ten; if she ain't happy before we finish the ride to-day, she can tell me so, and I'll take her wherever she wants to go. Bud, is it a go?"

"Lefty," said the marshal solemnly, "I'll trust you to play square with her, once you get her out of Number Ten. But — if you was to be crooked with her — and the news of it was to come back to Number Ten — the whole town would take the trail after you, Lefty."

"I know it."

"And I'd lead the gang."

"I know *that*."

"But," concluded Bud, "I know you're a square shooter. Lefty, her room is the first room to the right, when you come to the head of the stairs in the hotel. S'long, and good luck."

The killer hastily shook hands and then turned and swung into his saddle.

But Bud Levine stood staring after him.

"Poor old Lefty," muttered Levine. "He don't know her like I do. And Heaven help him! But, anyway, now I can sleep!"

Straightway he went to bed and was instantly lost in peaceful dreams, though all around him the rumors of battle drifted through Number Ten. Bud Levine had washed his hands of a problem greater than the taming of outlaws or the manhandling of killers.

Meantime, Lefty Harris swung from the saddle near the hotel and entered the building. The moment he passed the deep shadow of the doorway, the moment the inexplicable smell of the old building, strangely compounded of the keenness of alkali dust and the tracery of cooking odors wafted for many years from the dining room, fell upon his nostrils, Lefty changed with astounding suddenness.

A moment before he had been a lazy-eyed dreamer, careless, sleepy; now, the instant he passed the door of the hotel, his gait changed to a slinking alertness. His head turned swiftly from side to side; he seemed to be electrically in touch with all around him; for Lefty Harris was once more on an unknown trail.

Up that crazy staircase he slipped, and not a creak or a groan announced his passage. Steadily, without haste, he mounted to the top, and silently as a shadow drifted down the little hall to the first room on the right, where he would find the strange girl, Nancy, who had set Number Ten by the ears. At the door he paused for a decided moment, and in that moment of pause his senses, already keen beyond imagining, sharpened to a hair-trigger sensitiveness. Far off, some one stirred in a bed, and Lefty knew it; some one spoke in his sleep, and Lefty knew it; and from within the room which was his goal there stole out to him an utter silence, deep and almost ominous.

He turned the knob. No practiced sneak thief could have done it with more perfect silence. The door itself now opened inch by inch, steadily, silently, in spite of the rusted hinges. Lefty Harris was in the room.

There he paused once more, for a faint scent came to him, or something like a perfume, something wonderfully faint and sweet at once; and suddenly Lefty knew it was more than a fragrance — it was the presence of the girl.

He closed the door behind him. As he did so there was the faintest click, and instantly a dim white figure sat up erect in the bed. Behind her the dimly gray square of the window helped to outline her figure to his eyes, but he was certain that she could not see him against the black wall where he stood.

He remained perfectly quiet. If she should hear the slightest sound he knew that she would scream, for this was the nature of women. And men who are found sneaking into the bedchambers of women do not live long in the mountain desert. This, also, Lefty Harris knew.

"What's the game, partner?" queried a voice softly.

He drew a great breath. It was uncanny. Could she see in the dark? And why was there no outcry? A deep respect for the owner of that gentle voice swelled in the breast of Lefty Harris.

"A game for two," he said presently. "Talk soft, keep your wits, and don't get scared; or else the game is off."

"I'm not afraid. But why the soft foot?"

"Because if I'm known to be here, lady, I'll have Number Ten on my back inside ten seconds."

"Then why did you come?"

"Because I'm on my way, and need company."

"Well?"

"And I hear you're lonely, too, lady."

"This is odd. Who told you that?"

"I gathered it out of Number Ten — that you was lookin' for action, lady."

A pause; then soft, silver laughter. It flowed about Lefty Harris; it immersed him as cold water covers and takes the breath from the diver.

"What have you to offer?"

"A long trail."

"Where?"

"I don't know."

"How long?"

"I don't know."

"With whom?"

"You and me and two hosses."

"Who are you?"

"Lefty Harris."

"What's your business?"

"Anything excitin'."

"Where do you live?"

"On my hoss."

Another pause. And in that pause Lefty Harris, with superacute ears, could hear quick, audible breathing from the direction of the bed.

Then a command, a little sharper, but still in a guarded voice: "Lefty, light a match."

He obeyed without thinking. The flame spurted out from the head of the match in a blue flare and then steadied to a yellow triangle, wavering slowly.

"Raise the match and hold it above your face, Mr. Harris."

He obeyed again.

After a time he heard a murmur: "Why not? Why not go with him?"

But Lefty had revealed something else to himself when he raised that match. The light fell upon two gleaming eyes, upon parted lips, upon a white throat — he raised the match higher — stepped closer — staring. There was a sudden, muffled curse, and Lefty dropped the match to the floor. He had singed his fingers badly.

"Go outside," commanded the girl again, "while I get into my togs."

"You're coming?"

"I have to, don't I?"

He chuckled. "Sure. I'm makin' you go at the point of a gun." Then gravely: "You're goin' to take a chance?"

"I'm going to ride a day with you and see what happens."

Without another word Lefty Harris slid through the door silently and closed it soundlessly behind him. There he stood in the dark, his heart beating swiftly, a smile of which he was not conscious spreading wider and wider. It was more exciting than any adventure of men and horses and guns. It was unlike all that had happened in his strange life. But would she really come?

Soft noises, rustlings, the muffled click of boots being drawn on, and then in an unbelievable space of time the door opened again and she was at his side.

"Ready," she said. "Hurry, Lefty!"

"You got a hoss?"

"In the stables behind the hotel."

Then, in a daze, he went with her down the stairs and out to the barn behind the building. Still unable to think clearly, he saddled her horse, which she pointed out, and led it into the open. Without his assistance she sprang into the saddle.

If they had looked up they would have seen, perhaps, the figure of a man, dimly visible at a window that looked down upon the barnyard. But the thoughts of Nancy were riding already out along the trail; and the thoughts of Lefty Harris were reaching no further than the girl.

CHAPTER XXIV

At Billy's Lake

When the two jogged down the single street of Number Ten, the same happy haze still held the mind of Lefty. He could not understand it. He had gone to the hotel expecting that he would have to use the hint of his gun; but this strange creature had come of her own accord. And Lefty, searching through his mind for some similar type of woman, found none. As the marshal had said, she was unique. Was she a hardened adventuress? No; a single word spoken in that miraculous voice shattered the idea.

In spite of her daring, the impression persisted that she was totally ignorant of the world, totally fresh and new to it. Why else had she so unbelievably accepted him? Or was it that when he held the match above his face she had read his character and seen the honesty at the bottom of it. Besides, of course, she did not know of his repute.

A great resolution swelled in Lefty Harris to make that repute something of which she or no other woman would have to be ashamed. A strange instinct, long dead in him, for cherishing; an instinct which lies in all men, because they share all the instincts of women — girlhood and motherhood; this was the thing that boiled up in Lefty Harris.

He wanted to do some great, brave, and good thing. She trusted him; almost the first person in the world, she trusted him implicitly the first time she saw him. And he would die a thousand times before one article of her faith in him should be tarnished by his deeds. She would be to him a sister — at first.

Now, as these things, like a song in silence, a melody remembered, came in the heart of Lefty Harris, the dawn was growing over the hills, and already they could see in the distance that morning light gleaming on Billy's Lake.

It was a little pond just outside of Number Ten, and the source of all their water supply. Without it Number Ten could not have been. It was one of those miracles, a natural spring in the heart of the mountain desert, and the overflowing waters made a little lake, first discovered and used by one Bill — in the distant past; a pipe brought the water underground to the little town.

Also, by that growing light of the dawn, they could see the mountains growing up from the heart of the night which still lay thick upon the earth and splitting the upper sky where dawn would soon be clear and colorful; and by that light Lefty Harris watched the expectant, happy face of the girl. She was becoming a religion to him; all that was good in the man rallied about her. And then he turned in the saddle and looked back.

Far away, in the heart of the hollow, lay Number Ten, black as a stain upon the face of the earth; and along the path which twisted down to the town he made out a bobbing, dark object, very small, or else in the distance. Lefty Harris halted his horse to look.

Almost at once he made it out. It was a horseman riding at full speed.

"We're followed!" he exclaimed to the girl. "Feed your hoss the spur, Nancy!"

"Followed?" exclaimed the girl, and whirled in the saddle. She added calmly — with a touch of scorn, perhaps: "Why, it's only one man!"

"Ah!" murmured Lefty Harris

If that was the kind she was, he was the man for her, the best man in the mountain desert. No one man, or no two, for that matter, would stop him.

He turned his horse and faced the newcomer, and the girl reined off a little distance to give them room.

Neither of them thought of it, but another,

looking down on the strange scene, might have remembered the storied days of knighthood and errantry, when men fought together, and the woman was the prize to follow the victor unhesitatingly.

They could see the pursuer clearly now. He came bending far forward in the saddle, in order that he might cut the wind more easily. And there was no doubt about his purpose. He rode viciously up the slope and straight toward them. The current of the air flipped up the brim of his hat.

"Jerry Aiken!" cried Nancy.

"D'you know him?" snapped Lefty Harris. "Is he a friend of yours?"

"That depends."

A grim smile came from Lefty; it was all the answer he wanted.

"Hold up!" he shouted. "Rein up, unless you're looking for trouble."

The reply was a shrill yell which set Lefty's blood tingling. A gun leaped into his hand.

"No, no!" screamed the girl beside him. "Jerry isn't armed."

It was too late. Probably Lefty Harris did not hear, and Nan was too far away to follow her words with action in time; and Jerry was upon his foeman like a thunderbolt.

The moment the gun flashed in the morning light he disappeared from the saddle as though he had been shot down, and Nancy cried out in amazement and horror. But it was only an old Indian trick. With one heel caught over the back of his horse behind the saddle and with one hand twisted into the mane, Jerry rode invisible to Lefty, with his horse to shield him from the rain of bullets.

There was a curse from the killer. Automatically he fired at the place where the man should have been riding, and the lead chipped a chunk out of the horn of the saddle. The next instant the apparently riderless horse was upon him with a rush. Over the back, over the saddle whirled a figure that lunged straight at his throat, with the impetus of the galloping horse to give it velocity. Again the gun of Lefty exploded, but a reaching hand settled upon his wrist and jerked the gun out of its true direction, while the body of Jerry struck Lefty with stunning force.

It happened with bewildering speed. Jerry's horse plunged riderless past, and Jerry sat behind Lefty's saddle, his arms wreathed about the body of his enemy. There was a sharp struggle; the gun flashed and struck the ground; the horse, maddened by the wild struggle and the double burden, rushed madly forward and crashed into the water of Billy's Lake until the waves splashed around his shoulders.

Before he could turn and go back for dry land, Jerry had twisted the body of Lefty far to one side. And Nancy, reining at the edge of the water, saw the fierce, silent struggle, saw the maddened eyes of the fighters, saw Lefty's head depressed more and more toward the surface of the lake.

He passed the line of resistance soon. A last struggle, and then his head was beneath the water, and a yell of Indian triumph burst from Jerry's lips. It did not chill the blood of gentle Nancy Scovil. It made her heart beat with a wild exultation. It seemed right and natural. She had no sympathy. She only rejoiced in the wildness of the struggle.

But now the efforts of Lefty Harris grew feebler and feebler. Suddenly he lay limp in the arms of Aiken, and then two arms were thrust up from the water in mute symbol of surrender. And yet, for a moment, Jerry kept him submerged. Did he intend to kill the man?

No; now he sat erect and jerked across the pommel of his saddle an inert figure streaming with water. In this fashion he rode back to the shore and flung the helpless body upon the ground. It lay crumpled where it struck.

"He's dead!" gasped Nancy.

She had started to dismount, but the command of Jerry Aiken stopped her like a strong hand.

"Stay where you are. Leave him to me."

"But he's dead."

"Then you can't help him. What's he to you?"

What had come over him? He sat his saddle with the air of a conqueror. A new sternness and yet a new gayety was in him. It shone in his eyes; it sat about the firmness of mouth and chin. It was the same devil-may-care Jerry who had beaten the mob in Grogan's, outraced their horses up the street, and whipped into her room the night before.

A groan came from the fallen man. Swaying from side to side, he sat up, bracing himself with both arms, his dripping head hanging down.

"Now," said Jerry, "you come with me."

"Where?" she asked, and she wondered because she accepted his dictates so much as a matter of course. Perhaps it was because there was so little hesitancy in his manner, such firm assurance.

"Up there first. Then I'll look around at the world and decide where we're heading."

She followed the direction of his waved arm.

High above them the rose of dawn lay upon a flat-topped mountain, though the world below remained still semidark. And Nancy Scovil threw up both her arms toward it. She spurred her horse, and they galloped together, side by side, toward that goal. Both their mounts were pouring sweat when they drew rein, of one accord.

They seemed on the very crest and ridge of the world. Their own mountain outtopped all within their view. Far, far away rolled blue, misty ranges, still untouched with that rose of morning. About them the land fell away in steep, dropping cliffs of solid rock and jagged ravines. It was a land made for giants. There was no mark of man upon it.

And into their faces blew an air of incredible keenness and freshness.

Behind and below them lay their past lives. John Scovil, with hanging head and staggering horse, rode the last stage of his long night journey. And he had one thought in his mind: to escape from this land of madness.

Nearer to them stretched Number Ten in a bruised and broken slumber. Bud Levine alone was happy, for he had washed his hands of a great burden, he had passed on a trouble like a burning cross to call other men to war. But through the rest of the town men with bruised heads and sore bodies slept with their jaws hard set and dreamed of battles and victories and the smashing of bones. And in the jail Red Mack and Pete the Runt slept foot to foot with the hardness of the stone biting through their meager blankets.

Of the party which had started so gayly in the middle of night, Jerry and Nan and Scovil and Red and Pete, this was the result.

The two on the mountain could not see all these images. All they knew was that much had been put behind them. Jerry was staring over the mountains like a conqueror over a new land; and Nancy was staring into his face, as if she sought there an interpretation of it all.

"Come!" he said with a curt gesture.

She reined her horse close to him; his arm went about her and drew her strongly close to him.

"Jerry," she said suddenly. "Let me go."

"Not a hope of that."

"But I'm choking."

"What's wrong?"

"That Florida water —"

"It's your own choice," chuckled Aiken, "so make the most of it. I'd never have picked out this stuff for myself."

She laughed, muffled.

"Why did you start without me, Nan?"

"I don't know. Chiefly to see if you'd follow."

He smiled grimly.

"You'll do the following after this, Nan."

"I suppose so."

"I'm a new boat, Nan. I've been christened with Florida water and now I'm ready to put to sea."

"And go where?"

"Somewhere out there — into the sunrise, Nan. What would you call that country yonder?"

"Don't you know? That's the Land of Happiness."

"Then we're going for it. I've not the least idea what's in it."

"That's the best part. But what will we live on?"

"I've a gun and powder and lead. I've salt in my pouch — and Florida water on my trousers. We'll live off the land as we go. But we need a commission first. We've got to get married first."

"Of course. But let's talk about stupid things later on. You see that rock at the edge of the plateau yonder?"

"Yes."

"I'll beat you to it."

As she spoke she spurred her horse, and with a ringing shout Jerry raced after her. Over the eastern mountains the sun pushed up a rim of gold, and clearly against that stream of fire they showed as they dipped over the rim of the plateau. Her hair had blown loose, she was half turned back to him, and her laughter blew like music behind them.

So they swept over that mountaintop and glanced down toward a world that lay at their feet.

Max Brand is the best-known pen name of Frederick Faust, creator of Dr. Kildare, Destry, and many other fictional characters popular with readers and viewers worldwide. Faust wrote for a variety of audiences in many genres. His enormous output, totaling approximately thirty million words or the equivalent of 530 ordinary books, covered nearly every field: crime, fantasy, historical romance, espionage, Westerns, science fiction, adventure, animal stories, love, war, and fashionable society, big business and big medicine. Eighty motion pictures have been based on his work along with many radio and television programs. For good measure he also published four volumes of poetry. Perhaps no other author has reached more people in more different ways.

Born in Seattle in 1892, orphaned early, Faust grew up in the rural San Joaquin Valley of California. At Berkeley he became a student rebel and one-man literary movement, contributing prodigiously to all campus publications. Denied a degree because of unconventional conduct, he embarked on a series of adventures culminating in New York City where, after a period of near starvation, he recieved simultaneous recognition as a serious poet and successful popular-prose writer. Later, he traveled widely, making his home in New York, then in Florence, and finally in Los Angeles.

Once the United States entered the Second World War, Faust abandoned his lucrative writing career and his work as a screenwriter to serve as a war correspondent with the infantry in Italy, despite his fifty-one years and a bad heart. He was killed during a night attack on a hilltop village held by the German army. New books based on magazine seriels or unpublished manuscripts continue to appear. Alive and dead he has averaged a new one every four months for seventy-five years. In the U.S. alone nine publishers issue his work, plus many foreign countries. Yet, only recently have the full dimensions of this extraordinarily versatile and prolific writer come to be recognized and his stature as a protean literary figure in the 20th Century acknowledged. His popularity continues to grow throughout the world.